RUNNING TO STAY
UPRIGHT

A NOVEL

Sharon Wright

Books that nurture the soul

ISBN: 978-0-9910861-1-5

RUNNING TO STAY UPRIGHT

COPYRIGHT © 2014 by Sharon Saltzgiver Wright

All rights reserved. Except for use in any review, the reproduction or utilization of this work in whole or in part in any form by any electronic, mechanical or other means, now known or hereafter invented, including xerography, photocopying and recording, or in any information storage or retrieval system, is forbidden without the written permission of the publisher, Bellastoria Press, P.O. Box 60341, Longmeadow, MA 01106.

This is a work of fiction. Names, characters, places and incidents are products of the author's imagination or are used fictitiously and are not to be construed as real. Any resemblance to actual events, locales, organizations, or persons, living or dead, is entirely coincidental.

Cover design by Corrinne Hamilton
Front cover photography by Ben Wright
Blueprint drawing by Melissa Kane

BELLASTORIA PRESS
P.O. Box 60341
Longmeadow, Massachusetts 01116

For Denise Marcil,
who lives with such grace

43 Winding Path Drive

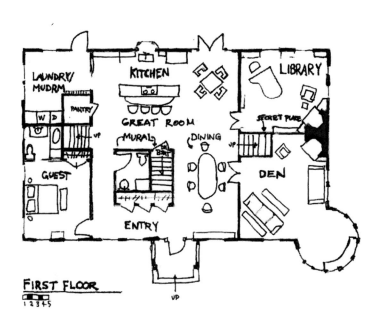

First Floor

Second Floor

Chapter 1

Liz jolted awake, her heart pounding. When she remembered what she had to do today, she wished she could roll over and go back to sleep...for about a year.

Sliding her legs out from under the covers into the winter chill, she sat up at the edge of the mattress, feeling as though she had on a baseball cap two sizes too small. She sighed, traded the down comforter for her slippers and chamois bathrobe, and trudged away from the warm bed that was still calling her name.

Charles, her high school sophomore, came skidding around the corner from his room. "Mom, I forgot to do my *Romeo and Juliet* thing. I need a paper plate."

"Ugh. I need tea...I think you just shot my brain out the back of my head."

"Mom, I'll get a zero."

"You should have thought of that last night. It's time for breakfast."

His eyes rolled as she turned to knock on the bathroom door. "Francine, we're going down."

A series of crashes, a screech, and the bathroom door flew open. "There's no water!" Half of the red hair Francine had inherited from Liz was a frizz; the other half, a pigtail.

These days red hair seemed to be all they had in common. Liz envied how Dan could effortlessly fly along with their middle child while she was left to stumble along behind, trailing a series of afterimages.

"Mom! How can I get ready for school without water? Britty and Ashley and I are going Lady Ga-Ga today."

Liz wondered if M-O-M could be uttered without its being bleated, and if this intel meant Francine's head would sprout some sequined protuberance after breakfast.

"I'll see what's up with the water."

"But Mother! YOU won't be able to fix it!!"

"Thanks. Go eat."

Francine downshifted to a coo, "Mums, could you just bring me up a cup of tea? I'm not hungry."

"No. Breakfast is..." Francine joined in a mocking drone, "...the most important meal of the day."

Liz blew her nose into a tissue retrieved from her robe pocket. "Anyway, as you reported, we have no water for tea." This provoked an aggravated moan and stomp downstairs.

Hesitating at the top of the stairs to put a buffer between herself and the descending adolescent scorn, Liz straightened the photo of a white-washed town above the Aegean Sea that Dan had taken during one of their pre-kid explorations. She'd been a corporate executive then, with 5-star hotels, floor tickets to rock concerts, car service, bonuses, and eager subordinates, which she'd given up for diapers when Francine, their second child was born. The abrupt shift to the mind-numbing repetition of teaching manners and playing "I see with my little eyes..." had been rugged going but working with Dan in his architectural business had helped. So it was laughably ironic that now, when she might be going back to a corporate job, all she could think of was the commuting, the politics, and the exhaustion. Even crap like this morning seemed like a luminous treasure.

As she started down the stairs again, her footing faltered, almost slipping off the tread. She put her hand out to brace against the wall and sighed. She hadn't told anyone about her job search because that would have meant admitting out loud how bad things were. She rubbed her forehead. It was her fault. Her problem to sort out.

Today though, she was going to tell Dan. All of it.

Charles clambered down the staircase directly across the double-height Great Room from the one she'd just come down and scooted into the pantry by the back door. She crossed through the sitting area into the kitchen and reached up to get cereal bowls from the bamboo cabinets that Dan had installed lower than standard height to accommodate her 5'2" reach.

He'd custom-designed the whole house for them, from the granite countertops quarried in his New Hampshire hometown to the mural he'd painted on the wall above her head of the woods across the street. But now, thanks to her, they might lose everything to the bank in a few months. She rewrapped the tie on her robe, tightening its hold. She had to act normal.

The kettle whistled. "Charles, where'd you get water?"

His auburn shoulder-length hair draped like a tent over his tureen-sized bowl of Crispix. "Outside. Scooped up snow."

"Brilliant."

Charles shrugged.

"Just hoping that pumping you with caffeine might get me my much-needed paper plate. A total Me move, Mom."

"Well played, my young Padawan." Liz lifted down four of the pottery mugs Francine had made. "Do you guys want English Breakfast or Hu-Kua? Oh wait, we only have PG Tips left."

Charles shook his head. Francine bubbled, "Tips is good, Mumsie." Well, at least her pubescent flares were brief. "And thanks for making Kashi last night, Mummers." Or maybe this shift meant she now wanted something.

"You're welcome." Setting the tea to steep, Liz took the phone down cellar to check the circuit breakers and then called the service number on the water pump. A woman with a voice that sounded like walking on gravel assured Liz that someone would come later that morning.

Trudging back up the cellar stairs, Liz joined Charles at the island with her microwaved Kashi. "Wasn't this assignment in your planner?"

"I didn't look till this morning."

"Charles, you're supposed to check your planner every night."

"I had play rehearsal, and Duncan needed help getting a game up on the computer. Then, we kinda got playing till dinner."

"What about after dinner?"

"I dunno."

"Go get dressed." Francine, loving this exchange, smirked at Charles as he shambled upstairs to get dressed. His response was to swipe her legs off the arm of the chenille-covered chair she was flopped across.

Liz's childhood had been so different, coming home to find her mother passed out on the floor next to a spilled glass of scotch, the ice melting into the rug and dried vomit clotting her hair. Unfairly familiar smells when other kids got to open their front doors to roasting garlic or logs burning in the fireplace.

She pressed the palm of her hand against the small of her back and got up to retrieve the lunches Dan had made, put them in the kids' backpacks, and search the pantry for a paper plate. Moving the step-stool over to the paper goods, all she could find were small waxed ones with Christmas trees on them. She called over to Charles, who was now dressed and back downstairs, "How about tracing a plate on card stock?"

"Brilliant." He grinned, mocking her earlier compliment about his melting snow, and slung his backpack onto one shoulder, plate to trace in hand. With the shuffling glide endemic to teenage boys, he headed out to the second floor of the detached garage to get card stock from Evergreen Design's office supplies.

Liz heard Duncan, who was seven years old and still nestled in that blissful period between the terrible twos and the terrifying teens, run from his room to dive on top of his slumbering dad for their morning wrestle ritual. She set aside Dan's tea to steep.

"Mother, where's my blue suede skirt?" Francine's frantic appeal hurled down the stairs.

"Last I saw, it was under your bed." With a growl, Francine stomped back to her room in the turret's second floor. Why that girl's heels weren't bruised purple was a mystery, but it was no surprise that she couldn't find something in that maelstrom. Dan had designed their bedrooms for sleeping or solitude, free from clutter, distractions, and all electronics, to encourage everyone back into the common rooms. But even though Francine buried his spartan approach, her room's sliding mountain of claptrap was just as effective in forcing her back downstairs.

Dan had built them a house that was one part masterful design to two parts magic, creating an integral part of what made them a family. It was the only place Liz had ever lived where she'd felt at home. Her breath caught in her throat, as the simple truth flashed its stark report. This anxiety about going back to work in Boston was rooted in her not wanting their kids to feel abandoned like she had. But by avoiding going back to work in Boston for so long, she'd brought her childhood to their doorstep. Her fingers clutched her mug as Duncan and Dan rumbled down the stairs. She plastered a grin on her face, having learned long ago how to stuff and smother her emotions. Stuff, smother, and smile.

"Hey Mom, why didn't the hungry shark attack Sally when she was swimming nearby?"

She cleared the fear from her voice with a cough. "Umm, because it was a sand shark?"

"Nah, it was a MAN eating shark," Duncan crowed. "Sally's a girl; the shark's a *man* eater—get it?" Dan tousled his son's hair as Duncan sat down at the table to drink his orange juice. Liz poured her youngest's cereal and milk.

Dan gave her a kiss. "Morning, Babe. How'd you sleep?"

"Fine."

"Hey Mom, look!" Duncan pointed up at the mural: hawks soared; a newly hatched duck family waddled in a line beside the pond; turtles sunned themselves on a log; a buck watched from within the darkened woods. "The deer has Happy Magic in his eye." Light streaming through the skylights and the chandeliers Dan had made out of welded metal and crystals splashed a tiny spectrum onto the painting. For years, the kids had stepped on these mini rainbows with a sing-song "Happy Magic!" for good luck.

"Lucky Bucky."

Duncan lit up at his mom's silly rhyme. She turned to yell upstairs, "Francine, time to go." Her voice deepening as she punched out the "go."

Duncan yelped, "I'll get her!"

Dan pointed, "Dishwasher."

"We don't have any water; the pump guys are coming later."

Unfazed by her information, Duncan spun around, discharged his dishes and ran upstairs to put his sister on notice. Liz followed him to the bottom of the stairs and screeched, "Francine, now! The bus will be here in two minutes."

"Where's Chuck?" Dan asked.

"He's out in the garage doing homework he forgot. Francine!"

Her daughter ran downstairs and past her with a quick kiss and petulant, "I feel so gross."

"You'll live."

"Don't worry. If you keep moving, no one will notice the smell."

She moaned, "Da-aad...I am so taking a shower in the girls' locker room as soon as I get to school," and with this last salvo launched, the door swung shut behind their red-headed pixie, adorned with a glittered paper tiara in rather weak homage to pop music's reigning GaGa.

Liz warmed her tea in the microwave and headed through the French doors into the den. Duncan, still at the magical age where he could solve a problem in long division but thought a new pair of sneakers would make him run faster, was kneeling on the turret's semicircular window seat, watching his brother and sister wait at the end of the driveway.

When the bus came, Duncan waved like a frantic mother bird distracting a cat. His older brother shot a quick look to the den window and nodded just before he boarded. Francine, the tweenie limboing betwixt child and woman, today gave her little bro a big wave and smile.

"Time for the lovey chair," Duncan crowed as he jumped into Liz's lap for the next morning ritual. Cradling him, his legs and arms sprawling out of her embrace, Liz ambushed him with a barrage of kisses, squeezes, and tickles from all sides; something she hadn't learned from her parents but from watching Dan with the kids. Duncan grinned with his whole face, "Will I still be your baby even when I'm bigger than Daddy and have a scratchy face?"

"You'll always be my baby, even when you start smelling like Charles." She was rewarded with peels of tinkling laughter. "Even when we aren't together, my love's wrapped around you just like this." She squeezed him to her chest, rather embarrassed by this desperate, preemptive plug for working full-time, although she wasn't clear which of them it was intended to comfort.

"Mommy, I can't breathe." Liz burrowed her nose into his tummy so that he wouldn't notice her distraught expression. "Can I go play the piano?" Liz nodded, and Duncan peeled himself out of the chair.

Holding her mug in both hands, she blew and watched her breath scatter the liquid surface. *Rhapsody in Blue* curled in from the baby grand piano in the library on the other side of the bedroom stairs.

It was the normalcy of mornings like this that made her ache to shield the status quo like an avenging angel. She tentatively took a sip of tea, but it brought little relief. Liz sighed, feeling brittle. Is this what happened when you lived a dream? When you got more than you believed you deserved? Lately, she'd felt as though she was only visiting a life that any day could be pulled out from under her, rolled up, and taken away. She stared out the turret windows at the bare grey trees scratching at the sharp blue sky and all she could think was that today was the day she would break Dan's heart.

She traipsed upstairs to get dressed. As she pulled on a turtleneck and jeans, "The A Train" lifted through the floorboards. After quickly running a brush through her short hair, she hustled down the stairs, calling Duncan to the bus.

They stopped by the garage, where Dan was waiting by the office door since Duncan was now too big to be kissed at the bus stop. Things were always changing, but now they were scrolling by at the speed of light. She should have Dan video her waving goodbye at the end of the driveway so that if she got a job in Boston, Duncan could remember how she used to be there when he left for school.

As the bus pulled away, Liz watched a hawk fly over the woods. Usually when she felt like this, she'd go sit on the big rock beside the pond to regroup, but today the short walk required too much effort.

She groaned out loud as she headed back to the house. She and Dan had played by all the rules: college, master's degrees, marriage, careers, kids. They'd worked hard, paid their taxes and volunteered. But then, one night, perhaps while they were sleeping or distracted by life's details, the rules of cause and consequence had shifted. It must have, because what was happening to them now was not how it was supposed to go.

Chapter 2

Home from errands that afternoon, Dan poured a potful of melted snow over a bouquet of organic carrots still sporting their dark green frills.

"What great color! I'm going to julienne these to go with the pork tenderloin." His enthusiasm was more like he was fixing the carrots and pork up on a date than preparing them for dinner. Liz looked over from her upholstered nest where she was ensconced with the mail. He grinned at her, "You look cozy over there."

She'd been trying to figure out which bills to pay and where the money was going to come from to do it. The electric bill blurred out of attention. Why hadn't they been able to get new clients? They'd been marketing Evergreen Designs with the ferocity of rabid dogs. And why hadn't she gotten them out of the stock market before it tanked? She shouldn't have broken her own rule and run up their credit cards. She should have done a lot of things differently, but hadn't.

She sighed and threw the bills in a pile on the floor.

A pot clanged on the counter, drawing her attention back over to her husband. What a lovely diversion. A sexy man in a denim shirt splotched like a memory quilt with the colors from countless oils painted. Watching him cook always aroused her as easily as when he kissed her neck in that searching, languorous way. She dreamily rubbed her neck, then ran her hand through her hair and extricated herself from her trench to move over behind the man and his vegetables.

As she stood behind him, her arms enveloped his, pressing her chest and hips against his back. He responded, pushing his palms down against the counter, rounding his spine. She curved with him. His head arched back. The deep murmur emanating from his throat was buried in the Bach being piped through the house.

They leaned into the other's quickening need. His hips gently moved to the classical adagio; hers followed. She sensed that small, still place within each of them begin to flare as a warm wash flooded her body.

She placed her forehead between her husband's shoulder blades while slowly sliding her hands down his torso. Her palms skimmed backwards across his buttocks before sliding down the backs of his legs along hamstrings taut from many miles run. Circling forward to his quads, her hands trailed upward, tantalizing. Her fingers bent and walked higher, slowly massaging inward.

The surrounding space thickened. Breath held—suspended—until it burst out in alarm at the loud banging of the back door. Before Liz and Dan could turn their heads, Donna was in the mudroom, appearing more like a bear from the woods than a woman in a fur coat and Bean boots.

Stamping off the snow, Liz's friend announced, "So, this is unemployment. Classical music, sex in the kitchen. Good to know, Pete could get the axe any day. Though I doubt he'd be so spontaneous in the sex department. Only the bed or shower, and I told him no more shower action until I get my own shower head. I'm so done freezing my tits off in the piddly spray that bounces off his lard-ass. Speaking of, got your call, here's some water."

Donna landed two gallon jugs of water on a shelf in the pantry. While she continued talking, she came into the kitchen with her arms circling in front of her as if clearing the air to make room for so large a presence. "Just had a meeting with Franco and the principal. You will not believe what my youngest has gotten himself into now." She picked up a chair at the table, spun it around, and thudded it to the floor. Still in her coat, Donna sat hard against the seat back. "Seems Franco is the Rodin that did the snow sculpture in front of the high school last week - an anatomically correct snowman and snow-woman doing it doggie-style."

Dan couldn't contain himself, dropping his knife into the sink, he had to lean on his elbows he was laughing so hard.

"How can you stand there laughing like a donkey when the spawn of my loins could be charged with an obscene public violation?" Dan stopped himself for a couple counts and then they both laughed even louder.

Liz, not seeing why this was so funny, didn't join in. "They're charging him with a crime?"

"Nah, I made that part up, but he was lucky our toaster oven didn't collide with his head when I found out. Really not good to have kids still home during menopause. He keeps threatening to move into Angela's dorm at Wellesley, although I think that has more to do with fantasizing about horny coeds than hanging with his sister or getting away from me."

Liz did not see any evidence that Donna was calming down. "What does Franco think?"

"Think? Does a teenage boy think? Oh, he was all 'Freedom of expression' and 'They don't appreciate art.' I told him 'Art my ass.' From the look he gave me, you can bet, the next time I piss him off, there'll be flyers all over town with my saggy butt in sepia subtitled *Art, My Ass*." Donna took her red and pink striped wool hat off her head, rubbed her thick, black hair roughly around her scalp, and then jammed it back on. "He's lucky his Dad's got his head so far up his own ass about the layoffs that he won't even notice. If Pete's home from work, he's either asleep or in the basement on the computer trolling Linked-in and Monster, in case he gets whacked. How about you, any job prospects?"

"Still waiting on Intech. Supposed to hear next week; looks good." Dan answered.

"Good stuff." Donna stood up and strode to the mudroom with a wave good-bye. "Later, Burgesses, or is the plural of Burgess, Burgi, or maybe Burgeon?" She vanished, her laughter billowing behind her.

Dan picked up the carrots from the sink and shook water off at Liz, "You, my love, attract the weirdest people."

"I married you."

"Well, you've also been known to pick some winners. Your friend Malia is as grounded as these carrots."

"Donna had a really rough childhood."

"So did you, and you're not a nutcase."

"Donna's not a nutcase. She's colorful."

"Liz, these carrots are colorful, that broad is certifiable."

When she'd met Donna eleven years ago at Alanon, Donna's rants had only been about her father and brother's drinking and abuse. Nowadays though, her rants ranged from politics to the declining quality of emery boards, not so much to find solutions but just because she needed to be heard.

With Donna's entrance and exit having exorcized their amorous mood, Liz put the kettle on to boil and headed into the den to start the fire. When her sixth match declined to light anything, Dan joined her with the teapot and mugs on a tray, rearranged the wood on top of some kindling, and had the Rumford fireplace blazing in minutes.

The family cat, Bassa, curled in Dan's lap, had been adopted from a shelter after their Egyptian honeymoon and named after the Arabic word for "the kiss." Sharing the love seat, Liz faced them with her feet tucked under Dan's bum; her shoulders stiffly scrunched toward her ears; her fingers reflexively curled into fists. She had to tell him now because the high school bus would be there in half an hour.

Liz took a deep draught from her mug to steady her nerves and almost spat the tea out when Dan said, "Good job on the bills. We still solvent, or do I need to join the world's oldest profession at Dunkin' Donuts?" Understanding that she didn't get jokes, he explained, "Pouring coffee, not prostitution." He smirked at her like a kid who had just discovered he could be clever.

Her stomach had become a black hole sucking away her resolve. She was supposed to be the brilliant business mind who got the jobs and enabled him, the artist, to focus on being creative, but this conversation was not going to do that.

She went straight to the point. "Our finances are in big trouble." The words bumped and collided, trying to get out around the lump in her throat. "I really messed up." She tried to swallow. "I've been scooping into our savings to meet expenses, and with the stock market in the tank, it's all gone. Both credit cards are maxed out; there's hundreds of dollars in interest and penalties every month. And this month we can't even make the mortgage. I've applied for a home equity loan, which isn't likely with the banks getting so tight, so if we don't sell the house, we'll be bankrupt by April."

The revelation lay there between them like a detonated dirty bomb, no survivors possible. His chest had stopped moving.

She swung her feet to the floor and stared at the fire for a few minutes, while he absently patted the cat. Then her voice continued in chunks, "If Intech doesn't come through, or we don't get something else, we will lose everything, even the house."

They'd been working on the Intech deal for six months. Bob, a friend of theirs and an Intech Vice President, had told them that the company had outgrown their facility and was thinking of building a new, three-building campus.

Dan's eyes instantly blinked alert when she mentioned Intech.

"I don't think we need to worry, Babe." He counted off his rebuttal on his fingers. "Bob said the President loved the ideas in the presentation, couldn't stop talking about the design. Even if nothing else comes along, Intech will be enough money to keep us going for a couple years." His voice was strong and free of concern. "Don't worry." He leaned over to tuck her hair behind her ear. "It will all work out." Dan's eyes sparkled the same way they had when they'd first met at the University of New Hampshire. Back then, she'd protested everything. A woman with any cause. She'd been passing out flyers to boycott milk because cows were pumped full of hormones and hooked up to machines that endlessly yanked on their teats after their babies had been taken from them to become veal. Dan had wandered over since his folks had a couple of cows. He'd walked up and really listened, and her righteous spiel had sputtered out within the depth of his understanding like a match tossed into a cool well.

But today fears for her family refueled her emotional blaze as Dan stood to throw another log on. She watched his back and annoyed, brushed her hair back over her ear. "I wish we had more than just Intech in the pipeline."

He came back to the couch. "You and your pipeline. All you need is one good deal, Liz, especially when it's as big as this one."

Too bad his positive thinking wasn't all it took because he'd have them rolling in money before you could say, "Shall we go to Paris for the weekend?" Unfortunately, what they needed was for him to actually do something. So often, Liz felt like she was the only adult in the house. Last week he'd hatched a plan to rent a U-haul, drive to his folks' in New Hampshire, cut down trees for firewood, and haul it back to sell. Liz had pointed out that renting the truck plus high gas prices would eat most of the profit, his folks might want their trees, and the wood would be too green to burn until summer.

The question, "Had she married the right man?" pressed hard against her chest. Would she have been better off with someone more serious? More reliable? Someone man enough to admit when there was a problem? There was only so much she could do. Right now Dan was reminding her way too much of her father. Her resentment seethed up from her core. The knuckles of her balled fists blanched white. She perched on the edge of the love seat, her feet punched down into the floor for fear of what would be forced out of her mouth if she moved.

Dan sat back down; Bassa reclaimed his lap, and Liz stayed put.

She had planned to reassure him, but his lack of reaction made her want the words to lash across his face so he'd wake up to her nightmare. She snapped, "I have an interview in Boston next week with First Insured Business. It's an entry-level position and won't pay as much as I used to make, but with health insurance, at least it would be something." The emphasis on the last word was bent to convey *because you're not doing anything*.

His exasperating response was, "Great! See, something will break."

This was not the reaction she'd feared, nor was it the one she now craved. He was oblivious: an insipid jackass instead of brawny rescuer or even sturdy support. Her anger escalated, thinking of how she'd been protecting him all this time, trudging alone through this stress for nothing. She felt dizzy, like this morning on the stairs, as if her spirit had suddenly evacuated her body to go somewhere safer.

He yammered on, "Everything will happen at once." He ticked off their future good fortune on his fingers. "You'll get this job, Intech will hire us, and then we'll have so much money, we can start a foundation for inner-city kids." Bassa bounded to the crest of the love seat's back in enthusiastic approval.

"What are you talking about? We're about to lose our house."

"Don't worry, Liz. It'll all work out."

She clutched at her failing self-control. "Don't tell the kids I'm interviewing."

"Why? They'll be proud of you; Mom saves the day."

"We only need someone to save the day because I got us into this mess."

"It's not your fault."

She ignored this. "So, you think it's a good idea if I work in Boston?" she asked a bit incredulously.

"Sure. I think it could be kind of fun for you."

Her mind clicked like a combination lock. Why didn't he feel betrayed that she'd be leaving Evergreen? Had he been wanting her to go work somewhere else? Before her niggling insecurity could explode into full-blown paranoia, Dan whooped, "Knowing you, you'll be President within the year and can hire Evergreen to re-do your building!" As irritated as she was, a small grin was knocked loose by his irrepressible optimism. "So Madam President, I'll take Francine to pottery and pick up Chuck from play practice; you can stay here for Duncan and put the dinner in for 45 minutes at 350. At least unemployment simplifies the scheduling."

"Yea, such great stuff this life of leisure." She tossed him a sarcastic smile.

"We're a great team, Babe." He tossed her back a sincere one. "This is just a temporary snag. We'll figure a way out. As long as we're good, nothing else matters."

"We're good."

"Always have been."

"Always will be." This exchange was a slight variation of the chorus they'd been repeating to each other since UNH, through times good, bad, sad or triumphant, through miscarriages, the birth of children, and the deaths of her parents. But today the familiar refrain seemed a bit limp. Liz curled back into the love seat. Dan picked up her foot to massage it, and they both watched the fire. This had all been very confusing. Not at all what she had expected.

Dan

He'd spent the three days since Liz dropped the bomb on him trying to digest the news, but he couldn't figure out how she'd let it get so bad, and why she hadn't told him way before this? Dan poured teriyaki sauce into the large Ziploc bag and added grated ginger, ground mustard, and pepper—a medley of his own devising. Easing in the pork that he had repeatedly stabbed with a metal cooking fork, he closed the bag and shook it before depositing it in the fridge.

He felt really tired. He'd go to bed as soon as Liz left for Donna's.

It would take a lot of pressure off if she got this job, but he'd need her when they got the Intech gig. How could he keep her at their little company, when she was capable of so much more? He didn't want her to resent him.

He still wasn't clear on how this had happened. Liz dodged him whenever he tried to bring it up.

He got potatoes from the bin in the pantry and began peeling them a bit more aggressively than was required. And what was that bit about losing the house? Liz wasn't one to be overly dramatic. He was worried about her. It wasn't like her to be so vague. What had happened? Was something else going on?

As he sponged off the counter, he wondered if she thought he was such a loser that he couldn't help? Or, even worse, that he was like a child that needed to be shielded from reality? It was bad enough not to be able to provide for your family but not to have your wife's respect made it worse.

Even if they sold the house they'd barely clear any money in this market. They'd been here since before the kids were born; they'd written their names into the foundation with sticks. This house was proof that he was a good architect. It helped him keep believing that it was this shitty economy and not him that was at fault.

He glanced over at the chair across the room, but Liz had her eyes closed, her feet up on the low table and bills in her lap. He wouldn't bother her. He cut the potatoes into pieces and put them in the boiling water to cook for mashing.

It was all going to be okay. Liz always saw the glass as half empty. They just needed a stop gap until the Intech job. Hopefully, it would happen sooner rather than later because this sucked. Maybe, it would help Liz feel more secure if he brought in some money in the meantime. After he finished the dinner prep, he'd make some calls to architectural firms to see if they were hiring. There was more than one way to skin a...he looked down at Bassa lying at his feet...oh, sorry, Dude.

Chapter 3

The stars seemed cruelly bright in the night's frigid, black sheath. Liz stuffed her keys into her pocket where they'd be easier to find than in her big bag. Shrugging deeper into her coat, she pulled her scarf further up over her cheeks. She was the last to arrive. She'd dawdled at home, feeling guilty about skulking away, until Dan had finally gotten her coat and patted her on the bum to launch her out into the cold dark.

She looked up from picking her way along the icy path to Donna's house. A convivial yellow light reached out through the living room windows, quickening her pace. Warmth, welcome, and wine waited inside with her gal pals who were gathered to play as they did once a month.

The living room was already rocking when Liz stepped through the doorway. "Welcome to Shangri-la, Mrs. Burgess," Donna trumpeted, sporting a baffling ensemble of a sarong wrapped around her hips, a bathing suit top, and a pair of furry dog-shaped slippers on her feet. She shimmied to get the belt of round bells tinging; her soft, white belly jiggling along.

Liz grinned. "That's quite the outfit, Donna. What do you have on your feet?"

"Franco gave me slippers for Christmas that look like Nikki." At her name, Donna's Akita raised her head from her new, red plaid dog bed with great disdain. "As you can see, the diva objects to any resemblance. Right after I unwrapped them, she went over and pissed in the shoebox."

"Way to state your truth, Nikki!" The others grinned, enjoying Malia's parody of her typical New Age prattle.

The furniture, which looked like it had been transplanted en toto from Great-Grandma's, had been pushed back against the walls. A mountain of silk, taffeta and sequins buried the sofa.

Malia had added a pink bra over her black turtleneck from the mound of Scheherazade garments; a belt of bells secured pillowcases over her wool pants. "Guess what we're doing!" As she twirled for Liz, her signature chandelier earrings swung and silver bangles jingled at her wrist; her silver mane billowed and then tumbled in a cascade over her shoulders as she slowed.

"Belly dancing!" Molly cheered the obvious, her jeans exchanged for a sage green gypsy skirt covered with silver embroidery and sequins.

"I think I'll just watch." Liz winced at the collection of netting and neon strewn across the cushions.

"Come on Mrs. B., play dress up with your gal pals. Shake out that tight ass. Give it a chance to breeeeathe." Donna raised her glass of the eggnog and added, "Speaking of, thank God the holidays are over. Even my fat pants are cutting off the circulation to my V-jay-jay."

A cold blast blew Sarah through the front door. Announcing, "The instructor just pulled in," she shed her ski jacket to reveal a complete belly dancing ensemble. She shrugged at Liz. "When I got here and found out what we were doing, I had to run home; I don't get many chances to wear this."

"Bullshit. You dance for Joe all the time," Donna jeered.

Sarah laughed. "He'd have an aneurism. I got it for a Halloween gig." Sarah sang with a jazz band that performed at quite prestigious spots around New England.

"The audience must have gone nuts," Molly gasped. "You look gorgeous." The light blue costume was stunning against Sarah's tawny skin, an elegant blend of her Asian and African ancestry.

"Everyone, this is Dahlia," Donna announced as she took the instructor's coat. "Dahlia, you've got your hands full with this crew."

"I love your outfits. What fun!" Dahlia exclaimed. She had on a hot pink genie top and chiffon harem pants with rows of jingling golden coins; her stomach and breasts happily hung over the edges of her outfit as she fiddled with her IPod player and speakers. Liz admired her nonchalance at wearing such a get-up.

Dahlia chimed her finger cymbals. "Tonight, we will free your inner Goddess. We'll dance in celebration of our feminine power." She clattered the cymbals again, punching her hips side-to-side with each clang then motioned them all to the center of the room. "Let's begin with a warm up. This is 'Welcome of the Snake Priestess.' Just follow along." A reedy flute serpentined out of the speakers like a cobra. Dahlia swiveled her head, added shoulders, then rolled her ribcage, finally circling her hips so that her whole rolling body undulated in rippling waves. The friends giggled and teased each other.

Next was "The Carpet Weaver's Dance." Liz wished she could just toss the unused costumes on the floor and plant herself on the couch. Her torso was more like a block than the stacked swiveling segments all the other women seemed to possess. Even Donna, who was built like an NFL linebacker, was able to gyrate, not jerk.

During "A Harem's Feast," a lively frolic with cymbals, drums and wind instruments, the music began to swirl around Liz, slowly lifting her out of her body. She might not be as fluid as Sarah, but her parts began to feel less fused. She smiled and began to relax as she jounced to the irrepressible beat.

The group merrily danced along in a bumbling jumble. "Shake it, Baby."..."Everything's moving but my hips."..."Hey Liz, try this tomorrow in the kitchen."..."Ali Baba here I come."..."It'll take more than this to get Pete wanting to open sesame my treasure cave."..."Sarah, you'd even turn on the camels."

An hour later, Dahlia packed up her music, bowed with hands clasped, and sashayed her exodus from the newly anointed desert queens. They pushed the furniture back into the usual formation and curled up for conversation.

Malia began, "Tonight made me think about how we have so little ritual in our lives. With everything changing so fast, we need rituals to ground us so we can stay in touch with who we are as a people."

Donna put her glass down, snapping her fingers as if clanging Dahlia's cymbals. "Okay, here's a ritual for ya, VooDoo Doll. My New Year's resolution is to lose twenty pounds and keep my son out of jail or the morgue, unless I put him there."

Molly said, "I want to get our photos out of the laundry basket and into albums."

Sarah concurred, "Me, too, and I'd like to make more time for my music."

"My affirmation is to meditate forty-five minutes every day, sell $20 million in real estate, and stop cleaning Steven's room," Malia offered.

After Malia, Liz knew it was her turn. She shared her already abandoned goal of doing sit-ups every morning and then, even though she always felt disloyal talking about family issues with anyone except Dan, she took a deep breath and admitted, "And I resolve to do whatever it takes so we don't lose our house."

There was silence until Donna said, "What the hell are you talking about, Red?"

"Between the economy and my stupidity, I've gotten us into a real mess. Dan's sure we'll get the Intech deal so maybe I'm being an alarmist, but there's nothing else if that doesn't come through."

Her friends appeared to have collectively lost their breath. Molly was the first to scatter the silence. "I'm sure everything will work out. Dan is so talented."

"I'll sell Pete!" Donna enthusiastically volunteered to auction off her husband. "Nah, I'd have to pay someone to take him."

Liz glanced at Malia, who picked up her wine so that the glass obscured her face as she drank. When she lowered her glass, she locked eyes with Liz. "We're here for you, Love."

"This economy SUCKS! Washington sucks. Those greedy, Wall Street bastards suck." Donna seethed.

Their outrage was a salve; it justified her feelings of victimization and helplessness, her anger. She could tell her friends wanted to keep belaboring the topic, hoping to console her while they processed the news, but she cut it off by swinging the conversation over to the posting on the town website about the level-three sex offender living on Surrey Lane. They were slow on the uptake, not wanting to abandon her, a stubbornness that brought Liz more comfort than actually discussing her troubles.

Chapter 4

"Sign in, please, Ma'am." Liz rose on tiptoe to write her name in the indicated ledger. "Who are you here to see?" "Heather White at First Insured Business."

"Your license please, Ma'am." When Liz last worked in Boston, she was referred to as Miss more than Ma'am, and you could go directly to whatever floor you were visiting. She wondered if this uniformed speed bump would next ask her to empty her purse or step in back for a strip search. Thankfully, he just handed her license back across the yacht-sized marble block with its banks of phones and video screens.

Stepping gingerly across the slick tile floor, she entered the flow along the carpet path that had been thrown down that morning to protect employees and visitors from the hazards of melted snow on polished stone. She showed her pass to the security guard stationed at the elevators, whose inert eyes indicated that there was not enough coffee in the entire building to stave off the boredom of his job.

In the narrow chute between elevator banks, dark cashmere and wool-coated figures, all sharp-edged with newness, hovered in resigned anticipation of the day ahead. When the light and chime directed the unbundling herd, they corralled below the golden 15-25 into the waiting mahogany box. As they ascended, Liz watched another innovation that had been installed since her corporate tenure as an insurance executive, a mini-television scrolling news headlines. Liz wondered how a TV located where a person spent fifteen to thirty seconds could be considered a warranted expense.

After informing the 18th-floor receptionist whom she was here to see, Liz pretended to read the *Wall Street Journal* until the summoned Heather, who was little more than half Liz's age, charged at her with a virtuoso smile and a hand outstretched like a spear. "Ms. Burgess, welcome to F.I.B." FIB an unfortunate acronym for an insurance company. "I hope your trip from Sudbury wasn't bad. Did you drive in?"

They continued exchanging snow and commuting filler as they tunneled through the cube colony warrens. Tucked behind her escort's narrow back, Liz visualized alternative cubicle configurations that would increase communication and allow for more efficient traffic flow, something she'd picked up from more than a decade of listening to Dan work with clients while she did the books and billing.

As they briskly made their way, Liz heard the absence of noise, that sanctified hush often present among the seriously self-important. She noticed only one employee wearing beige, an errant blot in the blur of black or dark blue suits.

Here was a focused enterprise in top form: F.I.B.'s artwork, mica wall sconces, $450 chairs rooted around an expansive teak table in the glassed-in conference room, all testified to the company's success. The atmosphere here was like slipping on an old suit that had been buried in the back of the closet. Even Heather seemed familiar.

Seated on the firm, upholstered seat, Liz lengthened her spine. Showtime. Senior Human Resources Manager Heather tapped a copy of Liz's resume with her perfectly manicured, power-red fingernail. "So Liz, why do you want to come back to the corporate world?"

Underneath the *I don't really want to* that tsunamied her mind, Liz heard herself say, "I would like to bring the lessons I have learned from running every facet of a small business back inside." Heather's overlarge eyes pressed on every twitch Liz might make. "It will be nice to work for a company where there is sufficient capital to fund initiatives and where you don't have to reuse the paper towels." The omniscient eyes flicked. There was no chuckle from across the desk. "The benefits are nice, too."

Heather finally smiled at Liz. "F.I.B. does offer an excellent benefits package." Then switching as quickly as if someone had pointed the TV remote at her, she angled her brows together and developed jowls. "You make it sound as though your business is struggling. Does that mean that you would leave us as soon as the economy turns around?"

"Oh no! I mean, the economy is slow, but that's not why I'm here." Liz scooched to the edge of the chair so that her feet could reach the ground. She was going to pull this off. "My husband can handle the business; my kids are older. My objective in returning to the corporate environment is to be part of a large team again." She smiled at her inquisitor. "It is very isolating working at home." Liz's palms pressed down on thighs so tense that they'd begun to quiver. "Plus, it would be great for my marriage not to be with my husband 24-7." Liz's chuckle sounded like an overdone facelift. She could not believe she was pandering to this adolescent gatekeeper.

Heather accepted this answer. "You haven't worked in a corporate setting for a long time. Do you think you can handle the pressure? The long hours?"

Liz began to raise her hand to push back her hair, but pressed it back down on her slacks. The one thing she'd learned as a kid during her very brief enrollment at Miss Nancy's Ballet School—brief, due to no money nor talent—*when on stage, do not touch your hair or costume.* She sank her tone into her commanding business range. "Running the design business demanded the same, if not more, time and discipline as my previous corporate positions."

Heather wrote something down without taking her eyes off Liz. "Mm, hmm. Well, I have to be completely honest with you, Liz; as I said on the phone, you are overqualified for this job." She pushed away Liz's resume. "I'm afraid you would be bored, and no one's best interests would be served."

Panic rose, clanging against the inside of Liz's forehead. "I understand your concerns. However, I am willing to take this step back and pay my dues again for the opportunity to work for a company like F.I.B."

Heather picked the resumé back up. Liz's breath loosened a little. "You have been a VP of Risk with sixty people reporting to you, a Senior Client Manager, and in charge of an initiative to standardize evaluative ratios." Heather's tone made Liz's accomplishments sound like liabilities. "Most recently, you have run your own company." She put the resumé off to the side and folded her hands. "I am sure you'll agree that this position is not a match for someone with your level of experience."

Suddenly, Liz recognized where she'd seen Heather before. She was the incarnation of Liz's earlier corporate self, just as committed, assured, and standardized. She displayed the typical symptoms of an affliction so often contracted within the confines of prestigious corporations, attributable to an ego swollen from inhaling the rarefied atmosphere for too long. Liz knew exactly how to deal with this executive wannabe.

"My memory wasn't erased when I left the industry eleven years ago. I'm as competent now as I was then. In fact, being a wife, mother, and running a sole proprietorship has only sharpened my organizational and management skills. If I am willing to take this position at this pay grade, you should leap at that opportunity." When Liz finished, Heather looked down and adjusted her conservatively accessorized suit.

The rest of the interview reminded Liz of a piece of bread left out on the counter overnight. The reason Liz was not going to get this job had nothing to do with her initial anxious chuckling or with her emphatic tirade. H.R. Heather had decided long before Liz rode the elevator up this morning that Liz was too old and too experienced to be an Assistant Actuarial Analyst at F.I.B. Clearly, some directive protecting the firm from lawsuits had forced Heather to schedule this interview.

During her descent, Liz's grief-stricken stomach ossified, pulling her down faster than the elevator. The security guard stood in the now deserted marble cavern. Liz looked directly into his eyes. His brows flicked up at being seen, and he nodded as he wished her, "Have a good one," in the gritty sound a voice makes when it hasn't been used much that day.

Chapter 5

Outside the F.I.B. building, sunlight vectored off towering glass and fallen snow. Plows passed, scraping metal across asphalt. It was supposed to get windy tonight, so most of what little had fallen last night would get blown away, leaving only the hardened pack from previous storms. Liz wrapped the scarf Francine had knit for her snugly around her neck.

Heading to South Station, Liz looked around at all of the people who had jobs scuttling along the sidewalks and wondered why these people had been chosen to have 401-k's, secure salaries, and company paid health plans? They didn't look any more intelligent or deserving than Dan or she. Were any of them the ones who'd said they'd call her back and hadn't? Or were they the people who had not even acknowledged receiving her resumé? The ones who treated her phone call as a nuisance instead of a communication from a fellow human being?

Her stomach churned with something that felt more like pain than hunger. It was lunchtime, but she couldn't stop if she wanted to catch the next train and make it back to change out of her suit before the kids got home. She started to run, shrugging her purse back up on her shoulder whenever it started slipping. She wished she had on sneakers instead of brown leather boots, or possessed legs longer than the pair that came standard with a 5'2" frame.

That was when the tights she'd borrowed from Francine's drawer started to slide down. The crotch, which had never been quite all the way up, was now closer to her knees than her hips and was impeding her forward progress. What was worse, the tights were dragging her underwear with them. A grab through her thick wool coat was futile. She heaved her scarf, which had come unwound in the struggle, around and over her shoulder. With her right hand she reached across her body to hold her purse strap in place. Her left dove into her coat and somewhat successfully hauled up her sagging undergarments and pinned them to her hip.

By the time she collapsed into one of the many empty seats on the Worcester line, she was a sweaty, disheveled, gasping version of this morning's groomed, professional, hopeful self. She couldn't wait to get home, out of these tights and into the shower. Too bad only Dan would hear the story of her bedraggled sprint to the train; it would've been great to hear them all laugh about it at dinner.

She squinted out the commuter train's windows, which never seemed to get any dirtier or any cleaner than blurry and were so much like looking out through tired eyes. Her phone rang. She dug it out of her purse, saw it was Dan, and waited until the conductor finished his announcement.

The train started out of the station.

"How did it go?"

She unbuttoned the coat he'd bought her because he'd loved how its "color of fields in late July" went with her red hair. Liz would have called the coat olive-colored.

"Not good. Some self-important priss decided not to hire me because I am overqualified."

"Oh." There was a pause she couldn't decipher. Then, "They'll find something that's better for you."

"That's kind of what she said, but I wouldn't hold my breath." She handed the conductor her ticket. "What have you been up to?"

"I called some friends at the design center and UNH alumni and searched job sites on the Internet, and then I went to the gym as Herb's guest. I tried a yoga class, and my body feels really loose, like I'm twenty-something." Liz couldn't fathom how contorting her body into macramé would make her feel anything but agony. "I'm going to check out some networking sites Herb told me about."

After hanging up, Liz dropped the phone into the boxy black leather purse she'd gotten at Marshall's last year, where they *Sell Brand Names for Less*. She propped the purse and her folded coat against the seat back as a bolster and took out the sleeve of the sweater she was knitting for Charles. Her stomach relaxed and growled at the thought of the food it wasn't getting. As she knit, she thought about the interview, and veins of relief plaited her unemployment fears. She really didn't want to go back to the corporate tangle. Back to the politics. Back to leaving the house at 6:00 in the morning and not getting home till more than twelve hours later.

Liz completed four rows and increased a stitch. She should be able to finish the sweater this weekend and block it next week so that Charles would still have a couple of months of winter of wear if he didn't outgrow it. Her firstborn had shot up all of a sudden, and he was eating like a rescued feral pup. They grew up so fast. She'd miss so much if she worked in Boston. She dropped a stitch and her hands fell to her lap. The truth was she didn't want to go back to being who she'd been before. This realization felt like that splinter you get deep in the bottom of your foot from scuffing across the back deck. Meeting Heather had been like seeing a reflection of her former self.

She winced at the memory of how she'd categorized her coworkers as either promoters, competitors, or minions. She'd jeered at people who'd left for a child's play and reported them if it happened more than a couple times. She'd belittled people's work in front of others if she judged it as inferior. She'd snapped at people she deemed "laggards" and was feared for her searing, "candid" reviews, a reputation she'd been proud of instead of ashamed.

She'd been a selfish, arrogant, nasty bitch. It had taken her years to reconcile ever being like that, and like any addict in recovery, she was very wary of returning to the environment where she'd been an abuser for fear of triggering the same behavior.

Liz looked up. Someone was having a coughing fit at the other end of the car. Germs, bills, taxes, broken water pump, no income, the bank...it felt like everything was out to get her. She chewed her taut lips and concentrated on her knitting. Her needles clicked; the train whirred and thumped as she repetitively looped the yarn around and through, around and through, around and through. At the top of the sleeve, she began decreasing at both sides on every row to round the shoulder. A long breath audibly released from deep in her belly. Screw F.I.B.

She cast off the sleeve from the needles and twisted behind herself to get travel scissors from her voluminous tote now propped behind her so that her feet could touch the floor. The kids used to call her mobile cupboards, "Mommy's Mary Poppins Bag" because it seemed like she was able to pull anything out of it. She said it was because she was organized. They insisted it was magic. Dan had sided with the kids at dinner, "Yep. Love is the most powerful magic in the world. And since your Mom loves you to infinity and back, tomorrow she'll probably pull a dolphin out of her bag." It'd been another of life's riddles demystified over waffles and Vermont maple syrup.

Her phone rang, and she dug for it in her magic sack. It was the water pump company asking when she'd pay them the $950 for the pump installation. Her stomach congealed into a lump of fear. Where was she going to get that money? She stowed the phone and looked out the smeary train windows. A tight, prickling sensation clenched her chest. A ponderous sigh brought no relief. Her heart began to pound faster and faster. She pulled her bag out from where it was wedged behind her and hugged it on her lap. She began to sweat, even though her coat was still folded behind her. They were going to have to sell the Volvo and become a one-car family, so they could pay for the pump.

Charles

He swung the bulging pack over his shoulder as he slid out of the seat. His sister was bumping up the bus aisle in front of him. Steven's voice called from behind, "Hey Chuck, don't forget to check out that site. The graphics are fresh."

Chuck turned and nodded to the dark-haired boy he'd been friends with since kindergarten. He stepped over a kid's leg jutting into the aisle and tossed back, "I need help in Spanish. Call ya." Steven was fluent from visiting his Colombian relatives with his mom, Malia.

Chuck stopped to check the mailbox. The mail was still there. Man, Mom was really slacking these days. Something was going on. She'd left dirty dishes in the sink all night even though the water had come back on. Usually, she didn't leave them there for five minutes before diving into the rubber gloves. And she'd bought a lottery ticket the other day, which was messed up because she'd always gone on about how the lottery was a tax on the desperate and the mathematically impaired, and how the chances of winning were so infinitesimal you'd have a better chance of seeing a manatee walk down Newbury Street. Mom was a math whiz, so she'd know.

And she was like tensed out all the time, especially around Dad. It was weird because she was all super sweet but cranked at the same time.

He dumped his backpack in the mudroom, kicked off his sneakers, and threw the mail onto the kitchen counter. Totally starved, he headed to the fridge where he stood looking, trying to figure out what he wanted.

"Charles, close the refrigerator until you've decided. You're letting all the cold out."

He answered her into the fridge, "Mom, it's winter."

"Not in here, Fresh-head. Close the door."

He quickly grabbed pickles, peanut butter, grape jelly, and milk, which he dumped onto the island before he went for bread, a knife, a glass and plate. His mother took the glass from him and poured the milk.

He looked at her with a jolt; she looked really old. There were big, black bags under her eyes. Her hair was gray at the roots. Then, he noticed she had on her bathrobe. He tried not to have the surprise in his voice, "You feeling okay?"

"Yes. Why?"

"Just asking."

There was hurt in her eyes. "Why, do I look that bad?"

Oops, this needed quick damage control. "I just thought that if you felt up to it you'd make my sandwich."

"Very funny, Wise Guy."

"You want me to go out and meet Duncan when his bus comes?"

"He can come up the driveway himself." She retied her robe tighter. "On second thought, he'd love that. That's really nice, Charles."

"I'm upstairs till then." Chuck headed up to the computer room to check out the site Steven had mentioned.

Francine was already sprawled out on the couch watching music videos on TV. He took the remote from her and turned up the sound to drown out his voice from downstairs ears. "Go easy on Mom tonight."

"You're not the boss of me, Loser. Give me the clicker and go play your stupid computer game."

"I mean it. You give her any grief and she'll find out you're French kissing Aidan Aponas at school."

Francine shrieked, "Fuck Off."

Their mother yelled up the stairs, "I heard that. You get to clean the toilets for that one, Francine. And turn off the TV."

"All right." Francine jutted her head at him with a snotty look on her face to let him know that he'd pay later.

"Francine, get down here and clean the toilets right now."

She turned off the TV and sweetly sing-songed, "Okay, Mom." To him, she hissed, "How was that? Nice enough, Shithead?"

He grinned, "You kiss Lover-boy with that trash-mouth? Blech." He dodged away and headed to the computer on the other side of the stairway.

Chapter 6

It was the middle of February. There was sure to be a battle after school for the sole remaining slice of Dan's heart-shaped Valentine's Day cake.

Liz's energy had withered after the kids had boarded the buses that morning. Maybe after she finished cleaning the kitchen cabinets, Dan could build a fire, and she could lie on the couch under a comforter for a while.

With three kitchen cupboards emptied, she'd washed the shelves and was Windexing the glass-paned doors when the phone rang. She scrambled down from her perch on the counter and picked up the receiver just before the answering machine clicked on.

"Hello, this is Connor O'Neil at Intech Human Resources. Is Mr. Burgess available?"

"Could you hold for a moment?" Her stomach ossified into a constricted lump. The man's voice was devoid of hope. She took the phone to Dan, who was reading in the library, closed the French doors and returned to the cupboards where she stood straining to hear. The call was short. Dan put the phone down on the arm of the chair. She watched him through the glass-paned doors as he stared at the hearth in front of the vacant fireplace.

With a yelp, Dan threw his head back as his body crumpled forward, collapsing his torso onto his knees. Liz watched his back heave up and down in irregular bobs pocked by ragged, gasping breaths. She became glacial. She couldn't move. She'd never seen him like this, never these crushing sobs that blistered out from his whole body. Here was the breakdown she'd feared.

Her knees loosened. She rocked forward, stumbling toward the library. Yanking open the doors, she landed on the arm of the chair and laid her chest over him, clasping her arms around him as if he were a horse in flight.

As his sobs slowed, they rocked together. He sat up, and as he did, she slid into his lap, their arms crushing their bodies together. Their rocking, now less urgent, softened into a murmur and slowly became the gentle reflection of their growing acceptance. They remained like this for a long time.

Dan finally spoke, "I can't believe this. Bob made it sound like the job was in the bag." He swallowed hard on what looked like a cannonball in his throat. "I'll call him and find out what went wrong—later." Liz tightened her hold on him. Anything she might say seemed like the wrong thing. He pulled back and held onto her shoulders. "What the hell are we going to do, Liz?"

It was so hard to know what to do. What could she tell him? This was like walking on swollen feet. You knew it was going to hurt, but you also knew that the best thing was to keep moving forward to get the circulation going again. White, hot fear obliterated all blame or frustration. This was not the time to point out that they had no client prospects. Or to criticize him for his looney moneymaking ideas. Later, she could walk across the red-hot coals of bitter choices.

"Liz? Does this mean we have to sell the house?"

"I don't know." Her voice faltered. Between every hesitant syllable glared the fact that she did know and so did he.

"I feel sick." He looked like it. "Maybe a run will clear my head."

"It's freezing rain outside."

"I'll take my chances. You'll have my life insurance if I get hit by a car."

"That's not even remotely funny and not because I don't have a sense of humor." She swallowed hard. "Do not ever say that again. We'd be nothing without you." Her voice cracked on this last word.

He gathered her into his arms. "I love you, Liz."

"We're good," she tossed out the first line in their chorus as if a buoy was attached to it.

"Always have been."

"Always will be."

"As long as we have each other." His response was rote, not earnest.

"That's all that matters." They clung together again, but this time it was with gratitude for each other, as well as desperation at their situation. They looked into each other's faces and wiped away the tears. He murmured, "Can we go to bed? I need to hold you more than I need to go for a run."

They stood. She took his hand in hers. And he followed her upstairs.

She listened to her naked husband snore under the comforter beside her. She was so wiped out that she was wired beyond sleep. She might as well go out and get the mail.

The biting drizzle drenched her before she got to the mailbox. Her private place by the pond, where she'd retreated so many times before, beckoned with its stalwart promise of peace. She checked her watch and then skate-stepped across the icy street.

Everything that didn't move had been shellacked by the freezing rain. The going was slow. Each step began balanced on top of the icy crust and then punched down through the brittle top layer into the five or so inches of snow below. Her gait was like the stuttered buckling of an elderly man. She took her hands out of her pockets and held her arms out a few inches from her body to help steady her advance.

At her crunching approach, a rafter of wild turkeys jostled away in their schizophrenic danger-run, who-cares dodge. She stopped to catch her breath and pushed back the clump of sodden hair plastered to her forehead. A rabbit darted away with such speed it registered more as movement than animal. She bent to scoot beneath the three birch trees that buckled low over the path under their icy burden, and rounded the bend.

Her boulder's rough granite had smoothed to polished stone, its frozen casing gleaming in the garish ambient light. She leaned her seat against its icy sheen to look out over the frozen pond: a white, flat, open space cut by deer and fox tracks. Squinting against the sky's colorless glare, the trees on the opposite embankment blurred into rounded, sagging silhouettes as though everything was being pulled to the center of the Earth, drooping under the weight of too heavy a burden.

She'd lose this place, too, if they moved. She closed her eyes; the freezing drizzle prickled her skin. A shiver shot through her like a riff down a piano keyboard. She noticed that the back of her throat felt scratchy. She'd probably get sick. Not that it really mattered.

She pulled her hand out of her pocket to check the time again. Her skin had gotten wet through the material of her jacket. She didn't need to meet the bus; in fact, her kids would probably rather she didn't, but given her sore throat, she should probably head home anyway.

She stepped into her footprints, making the walk back easier even though her visit had done nothing to ease her heart.

The wind had picked up, causing branches to click together and the trees to groan out their complaints about the heavy load they were being asked to bear. Occasionally, a creaking rip followed by a muffled crash signified that a tree had given up the struggle. Each time the sound was like a lash, and Liz faltered outside her frozen footstep path for a couple of strides.

Chapter 7

At 7:30 that night, the family was in the den in front of the fire, burrowed under afghans and armed with hot Ovaltine. Bassa jumped up into Duncan's lap with the attitude of a presiding moderator. The only light other than the fire and some candles was from a lamp in the turret behind them.

Liz asked, "Everyone ready for tomorrow?" She sat on the edge of a chair with her slippered feet planted on the rug.

"I still have three chapters of *Shogun* for English." Everyone other than Chuck claimed to be done.

"Well, your Dad and I called this family meeting so that I could get everyone up to speed on what's happening." Bassa, who had been kneading Duncan's legs, turned in circles and settled. "As you all know, Evergreen Designs' business has slowed down with the economy, so very little money's been coming in for more than a year. Today we found out that we aren't going to get the big job we were hoping for. So since we've gone through our savings, we need to drastically reduce our spending."

Liz consulted her notes on the yellow-lined pad of paper in her lap. "No more expensive tea, organic veggies, or juice boxes. Dan, we need to buy in bulk and start using coupons. I am going to apply for the school lunch program, and we should move the office back to the house and turn off the power out there. No new clothes unless you outgrow all your old ones and then it's sales or the Salvation Army." She glanced at Francine, whose face was as stricken as Liz had expected. "No eating out or buying food at convenience stores. Our pantry or the refrigerator are the only places to get food."

She flipped the sheet to the next page. "At the end of the month, I am going to cancel cable and all mobile phones except Evergreen's. Be double sure to turn out all the lights when you leave a room. The Volvo is sold and being picked up on

Saturday." She folded her hands. "I think that's it, unless anyone else has any ideas."

Her plan was met with stunned silence. Even Dan looked dismayed. Liz wondered if she should have been a bit gentler in her delivery. Now that everyone knew the hole they were in, the enormity of it hit her even harder. She had thought struggling through it alone was the worst. She'd been wrong. Her fingertips softly drummed on the lined pad. As the silence stretched on, her heels jounced on the floor, sending the pad dancing on her thighs. The clock bonged a quarter to eight.

Duncan started in a small voice that grew in determination. "Dad, can you build me a table for the end of the driveway?" He picked up Bassa and hugged him to his chest.

"Sure, Buddy. What's up?"

"I'm going to have a store and sell my sheet music and Legos to make money for the family." These were Duncan's most valued possessions, so he must have thought they would bring the most money.

Dan rushed to reassure his son. "That's a great idea, Big Man, but you don't have to do that. Thanks for offering though. That's very grown up."

Liz quickly added her assurances. "Honey, we're just doing these things preventatively, like taking vitamins." She and Dan exchanged a look in silent agreement that this was not the time to bring up anything about selling the house. She glanced over at Francine, who hadn't said a word. Her daughter's legs were curled up under her, her arms crossed. Her face was stern, but she was chewing on a strand of hair, something she hadn't done for a long time. Liz would've felt better if Francine had been screaming at her.

Dan interjected, "We're all healthy and have a roof over our heads and plenty of food. This is a chance to simplify and not be running all over the place."

Chuck leaned toward Duncan. "Everything's sway, lil bro." He turned to his folks. "It's not your fault the economy sucks. It'll come back. Anyway, stuff's stuff; it doesn't matter." Chuck swung his hair back with a head flick. "This is one of those character-building deals you talk about, right Dad?"

Dan responded with a smirk. "You're already such a character, any more building and you'll become some giant, glowing creature, chanting forgiveness and throwing canned food at people." Duncan laughed so hard that Bassa frantically scrambled out of his clutch. Dan clapped his hands and rubbed them together. "Well, our family sage has spoken; thank you, Chuck. Cool it on the 'sucks' though. So, everyone clear on what we have to do?" Silence. "All right then, unless anyone has anything else to say, it's time for bed or homework."

When Charles had been really little he'd asked what it would be like if there wasn't any color and then answered himself that everything would be invisible. Dan had joked that their preschooler spoke in koans, the Buddhist teaching riddles, and anointed him the family sage.

Duncan asked, "Do you guys want me to play some Mozart? Mummy, you say it always makes you happy."

Dan answered for Liz because he must have noticed that she was unable to speak. "Go for it, Buster."

Chuck said, "I'd like that, too, Dunc. Can I come in and read? *Shogun* will rock with Mr. Mo."

They were in bed, propped up by pillows. Dan was reading or at least holding the book open. He hadn't turned a page for a long time.

Having finished *The Ten-Year Nap*, which, while well-written, had hit rawly close to home, Liz turned the page in the thriller Donna had recommended. Dan asked, "How's the book?"

"Just what the doctor ordered. How's yours?"

"Okay." He put his book face down on his lap. "That family meeting was rough."

"Sorry. I should have gone a little easier."

"You said what needed to be said. I think they'd assumed that not going to the movies or out to eat was enough."

"I kept hoping things would get better, for too long I guess."

Dan pushed himself up to sit against his pillows. "Looks like it's mac & cheese or rice & beans."

"Comfort food."

"Liz, just remember that you're not in this alone. If you tell me what's up, we can work it through." He closed his book and put it on the shelf next to the bed. "I was proud of Duncan thinking of opening a store to help, but it about ripped my heart out." He turned off the wall sconce beside the headboard and slid down between the covers.

"He is amazing. And of course, Charles responded with his usual old-soul wisdom." She closed her book. "Francine was abnormally quiet. Nice change but worrisome."

Liz turned out her light and rolled onto her side so that her husband couldn't see the tears rolling onto her pillow. She worked to keep her breathing steady. At least, while everything else threatened to change, she could pretend to still be the girl who didn't cry.

Chapter 8

Liz followed Molly into the Burgess' den, where a fire was blazing in the fireplace. The reflected flames sparkled in colorful hand-blown wineglasses.

Donna was haranguing the rest of the group from one of the club chairs she'd pulled in from the great room, "...expect us to be odor-free with hair like an air-brushed supermodel." She tossed her head as if on a photo shoot. "Proctor and Gamble's brainwashed us, so now it's politically incorrect not to be hyper-sanitized. Fuck that...I only wash my hair once a week."

Molly gasped as she warmed her back by the fire. "Donna, No!"

"Yep. Over-washed hair gets greasy cuz it's stripped dry; the oil glands gush trying to protect it. Better to just rinse it and give your scalp a good hearty massage." She demonstrated, plowing her fingers deep into her thick curls. "Get the blood to the roots. Whipping up a lather afro like the ads just washes money down the drain."

Sarah nodded, "Toothpaste too, you don't need that rope they show. The brushing and flossing do the job." No one questioned this since Joe, her husband, was a dentist.

"It's the perfect analogy for our culture: we wash out our natural oils and then spend a wad of cash on conditioners to put the moisture back in."

Sarah moved her sweater to make room for Molly next to her on the love seat. "Come sit. I just threw this here when I got a hot flash. Lately, I hardly sleep; Joe either, I bury him in covers then drag them back off."

"I haven't had them after acupuncture and a snake venom remedy," Malia suggested.

"Woot, sign me up for that." Donna lustily scooped another chip into the salsa.

"It's a tiny homeopathic pill. Actually, there's no venom, only its vibration."

"Well, vibration's my cure, I masturbate every day. Get yourself one of those cute little vibrators, girls, and zzztt, no more hot flashes. The only side effect..." Donna rocked, rolling her eyes and moaning, "...mind blowing orgasms." Her grin was so wide it split her face in half. "Got mine at a great store in Brookline - 'The Grand Opening.' Love the name. Run by a couple of lesbians, figure they've gotta be experts."

Molly's mouth went slack. Liz shook her head, and Malia nodded. Sarah chortled, "Donna, you are too much."

"Argh, getting old sucks. I walk around with minipads glued in my crotch cuz if I laugh too loud or sneeze, I wet my pants." Donna was on her roll; her face conveying so much expression it looked twice its normal size.

Malia raised her glass. "Here's to aging with grace and keeping our pants dry." They all toasted.

Donna raised her glass again, "Here's to aging at all; hell, it beats the alternative. Hey, Nancy Nicholson's sister does Botox parties, she should come next month."

"That'll give us a stiff upper lip." The others groaned at Malia's bad pun.

Molly sat up straight, her eyes spritely, "I'm so excited about the animal communicator."

Liz hadn't been able to think of an activity, and this woman, Danielle, had offered a free class since Malia had sold her house above the market.

"You warned her about this crew, right?"

"Hey, she talks to animals, probably a little bird told her," Donna snorted. When the doorbell rang, Malia popped up to welcome Danielle, a tall, slender, thirty-something with a face as fresh and freckled as an Irish country lass. Dan was taking her coat and another woman's, whom she introduced as Carin. Even younger than Danielle and about as short as Liz, Carin sported over-bright blond hair elevated in a spray shellacked swell and very generous surgically enhanced boobs.

She gushed to her ambushed hosts, "Thanks so much for letting me come. Danielle, like, blew me away, said my sister's dog Rudi was somewhere beside a green lawnmower, and they found him trapped in a neighbor's garage!" She plopped down in a chair and reached for a glass with the desperation of a man too long at sea. "May I?" She was pouring herself Chianti before Liz could nod. "It's so great to get out. I have a toddler from hell, a baby girl, and a husband who's worse than the two kids combined." She sat back and tipped her glass to the room before half of it disappeared in a desperate slug.

Donna nodded, "Men suck, and maybe the animals can tell us how to train them."

Danielle, the instructor smiled, "Maybe. Anyone have an animal you'd like to talk with?"

As if on cue, Bassa stalked into the room and flopped at her feet. "Well, hello!" Danielle leaned forward and scratched under Bassa's chin. He lifted his head and shut his eyes in feline ecstasy. "Okay, let's start with this gorgeous fellow here." She passed around paper and pens. "Begin by mentally inviting the animal to talk with you. Write down whatever pops into your head, no matter how silly it might seem. Then, when you're done, thank them. I've written some questions, and we can compare what we get."

Liz sat up straight, her voice edging into panic, "I thought you were going to do it, not us."

"I am, and if you'd like, you can, too."

"Are you afraid of what puss will tell us, Mrs. Burgess?" Donna smirked.

"No, no, it's okay." Liz sighed more loudly than she intended and ran her fingers through her hair as if plowing under her discomfort.

"Won't we bombard him?" Molly asked.

"Our collective intent actually makes the connection stronger. Animals psychically communicate on many levels simultaneously, even after they've crossed over the rainbow bridge."

"What the hell's a rainbow bridge?" Donna muttered to Malia, "I see why you're friends with this one. Woo, Doo, voodoo."

Sarah threw a pillow at her. "DiFranco, shut your trap and open your mind."

Inured to skepticism given her chosen profession, peace drifted off Danielle like a signature scent as she continued undeterred, "The animals love being heard. Have fun."

Liz silently asked Bassa the first question on the paper, "How does your body feel?" She felt an itch on the back of her left ear. After the next question, Liz looked up, and Bassa was vigorously scratching his left ear with this hind paw. Too weird.

After they'd shared their responses, Donna's Akita, Nikki, was next, even though she was still at home. Danielle relayed that Nikki wanted Donna to find something in the basement. Donna complained, "Pets become way too high maintenance when they talk. Kinda takes away the whole reason to have one."

When Danielle suggested that they connect with a 120-year old crocodile named Mr. Freshy, Donna couldn't stop laughing, which escalated to gasping for breath when she found out that he'd been worshipped by an indigenous tribe in South America and retired to a zoo after recovering from being shot. They thanked Danielle, and Donna offered to drive Carin home

"That'd be great. I haven't had this much fun in, like, forever." Carin poured herself another glass of wine and snuggled deeper into the chair. "Liz, your house is beautiful."

"Thank you."

"Her husband designed it."

"That is so cool. Where'd you get that gorgeous rug? My wood floors are killing my feet."

"From a refugee Tibetan family when we were trekking in Nepal; they'd woven it. There's one from Turkey in the library, and that small prayer rug is from our honeymoon in Egypt."

"That's so cool you met the people who made it."

"It might be for sale."

"Cool."

Liz caught Malia's wide-eyed look of disbelief and quickly asked, "Carin, are you home full-time with the kids, or do you have another job?"

"I quit when I had kids. Carl's pressuring me to go back. Like my whopping minimum wage would even pay for childcare."

"It's a blessing to be able to stay home."

"Although working would be a nice escape." Carin's eyes flicked before she continued. "Carl works at home and like, makes more of a mess than both babies, although today he grabbed the mop out of my hands to show me the right way."

"You're kidding?"

Carin continued smugly, "I wonder who's the idiot though; I stood there and, like, asked questions until he'd done the whole damn thing."

"Good for you."

"He started working from home when I was pregnant with Emma, and the first day he bombed in wanting lunch, like, just opening the fridge made me want to puke. I asked if he wanted a ham and cheese or fluffernutter, and he said he wanted hot lunches."

Donna went wild. "Hot lunch? What next, a blow job while you're dusting? Whatever happened to the good old days, when men came home, had two gins, and fell asleep in front of the TV?"

"My son's just as bad as his Dad. I'm trying to toilet train the little monster, and when I was on the phone with my sister, Carl Jr. went around the corner into the dining area and shit on the floor."

"Did you tell your husband his hot lunch was ready?" Donna asked. Everyone roared except Liz, who sat there with a confused look. No one could explain since Donna veered off on a new thread, "Did you hear about the rave on Grindstone Lane while the parents were in St. Kitts? About 400 kids heard about it on the Internet. Some boy from Weston o.d.'d. I just don't get this long-distance parenting. I'm not mother of the year but at least I'm here when my kids screw up."

Liz looked around at her friends' knowing, nodding faces. How easily they condemned these people's parenting. She needed to bring some balance to the conversation. "I feel sorry for parents with careers, they seem so exhausted and stressed out." She looked at Malia, a working single mom, for some support but got no reaction.

"Hey, they chose the bigger house and exotic vacations over their kids. No one put a gun to their heads."

Sarah leaned forward for some artichoke dip, "You can't pop into kids' lives for an hour or two and really know what's going on."

Liz felt defensive. "We don't spend hours together every day, but we're really connected. I think it has more to do with being aware and noticing than with the number of the hours you're around."

"Nah, you've gotta be around to jump on those teaching moments."

"Why bother having kids if you're going to have other people raise them? So, like, you can have a picture on your desk?"

"And I love these two-income families pulling in six figures who hire some cheap nanny who can barely speak English and didn't graduate from high school to take care of their kids as they wave goodbye from their Lexus." Donna and Carin were like a debate tag team.

Liz stared hard into her wine.

"My mother always said it was easier in Vietnam." Sarah turned to Carin, "My dad met her during the war. She said women didn't have all these choices, and it was a lot simpler."

"A lot of women who come to the crisis center stay in bad situations because they don't think they have a choice." Molly had been a social worker in Kansas before moving here; now, with her step-daughters school age, she had begun volunteering at the women's crisis center.

"That's different." Donna put her glass down so she could throw her hands around as she spoke. "I just love the term 'working mother.' What the hell have I been doing, blowing runny noses, budgeting, cleaning, scheduling, driving, teaching, shopping, feeding, yada, yada, yada...Working my ass off, that's what."

"They act as though we're planted on the couch watching reality TV and mashing chocolate-covered potato chips in our mouths." Carin, again picked up Donna's rant.

"I was standing with this woman and a guy at a party, and she started talking about the economy and before I knew it I was looking at her back. Unless they want to know what teacher..." Liz tuned Donna out when she heard Dan coming back down the stairs. She shed her blanket and popped off the settee. Balancing her glass and the empty dip bowl on the tray, she escaped the frustrating yak through the French doors. Her mother had stayed home and been awful, while plenty of women with careers were great mothers. Some women were better mothers because they worked. She'd worked the first couple years of Charles' life, and he'd turned out great.

At the sound of her shutting the doors, Dan turned toward her from making himself a mug of tea and grinned. The scent of chamomile blended with the fresh zeal of their earlier basil and lime chicken. Suddenly, she felt really tired, "Are we keeping you up with our noise?"

"Nah, just couldn't sleep." He planted a kiss in her hair. "Having fun?"

Liz refilled her glass with water and squeezed in a lemon slice. "Do you think they'd notice if I went upstairs with you?"

He lightly brushed the back of her neck with his fingertips, "I would."

She kept her eyes low as she kissed him, so he wouldn't be distressed by the sadness and fear he'd see there.

Thankfully, when she returned to the den, the women had moved on to movies and the Oscar contenders. Carin looked up at her entrance, "Liz, what time is it?"

"Almost eleven."

"Oh my God, the gremlins will be up in six hours." She bolted upright and spun toward Donna, "Can we go?" The Swedish grandfather's clock began to clang out the hour, and Carin was out of the room after a hasty good-bye before it stopped tolling. Donna and Liz quickly followed her out, Liz half expecting to find a glass slipper in the mudroom.

Chapter 9

When Liz returned from saying goodnight to the others, Malia was ferrying the dirty dishes into the kitchen and rinsing out the empty wine bottles. "Oh Malia, I'll do that. It helps me wind down."

Malia shook her head, sending cascades of silver-white hair shimmying, and continued cleaning. "I'm almost done."

Liz envied how casually Malia inhabited her ample body, filling it wholly and without apology because she understood none was needed. There was none of the brittle, weary resignation so many middle-aged women embodied.

Malia dried her hands on the cotton tea towel hanging from the oven, her stack of silver bangles jangling along her arm. "That was fun tonight. Carin was 'like' 'cool.' But she's going to be in tough shape tomorrow with such little ones." She retrieved her sweater and purse from the club chair she'd pulled back into the Great Room from the den and headed for the pantry to get her coat from the antique carriage seat. "I'm sorry that you may have to sell your things."

"It's more upsetting thinking about all the money we've spent on crap over the years. If we had that money, it would mean another month, even another year in the house. Really stupid."

"I'm sorry."

Liz studied the travel photos on the wall, chewing her lip, her hand resting at the base of her throat. "Do you think you could teach me to meditate?"

Malia paused and then jammed her hands further into her mittens, "Anytime, Love." She was no doubt trying to hide her shock at this extraordinary inquiry. Liz rarely brought up Malia's interest in meditation, Reiki, or floral essences, so this request told Malia just how desperate she'd become.

Still avoiding Malia's eyes, Liz took her down-filled jacket from the hook. "I think I'll follow you out and go for a walk."

She tugged on the woolen ski hat with the ear flaps and top tassel she'd knit and pulled it firmly down on her head.

In the driveway, Malia turned to embrace her. "I love you, Lizzie."

When Liz started to pull away, Malia continued to hold her beyond the standard good-bye, hewing a crack in Liz's withholding so that she quietly admitted into her friend's shoulder, "It was hard to hear them trashing mothers who go off to work because I may have to, and it's killing me." Malia gave her an extra squeeze as she asked, "Why do people do that to each other? It's so judgmental. Didn't it piss you off?"

Malia, a divorced mother and real estate agent, released her hug but continued to hold Liz's mittened hand in her own. "No, I know that they think I'm a good mom. They were just trying to convince themselves that they've made the right choices."

Liz looked down at her foot and scuffed at some ice on the driveway. "I think most working parents would rather be home with their kids if they could."

"And a lot of at-home parents would like the chance to get out, earn some money and flex their brains. Both the at-home and work points of view are valid. Both have their benefits and their challenges."

Liz dropped Malia's hand and collapsed back against her car, crossing her arms. "I wish things could just go back to how they were."

"That can feel better because it's what you know. But, it's easy to get stuck in what's familiar. We mistake a habit for comfort, but going forward can be good, better even."

Liz didn't want something new. She wanted what they'd had. It'd been really good. What a stupid thing for Malia to say, so much for her empathy. She looked at her friend almost coldly. "Well, in keeping with going forward, could you list our house for sale, just in case?"

"Of course. Hopefully you won't need to do more than that."

"Hopefully."

"I'm curious. Why are you worried about going back to work?"

Liz listed her reasons: missing the kids growing up; feeling like she was abandoning them like her parents had; Dan thinking he'd failed. "But I think the scariest thing is that I might go back to how I was before. I like who I am now and looking back...that other me was really awful."

"What were you like?"

"Shallow, driven, all about work. I once asked a guy to do something, and he said he would but that he was on the way to be with his wife who was in the Emergency Room. I very magnanimously told him, okay, but I wanted it by the morning. Can you believe that? Nothing like: I'm sorry, how is she; or, don't give this another thought. I was horrible. It's taken me years to get over who I was in that environment."

Malia reached to clasp Liz's hand in hers again and gave it a pat. "Maybe you'll find that you have a different definition of success this time. Liz, you're at a different place in your life. Have faith in yourself. Besides, your kids won't let you get away with that."

"True." Her voice became a little stronger.

"You and Dan are doing all the right things. Something will come." Malia gave her another hug. "I love you. I'll call you tomorrow."

After Malia's car backed down the driveway and her taillights disappeared around the bend, Liz crossed the street and scurried into the woods before another set of headlights could slice apart the dark.

She followed the muted moonlit path that hemmed the pond's edge with measured steps, the old snow protesting with terse screeches under her boots. She had come outside, hoping the sharp thin air would clear her head, but instead it had only dried out the inside of her nose. She pressed a mitten over her face and exhaled moisture and warmth through her mouth.

The path continued on beside tall, thin trunks; gray ghosts rising from the white underworld as they creaked out their complaints about the cold. She passed the spot where local kids came to party. Her kids should come pick up the trash before it snowed again. Curling her fingers inside her mittens to warm them, she flinched at a loud crack from the frozen pond that flew past like an arrow.

Almost there. She saw the three birches shivering silver where they marked the last turn. Liz put her hand on a trunk angled over the path for balance.

Her rock was ashen in the moonlight, dark lines and smudges revealing its cracks and contours. Looking out over the pond, Liz leaned a hip against her igneous friend and crossed her arms. In summer, the moonshine shimmered a path across the water; tonight, it was an indistinct blur on dusted ice. Boston glowed faintly orange over the trees that toed along the pond's opposite bank. An exhaled sigh gathered in front of her face before the crystal mist dwindled into darkness.

She slid her back down the rock face into a squat, hugging her folded legs, her chin shelved on top of her knees. When would this nightmare end? What is going to happen to them? A blast of winter wind icily clawed at her and screeched onward. Dried cattails murmured nearby in the sudden rush like stunned witnesses.

She indulged herself a few of what Malia called cleansing breaths, but nothing inside shifted. She remained implacably jagged. Wearily she sat on the hard snow and laid her shoulder and cheek against the rock, which instantly bit into her skin with cold teeth. The pain cut through her confusion. Everything except the burning freeze was seared away.

A slight movement caught in her periphery. She pivoted on her haunches.

A massive buck with a rack of antlers four feet across with twenty or so points stood at the edge of the woods, not even six feet away. He towered above her as she squatted, exposed and now pinned against her rock. He was so close, she could hear his breath frosting the darkness.

Black eyes, simultaneously fierce and soft, conveyed a knowing born within the ancient forests. His gaze locked in hers.

A magnificent statue except that his ribs expanded and contracted like bellows, fanning his flaring nostrils. Her own ribs had stopped moving. A long strand of moments strung together left no temporal markers to track how long she and he were bound. Then, without ceremony, the buck lowered his head slightly and slowly swung to dissolve back into the deep.

She watched the woods long after he had disappeared. Such magnificence. It felt as if she had been seen, acknowledged, and accepted. Enchantment dusted the frosty air. There'd been no need to speak, communication had flowed naturally beyond the limitations of speech. Had Danielle bestowed this gift tonight during the animal communication class? Had a call gone out to this regal beast during their game?

The cold had sunk through to her bones. Her body trilled with a subtle shivering that quickly escalated into a teeth-rattling tremor. She rose and began jogging back along the path for about ten strides before she hurtled into a full-out sprint.

When she burst into the mud room, exhausted, her breath clawed at the air in painful gasps. This was the best she'd felt in months.

She headed up to bed, leaving the kitchen sink full of dirty glasses.

Donna

Donna stripped off the fleece pullover to no avail. Heat emanated from her core. She stepped outside into grayish daylight, fully expecting to see steam rise from her body. Sometimes being a woman really sucked. In fact, it sucked more than it didn't. What was the name of those snake mucus pills Malia went on about? Bring 'em on. She fanned her hand in front of her face to force in some coolness, then inhaled deeply, which instead of relief felt like sucking water up her nose. Her lungs expelled the frigid incursion in a series of bitter coughs.

Nikki echoed with barks from inside the storm door. "I'm comin', Girl." Donna ducked back inside and grabbed the leash from its peg. The dog jabbed Donna's hip with her nose. She responded by vigorously rubbing Nikki's head and sighed.

She felt old, used up, worn out. She felt irrelevant. She didn't recognize the "stars" in the grocery store tabloids anymore or understand this new OMG talk or even like the music. No longer full of zip, she had to push through a solid wall of fatigue just to get through the day. But she could do it; grit was in her blood. Her great-granny's husband had been killed by the White Russians in the revolution, and the family matriarch had strapped her two kids on her back and pulled a loaded cart over the Urals. Even in her nineties, if anyone tried to help her, the old Slav would proudly pound her withered chest and proclaim, "Strrrr-ong like bull!" This thought provoked a wry smile as Nikki galloped ahead thrilled to be outdoors. Donna called her back to her to clip on her leash.

Liz was stubborn, too. Maybe she'd swing by Liz's house later and pretend to be on a rampage about menopause or Franco or something and bring some soup over. She'd keep watch over her friend. After all, she, Donna, was strong like bull. She had to be.

"My life sucks, Girl." Nikki padded alongside: head high, chest thrust, eyes alert. "The kids don't need me. Pete's a fucking ghost. Haven't seen his dick in months. I could run around the house naked with peacock feathers stuck in my ass, and he wouldn't notice." She reached down and soundly thumped the thick fur on Nikki's massive back as they walked. Anything she and Pete had together was gone. And she didn't know why.

It all felt too raw, too big a knot to begin unraveling. The anger that had driven her since she was a kid leapt higher, fed by the shelter of her defenses.

They turned onto Guzzle Brook Drive, beginning the loop back home. The large suburban homes installed within ample tracts of snow-covered lawns silently watched them pass. The bottom of Donna's feet scuffed up the sanding truck's gravel. She quickened her steps. Maybe she'd pop in on Carin this afternoon after Liz's. She reminded her so much of herself at that age: strong, prickly, using humor as a shield.

It was exhausting always being the warrior. Always to be so strong...so angry. But when you have been one way for so long, it becomes impossible to imagine another way to be. If she wasn't angry, she would probably disappear.

Chapter 10

It had taken Liz about half an hour to get to Bernie's Automotive Supplies. She was waiting for Bernie in a narrow room behind the showroom that smelled of dust, mildew and oil. The coffeepot on the card table was stained from countless brewings. A handful of hard plastic seats, their backs pressed up against opposite walls, faced off from only a few feet apart. At one point, a tall man came in to get two doughnuts from the box on the table. Other than that, Liz had been alone since the salesman had deposited her here and gone to get the boss.

She flipped through a copy of *Field and Stream*. Bernie was already 25 minutes late for their appointment. She was half reading the reprint of an editorial by Theodore Roosevelt that the magazine had originally published in 1927, when someone aggressively twisted the doorknob.

"Let's go," was more of a growl than a request. She followed a bulk she assumed must be Bernie down the hall, past the open door of a darkened restroom that reeked of the cheap liquid hand soap so popular with gas stations and fast food chains. He abruptly turned into an office. His swivel chair groaned and the coasters squeaked as he sat down behind his cluttered metal desk and motioned her to a chair exactly like the one she'd just left.

"What makes you think you can be an office manager?"

Okay, so he was getting right to it. She fought not to wince at his thinning, greasy hair, improbably dark and combed sideways over his scalp. "Fifty people reported to me when I worked in the insurance business," Liz began. "I managed budgets and increased business 125% in one year. Most recently, I've been the office manager at a small company where I ordered office supplies, billed clients, did the scheduling, marketing, accounting, and trouble shooting, as well as oversaw all technology acquisitions."

"Yeah, but why do you think you can do this job?" His blotchy, puffed face looked like a baby's rash-covered butt with eyes.

Determinedly, Liz connected the dots for her potential boss. She reiterated the skill sets mentioned in the ad and explained how her experience qualified her to fulfill them.

Powdered sugar from one or more of the doughnuts liberally speckled his beach ball belly. "Your only experience is in insurance and architecture. We sell auto supplies, not some white-collar bullshit. This is real work. Inventory-driven. If our customers don't get what they need, they lose money, we lose them, and I lose my shirt."

"Whatever you need done, I can do it."

"I decide that, and I don't think so. You aren't qualified for this job." He pounded his desk. Liz was sure that if she pushed back his pudgy face a Pez would pop out. "I don't know why you applied or which idiot thought you should come in and waste my fucking time."

Well, if he hired idiots, he was right; she didn't qualify, but why did he feel she wouldn't be able to answer the phone or order coffee and paper clips for a four-person business? The pathetic truth was that if he'd hired her, she would have gladly worked for this lumbering tyrant so that she could support her family.

Reeling from the revelation of how far she had sunk and how powerless her desperation had made her, she clutched the chair, paralyzed, staring at this barbaric troll. After shuffling through some papers on his desk and dialing the phone, Bernie noticed that she was still sitting there. He scowled at her, then spun his chair to face the filing cabinets while yelling into the receiver, "Kevin. Where the hell are the 20-47s? What the fuck are you assholes trying to do to me? I've got customers..."

His harangue pushed her up from the chair and down the hallway. In the parking lot, her hands shook as she pressed the key's button to unlock the car door. Her stomach clutched as if Bernie had kicked her hard in the gut. Her leg trembled as she pressed the gas pedal. Focusing every nerve fiber, she concentrated on backing out and going down Route 9. Pulling abruptly into a Super Stop & Shop, she cut the ignition.

Shoppers pushed carts and unloaded their groceries. Her cheeks felt warm, and she realized she was crying. She collapsed, her forehead pinned to the steering wheel, overcome by a grief so bruised and swollen it bled out from her body in snot-running sobs. All of her senses collapsed inward so that her primal wailing bleated against the inside of her skull. Drool strung down into a puddle on her pant leg. She didn't move to wipe her mouth.

When she lifted her head for air like someone drowning, an older woman glanced nervously at the movement inside the car and hurried past with her head down. Liz closed her eyes, flailing her head from side to side as if to banish the sight of the woman's fear, but the suffering was inside.

Thoughts began to come unbidden from some black, subliminal place. *She could stab her travel scissors into the soft underside of her wrists. She could go home, draw a warm bath and slide beneath the surface, sucking the water deep into her nose. She could accelerate around the parking lot and slam into the store's gray cement wall.*

Bleak temptations.

She could not be trusted with silverware tonight. She could get bottles of aspirin and vitamin water in the grocery store and empty them into her stomach. She allowed a hollow, macabre sneer at the irony of health aides dispatching death. In a way they would be the ultimate cure all, definitively ridding her of this pain. This deliberation slowed her sobbing as if it offered a plausible course of action to be considered.

The air in the car had become cold. She dragged the sleeve of her wool coat across her face, then turned the key in the ignition, the hard plastic cool against her thumb and forefinger.

Going home was not an option, so she drove for Malia's like someone possessed. She'd take the Mass Pike instead of Route 20, so she couldn't swerve into oncoming traffic.

Chapter 11

The light blue ranch looked as if it had shrunk trying to get away from the cold. The snow squeaked bitchily underfoot as she strode to the back door that everyone used except for UPS and FedEx. She stood on the step, but before she could knock, she noticed Malia in the sunroom in sitting meditation, so she walked into the backyard and dropped onto the snow-covered garden bench.

As she watched, Malia's stillness suffused through her as if a cord brokered the distance between them. She felt her tension give way to an uneasy resignation and then to a kind of arbitrated tranquility. When Malia finally opened her eyes, they widened in surprise. Hastily hoisting herself up from her floor pillow, she pointed Liz toward the kitchen door.

"Liz! You must be freezing! What are you doing out here, Love?" Her concern was gentle, cautious. She ground Colombian beans she'd brought back from visiting her family and set the coffee to brew. "I was just sending you some healing energy during my meditation."

"I think I got it."

"Lovely."

"I really needed it; the interview did not go well, and after...I was having some very scary thoughts."

"You were?"

"About hurting myself."

Malia froze for a moment, holding the empty mugs, and looked intently into Liz's eyes. "Thank you for choosing to come here." She continued making the coffee but now it was with an earnest focus.

Liz began to shake again as it registered that she was now safe; an inner wind howled through her mind, and Malia's kitchen started to dissolve. Malia was next to her, her arms around Liz's waist before Liz's knees let go, guiding her to the wicker settee in the sunroom where she tucked her into pillows and a comforter. Liz closed her eyes until she heard Malia return with the coffee.

"Here you go, Love."

"Thank you, Malia."

"No. Thank you." A long silence followed that was neither comfortable nor uncomfortable.

They slowly sipped their coffee until Liz softly said, "The guy was an absolute putz. Said I'm not qualified to work in auto parts."

As Liz replayed the interview, Malia tucked her feet up under her in the rattan chair, swept her hair up into a diaphanous white, silver-gray swirl and secured it with two clips. Malia's brusque response was, "Well, I don't like to judge, but the man is clearly a moron with self-esteem and anger issues and no doubt a teeny-tiny penis." She grinned when Liz smiled and then promised, "And I won't be magnanimous and say that it's probably better that you're not going to work for him because I know how badly you need a job. But how he treated you was abominable. I am so sorry, Liz."

"Thanks." Liz gave her a little lopsided grin, "I love how you say the word, abominable. It sounds so lovely in your accent."

"Well, he wasn't lovely, so how about 'he sucked'!" They both chuckled morosely. "Do you want me to call Dan to let him know where you are?"

"That'd be great."

Malia returned and informed Liz that she'd left a message. Liz raised her head up off the pillows but dropped it back down into the downy cradle. Staring up at the wood rafters, she moaned, "Malia, what have I done to my family?" Her voice thinned like a taut wire. "I totally messed everything up. And then, my pride and fear kept me from asking for help." She spun up to sitting still swathed in the comforter with her feet square on the floor. "I blew the investments. Now, I can't get a job." Her knees bounced up and down. "I should have done anything except what I did."

"Your family is fine. Look at them when you go home. Really take in their health, their beauty, all of the love. They are thriving, Liz."

Liz took another sip. The coffee softened the lump in her throat. She set down the mug and repeatedly pushed the palms of her hands down her thighs as if wiping them off on the blanket. Frustration with herself and with the world chafed her tongue, so it felt swollen, too big to fit the words and so she mumbled, "I cannot believe I was having thoughts like that."

With soft-eyed acceptance, Malia opened her hands in her lap toward Liz. Liz knew that she was probably shooting healing energy at her, but she didn't scoff. Today she'd take any help she could get, no matter how dubious. She stopped rubbing her legs and held onto her knees, distractedly squeezing them in an arrhythmic pulse.

"Why don't you call your doctor and see about some meds to help get you through this? You're under incredible stress, plus you're menopausal and not sleeping, and you have teenagers; a sure fire recipe for the reaction you've just had." Malia took a deep, slow breath. She reached across and handed Liz a tiny, brown bottle with a bright yellow label and black rubber dropper bulb. "It's a floral essence blend called 'Rescue Remedy.' I can't get through a closing without it. Put three drops under your tongue."

"Thank you." Desperation and trust colluded to precipitate Liz's unquestioning application of this New Age elixir. She leaned back into the pillows still holding her mug in her lap, her fingers wrapped around its warmth. "If it were just Dan and me, we'd go live on some South Pacific island until things turned around. But the kids...it's so awful. Duncan refuses to take piano lessons anymore. Charles was limping because he didn't want to ask for bigger shoes." She reached over and placed her mug back on the table. "I feel like we're careening to oblivion." Liz rolled her lips against each other between her teeth; her balled hands squeezed at the comforter as her eyes darted around the room. "Everything is completely out of control."

"I understand." Malia's body, her eyes, her whole being was a welcome refuge where Liz's feelings could rest.

"When will this end?"

"In order for it to manifest, be really clear about what you want to happen."

"I don't know what I want except for it all to go back to how it was."

"Until you know, you can just ask for your family's highest good."

Liz sighed and stood up. "Thanks for everything. I feel a lot better. I think my highest good right now is to head home and lie down."

Chapter 12

When Liz got home from Malia's, Dan wasn't there, with no note on the counter. She scrunched her eyebrows and lips as she shed her outer layer of coat, hat, and boots and tried to puzzle out where he could be. He didn't have a car, and his running shoes were in the mudroom. The only message on the machine was the one from Malia.

After such a grim morning she just lit a couple of candles, avoiding the frustration of trying to light a fire. She put the phone on the floor next to the love seat and crawled under the comforter they called The Puff to lose herself in an English mystery set during the Napoleonic Wars. Bassa kept her company curled on the red fleece by the fireplace. All was silent except for the hum of appliances and the intermittent clicking on of the heat. She was in the middle of a titillating scene involving a garden hedge, a lowered bodice, and a roving tongue, when the phone rang.

But the voice that greeted her wasn't Dan's. "Hey Liz, I need your help!" Carin's voice was muffled under whirring road noise. "Carl gave me $7,500 for an Oriental, and I've been scouring rug stores for, like, the last two days but nothing's anywhere near as cool as yours. Have you decided to sell it?"

Liz almost dropped the phone. She excitedly wriggled her fingers, drumming them on top of the comforter as her mind raced. If they sold the rug to a store at some point, they'd only get wholesale not the retail price, but she hadn't seriously considered selling it yet. Carin continued undeterred, "If you'd like to, I could stop by and pick it up."

"I could drop it off tomorrow." That way she could check with Dan tonight.

Carin's voice nervously skipped faster. "I really need it today. Carl's boss and wife are coming to dinner tonight, and I have orders from him to get a rug, and I haven't like done the grocery shopping or cleaned." Carin's voice tightened with panic. "I'm desperate, and your rug is really sweet. Please, Liz?"

She should talk it over with Dan, but this was a lot of money. Carin had to have it today; her husband probably wouldn't be interested after the dinner with his boss. Too big a risk to take. They needed this money to buy them more time.

"Sure. That'd be fine."

"Oh, I am so excited! Thank you, you've saved my life. I'll turn this bus around and be there in like fifteen minutes."

"Could it be more like an hour?"

"You bet. Perfect. I'll get the food first."

Perfect? Liz didn't think so. Dan would flip out if she sold the rug without asking him. Hopefully, he'll come back soon. But what if he came back while they were carrying out the rug? Her stomach flipped. This was a nightmare. And a dream come true.

The phone was still in her lap. She picked it up and left a message on Herb's machine, then she tried their neighbors the Uppingtons and the town library. She couldn't imagine where he was.

She called Malia, blurting out, "Hi again, it's me. I'm fine. But Malia, I just told Carin I would sell her the Tibetan rug."

"What?" Malia's shock made Liz feel even worse.

"I had to. She offered me more than two mortgage payments. Dan is going to flip out."

"He doesn't know?"

"No. I can't find him. Carin has to have a rug today, and his crazy schemes aren't bringing in any money. He's making me nuts."

"He's trying to help." Malia cautioned. "Dan's creative and optimistic, which also means he schemes and dreams. We all act within the arc of our personality. The two sides of our soul's equation have to balance, so our behavior's consistent even when it's not ideal. Condemning people for that is like the woman who marries an executive because he's ambitious and makes a lot of money and then is upset because he spends all his time working."

"Fine, but where is he? Argh."

"Would you like me to come over and help with the rug?" She must be worried about Liz being alone because of this morning's suicidal thoughts.

"I'm fine."

"Have you called the doctor?"

"I'll call my GYN, and Donna for the name of the shrink she took Franco to that time."

"Great. I'll call back after dinner to see what they say. Do you have a paper and pencil? Here's the number of my acupuncturist..."

After they hung up, Liz decided it'd be more helpful to call her old employer Mutual Benefit about a job before calling the doctors. She asked for Ted Norton, who'd reported to her fifteen years ago and was now a V.P. "Hi, Ted. It's Liz Burgess. How are you?"

"Liz! It's been ages. How are you?"

"Fine. How are you?" Liz carried the phone upstairs to her bedroom as they spoke in case Dan came home during the conversation. She paced around the bed, clutching the phone as if it were a ferret that might escape.

"Great. You still running your husband's business out there in the 'burbs?"

"For now. Although that's why I am calling. I'm looking to get back into insurance full-time." She plowed on without pause so that she wouldn't lose her nerve. "You have anything I could do?"

"I'd love to have you here. Unfortunately, we have a hiring freeze. I'll see what I can do though. There's no doubt that we could definitely use you. Just politically it will be tough; the freeze..."

She interrupted his uneasy explanations. "Ted, I totally understand. Seems that way everywhere. If things change, could you let me know?"

"Absolutely. You'll be my first call. That's great that you're thinking of coming back."

"Thanks, Ted. I appreciate that."

"No problem. Call me if you're ever in town."

"Absolutely. Thanks, again." Liz clicked off the phone, tossed it onto the mattress as she sat down and flopped backwards. Sighing loudly, she stared at her bedroom ceiling, a scream starting to build until the doorbell sliced it down to a loud moan. She sat up and with curled fists punched down into the bed to launch herself up.

"Hi Liz! I am so excited. If I remember it right, your rug is like the best."

Liz led Carin into the den. "I was thinking we could lend it to you for tonight, and you could see if your husband likes it."

"He wants a rug there - or else. He'll kill me if I don't get one." She clapped her hands. "Yes! It's even better than I remembered. Oh, this is such a relief!" She opened her purse, pulled out her checkbook and pen and went over to an end table to fill it out. "Here you go. Thank you so much. You've saved my life."

Liz silently added—and perhaps ended my marriage. They rolled up the hand-woven treasure and loaded it into the back of Carin's black Lincoln Navigator SUV, the mammoth vehicle easily swallowing the large carpet. The whole time, Liz had an eye out for Dan, feeling more like she was stealing the rug than selling it and wondering how she'd explain what was going on if he showed up. When Carin pulled out of the driveway, she began to breathe again with the knowledge that the end—a very large check—justified the means. Liz rushed inside for her bag and furtively jumped into the minivan, heading for the bank as if she was peeling away from the scene of a crime.

Chapter 13

Liz was back on the couch trying to read her novel when she heard the back door open. Not even tearing bodices or galloping midnight escapes had been enough to hold her attention while she worried about how to tell Dan about the rug. She vaulted to her feet; Bassa scrambling as the comforter and book went flying. "Where have you been?"

He was still in the pantry taking off his coat when he turned his twinkling eyes toward her. "Herb took me to the gym as his guest." He moved toward her with his arms wide for a hug. "I have great news, but how'd the interview go?"

"I was worried; you didn't leave a note."

"Sorry, I rushed out." His arms dropped to his sides.

"What's the good news?" She'd better cool the inquisition.

"Oh, yeah! Pamela, the owner of the F. Scott Gallery, was in yoga, and we got talking, and she wants to hang one of my paintings."

"Dan, that's great! How much is she going to sell it for?" From his face it was obvious that she should have just congratulated him and not asked about the money.

"She hasn't seen it yet."

"Right. That's really exciting."

"So, how'd the interview go?"

"Not good. The guy thought..." The phone trilled, and Liz lunged for it in case it was Carin.

"Greetings, Mrs. B." Donna. "How's it hangin'? Anything looser than yesterday?" Liz was perplexed, thinking this referred to her life until it registered that this was Donna, and her inquiry probably had more to do with her boobs or buttocks.

"Hi Donna." Liz turned on the faucet and began filling the tea kettle.

"Are you going to the school board meeting tomorrow night? I am so bullshit they're cutting art and music."

"Mmm."

"Franco would be a drug addict without art. Even if these kids become accountants, playing the flute will make them better CPAs."

"They probably define academics as reading, writing and arithmetic for budget reasons." She knew firsthand the stress of trying to balance a budget and falling short.

"We have budget issues cuz school administrators pay themselves too much, and the teachers' union has us strapped with insurance and pensions."

"But we have to pay them."

"What about the kids? And our future? How will we end war if there are no great tenors to stir our passions? We need to be inspired to evolve. If guys can't burn off their testosterone on the football field..."

"What the...?" Dan had gone into the den. "Where's the rug?"

"Donna, I've got to go."

"Okay, Mrs. B. Later."

Liz hung up and hurried in for damage control. Dan was pointing to where the rug used to be. "Why are you getting the rug cleaned when we have no money?"

"It's not getting cleaned." Her tone had become bitingly indignant with his accusation. "I sold it to Carin. The money will cover a couple months of expenses."

"What! You sold the rug? Without talking to me?" He started ticking points off on his fingers, "We bought it in Nepal...over tea...from the people who made it...in their home. I can't believe this. What the fuck, Liz?"

"Tough times call for tough decisions. We really need money, and a buyer popped up who would have bought something else if I'd hesitated. To anyone with half a brain that spells sell."

"Oh, so now I have half a brain? Is that why you've been treating me like the family moron?"

"You're not a moron." The connections he was making weren't logical. His reaction was way overblown. Couldn't he see reason? She'd had no choice. "Dan, I had to sell it."

"Can we get it back?"

"No. I cashed the check."

"What? Without talking to me? Selling the rug may be logical, but it was wrong to do." Something shifted on his face. "Are you punishing me?"

She hadn't considered that. Had part of her done it as some kind of passive-aggressive jab? She scrambled to recover. "We haven't made money for twenty months! We're crushed under a mountain of debt. Bill collectors call at all hours." Her voice dropped an octave. Her jaw froze, forcing the words out through rigid lips. "I cannot take it anymore."

"Well, I can't either. Again with the not talking to me."

"I tried to find you. You didn't leave a note."

He walked away from her. "What's going on here?" His words skidded back at her. "This sucks. What the fuck?" He rammed his body down into one of the den chairs, his hands massaging his knees as if they were sore. His voice became a rasp, which hardened as he continued, "What's happening, Liz? We talked about everything. We were partners. Now, I don't even know who you are."

With every sentence, their voices were getting tighter and louder. Liz paced back and forth in front of where Dan was sitting. Suddenly, he jumped up and held her by the shoulders, shaking her slightly with the intensity of each word, "Screw the money. Since freakin' college you've lectured me about trust and communication and honesty. What was that, just a bunch of bullshit?"

She abruptly circled her arms outward to break his hold. "No! I have been trying to protect you."

"What am I—four?" He made his voice mockingly singsong and pranced his fingers around in the air as if working marionettes. "Who do you think you are, the all-powerful Oz, controlling everything from behind the curtain?" Then he stood up straighter to say in a deep voice, "It's not possible, Liz. When you try to control everything, everything controls you."

"I am trying to save this family and our home, Dan. We have no money." Her voice was petulant, shot through with impatience; she could tell he read it as sanctimonious condescension. "If we do not get money fast, we are going to lose this house." As she said this last bit, she stomped her foot and pointed at him, then her head popped back a little in surprise with the realization that she was rubbing his face in exactly what she'd hid from him for months, but it wasn't enough to stop her, all her silent frustrations madly shoved at each other in the rush to be the first to jump out of her mouth and be heard. "An opportunity for some cash came our way." Anger swirled hot on, her tongue searing her words. "It would have been stupid not to grab it."

"Stupid, again?" His pitch was nearly falsetto.

"Argh. You know what I mean."

"There had to be other options."

"No."

"So says you. But you are not always right, Liz."

Defensiveness tasted like bile in the back of her throat. His accusation had skidded too close to her own self-recriminations. She repeatedly slapped the back of one hand down into the palm of the other. "Here was a way I could keep the family afloat for awhile just by selling a thing, which, I might remind you, you said was an investment when we bought it."

"Well, that 'thing' was a part of our history. Part of who we are. I know you pride yourself on not being sentimental, but a little emotion once in awhile, Liz, would be nice." An animated silence sparked the space between them. Dan barreled on, either in hopes of burying what he'd just said under a torrent of words or because he was as much at the mercy of his emotions as she was now a pawn of hers. "First, you don't tell me anything, now you do this. I know we don't have any income, but this involves both of us." At "both of us" he pointed back and forth between the two of them in rapid succession, and then, with each next syllable jabbed his finger towards her, "Not just you."

"So, what would you suggest we do, Dan? Sell the lawn? Cut down trees? Bake bread and sell it to the neighbors? What's your next brilliant idea? Set up a face-painting booth in front of the house?" Dan walked over to the fireplace, put both hands on the mantle and leaned over to look into the dark space, every muscle tensed. She pounded on, hurling spiky words with poisoned tips. "We need money, Dan, not pie-in-the-sky fantasies. While you sit around and dream up ridiculous schemes, I had to do something."

Dan spun around, clapping his hands together; his face red and swollen. "That's bullshit. I've been working my ass off to get business for Evergreen, and you know it." He ticked his points off on his fingers again. "Plus I have to keep everyone up and happy. I do the shopping and cook. I wrack my brains to come up with something, anything, I can do to get us out of this mess. I hardly sleep." He threw his hands down and walked away from her toward the turret. "Sure some of my ideas won't work, but at least when something pops into my head, I run it by you. I don't sneak around behind your back. You didn't tell me about what was going on until we were so screwed that it'll take a miracle to get us out of it, and I'm supposed to be all calm and happy like always. The whole thing is such complete and total crap. And I am sick of it." He rounded, walking rapidly back toward her. "If you're not happy with me then talk to me about it!" He hit himself in the chest on "me" and they glared at each other.

Liz sat down, slumping her shoulders against the back of the chair. She crossed her arms, and Dan threw his into the air and stormed from the room. "Fine, don't talk to me. I'm going for a run. No, I'm exhausted—a walk. Damn it, I'm out of here."

After he left, Liz went from room to room on the first floor, abruptly adjusting things that were out of place and punching pillows. She considered calling Donna to vent, but Donna was much better at ranting than listening. Malia would only get more worried after what Liz had shared with her this afternoon. Calling her mother-in-law, Elaine, when she was like this would upset Dan's mother more than it would calm Liz down. So she

Running to Stay Upright

kept punching pillows. The kids would be home soon, and she could bury herself in their noise.

Chapter 14

That night the candles were lit as always even for scrambled eggs on a Wednesday. Dan told them all about his futile efforts in yoga that afternoon, spinning it into a hysterical contortion story that ended with the instructor having to extricate him out of a pose. In an effort to mend things with Dan, Liz told the kids, "Your Dad hooked up with a gallery owner at yoga, and they're going to sell one of his paintings."

"That is awesome."..."Good job, Dad."..."Cool!"

In celebration, Duncan chirped, "Let's play Sparkle!"

"Oh Dad, do we have to? We play that stupid spelling game every night," Francine whined.

Liz snapped, "Francine, it is not stupid."

"Argh! Why can't we just eat when we're hungry in front of the TV like Britty's family? They're going skiing at the Balsams for winter vacation; all we do is stay here and play Sparkle." The light mood quickly excused itself, and a dark scowling presence took its place at the table.

"Shut up, Idiot," reprimanded her older brother.

"Don't call me an idiot, Turd." Then even louder at Liz, "And don't call me Francine, I hate it. You think you're such a great mom, and you don't even know I want to be called France." She stabbed a finger roughly in her brother's direction. "And he wants to be Chuck, not Charles, like he's English royalty or something. You're so stiff. You have no sense of humor. Why don't you ever lighten up?" Her features crunched into the middle of her face. "My friends are afraid of you, you know."

Liz felt like her chest was a sieve with icy water pouring through. Her eyes darted around the room afraid to land. "No, I didn't know that."

"Francine, stop! Your mother's been running around all day to interview for a job she'd hate, for us."

"Did she get it?" Duncan't face brightened.

"No," Liz confessed.

Francine muttered, "See, she couldn't even do that."

Before his daughter could stand all the way up with her half empty plate, Dan bellowed, "Sit. Back. Down." Francine's quick plunk back down into her chair was followed by a heavy pause, then Dan's emphatic, "I never want to hear any of you ever talk to my wife like that again. Francine, you are acting like an ungrateful, selfish brat. Don't you ever treat your mother with anything but the utmost respect. Am-I-Clear?" Stunned silence rushed in behind the novelty of their father's raised voice.

"I'm sorry." Francine whimpered, dismayed and contrite.

They pretended to eat for awhile; the eggs becoming rubber in Liz's mouth. Chuck mumbled, "Mum you can call me whatever you want. Geez, you named me."

After an eternity of the silverware's clink and scrape, Dan finally said, "Anyone who is done is excused." Liz was the first one to move. She robotically took her plate to the counter and went up to her bedroom.

Without turning on a light, she pulled back the covers from her pillow, rolled onto the bed, and stared at the dark ceiling, wiping the tears with the flat of her hands. Malia had said that if you follow anger down, you'd find either fear or sadness, and Liz had been having both of those in such extremes that they were leaving bits of herself dripping down the walls.

When had her daughter—whom she'd taken into Boston for tea at the Ritz, sung with in the car on the way to pottery class, and held sobbing when not invited to a party—become so estranged? She pointed her feet, stretching her toes, and then coiled her body into a fetal curl with her fists tucked in at her chest. Why hadn't Francine defended her? Did she dislike her that much? Liz froze: Did Francine feel the same way that Liz had about her own mother? Panic and grief flashed red inside her head. Liz's self-image morphed into the stone-faced witch Francine's friends must see. She rocked back and forth. Was she that formidable? That awful?

This was ridiculous. This wasn't solving anything. A couple more hours and she could go to bed, but now there were things to be done. She got up and headed to the top of the stairs and stopped at the sound of anguished voices in the great room below. She heard a fork clatter onto a plate. "I'm so sorry, Daddy."

"I know, Honey. We're going through a tough time right now. Everyone's under a lot of stress."

Francine's sobs were making it hard for her to talk between her serrated breathes. "I cause all the trouble. You guys would be better off without me." The hairs on Liz's arms rose as she heard her daughter unknowingly echo her parents' self-destructive threats.

"We wouldn't be us without you, Pixie girl. You're just growing up and that can be really hard. We understand. Why don't you go up and give your Mom a hug?"

"You think it's okay?"

Liz turned and quietly scurried back into her room. She shut the door, turned on the lights and headed for the bathroom to splash water on her face.

At Francine's knock, Liz called out for her to come in. Liz saw Francine notice the dented pillow and rumpled comforter. "Mummy, I am so sorry. I'm so mean." They came together and hugged, then with her arm around her daughter's shoulders, Liz eased them over to sit on the edge of the bed.

"Francine—I mean France—you aren't mean. Everyone says things they wish they hadn't."

"It just came out."

"I did the same thing to your Dad this afternoon." Liz stroked her daughter's hair, not reacting to Francine's surprised expression. "I'm still learning, too, but I can't read your mind. I had no idea you wanted to be called France. Are your friends really afraid of me?"

"Mmm, some of them."

"Well, I'll talk to Malia about how to be more warm and fuzzy. Maybe I'll wear an apron and bake some cookies."

"Ugh, Mom, just be yourself."

"You sure?"

"Yea...but cookies would be nice." She grinned.

"Keep reminding me to call you France. It may take me awhile."

"K"

"I love you, France." Liz gave her a squeeze. "Is it all right if I still call your Dad, Dan, or does he have a secret name, too?"

"It could be B.M. for Big Man." They giggled lightly.

"Duncan would love the bathroom humor." She gave her daughter a kiss on the top of her head. "How much homework do you have?"

"I did most of it in study hall, but I have a chapter of Social Studies."

"Well, I'm going to take a hot bath, and then how about a game of Five Crowns when you're done?"

Liz started the tub and went downstairs to make some tea. Dan was loading the dishwasher. In a low voice she said, "Thanks for sending France up." He nodded, focused on the dishes. "Where are the boys?"

"Chuck is on the computer, and Duncan is..." He pointed to Duncan's secret place, a crawl space under the bedroom staircase.

Liz's eyebrows shot up. "Is he okay?"

"I think he'd like to talk to you." Dan's face looked as though it'd been turned inside out. Alarms went off in her chest.

She knocked on the small door hidden in the library wall. When Duncan answered, she scooched down to address her youngest son. He was buried in pillows and blankets and holding KoKo, the stuffed gorilla he'd had since his crib. She crawled into the battery-powered glow and shut the panel behind her. He looked very small, his face stricken. "Mommy are you dying? Is that why they didn't give you the job?"

"No! Duncan, why would you think that?"

Trying to be his most grown-up, he ticked his reasons off on his fingers like his Daddy did. "You go upstairs without doing dishes—a bunch. You were in your bathrobe after school the other day. You didn't close the garage door. And Daddy just got a phone call about you and sounded really scared."

"Sometimes the most convincing evidence can lead us to the wrong conclusions, Pumpkin. Mommy just needs some sleep, that's all. You know how you feel when you're tired, and then the next morning everything is fine?" She pushed back Duncan's bangs and kissed his forehead, wondering what call Duncan was talking about. "Could you play the piano for me? I'll be able to hear it during my bath."

Duncan sat up, brightening, "What should I play?"

"Anything."

He pushed open the wall panel, "I'll play Mozart; you always like that." Duncan crawled out of his cubbie and fairly skipped over to the piano.

What phone call?

Dan wasn't in the kitchen. She checked with Chuck who was on the computer. Dan wasn't in the den, either. She jogged up the stairs to check on her bath when Dan's voice came from their darkened bed. The tub had been turned off. "Liz, Malia called. Are you okay?"

"Yes."

"She said you were thinking about hurting yourself after the interview."

She crossed to where he was sitting on the bed and saw the tears on his cheeks reflected in the light coming from behind her. She framed his face in her hands, wiping away his tears with her thumbs. "A lot of it was hormones. It all just got to me."

"You see how much the kids need you—and me? How I can help? Just ask. Anything."

She sat next to him. "I'll try; old habits die hard. When I was a kid, I had to keep it all in."

"I know." He wiped his face dry with both hands. "But don't you know by now that you can count on me?"

"Yes," her voice was barely a sigh as she stared desolately at the floor.

"You told me not to even joke about ending my life."

"Yes." She crossed her arms, running her hands up along her triceps to hang from her shoulders. "And I say to communicate and trust and haven't. I'm sorry. I can't seem to do anything right."

"Stealing lines from your thirteen-year old?" An ironic chuckle. "You don't have to always be so strong, Liz. You don't have to be anything all the time. I'm here to help you." She slid into his lap. The last time they sat like this they'd just heard they weren't getting the Intech job. That time felt like desperation, this felt like release. They dissolved back into their bed still entwined and lay there, holding each other, tears now sliding off both their faces. The piano stopped. They heard the kids getting ready for bed.

She said, "I've cried more in the last few weeks than I have in my whole life. It's exhausting."

"It's okay though."

She pushed his hair back, "I hope so."

"Shall I go check on the kids?"

"Sure." He slid off the bed. She stared at the ceiling for the third time that day. This time all she wanted to do was sleep.

But she got up again to let the water out of the tub and went to play cards with her daughter.

Dan came out of the closet in his flannel pajamas. "We're all closed up for the night." He picked up the book, *Brunelleschi's Dome*, and flopped onto the bed next to her so that the mattress came at her like a rogue wave. "How much did you get for the rug?" Liz tried, not too successfully, to hide her pride when she told him the price. He was literally open-mouthed and wide-eyed. "$7,500! We only paid $300. That's a return of, of..."

"24 times our investment."

"Love that human calculator thing." He rolled over to her. "When we're working again, we can go back to Nepal with the kids and get another one."

"Deal." She refrained from pointing out that the trip alone would cost a lot more than paying many times the retail price for a rug down the street. That wasn't the point. With his arm around her, she snuggled her head into the crook of his shoulder. "Why do you think Francine's friends are afraid of me?"

"I don't think they're afraid of you, probably just intimidated by a strong, very bright woman because they don't know who they are yet."

"But I don't want them to be intimidated."

"They're just kids, Lizzie."

"And I'm a witch."

"You just see the world in a very pass/fail way, and they're scared they won't measure up. It's good for them to be challenged like that."

She sighed and wriggled, trying to burrow in deep beside him. "Dan, I wasn't really going to do anything to myself after the interview. But it was pretty scary. Driving down the Mass Pike, I thought that if I just jerked the wheel a tiny bit, I'd be under the semi and it would all be over. And what was even weirder was that what stopped me wasn't death or loving you and the kids...I decided I couldn't do it because you'd all be left without a car since we'd sold the Volvo." She started laughing.

Dan pulled back and scowled at her, but she just laughed harder. She couldn't stop. He chuckled sporadically with her like an engine trying to turn over. When she finally caught her breath, he said, "I love you, Liz. We're good, Mrs. Burgess." She was too emotionally drained to finish their traditional chant and closed her eyes as her husband covered her face with kisses. She needed to reconnect with Dan, to lose this day beneath a storm of physical passion, to forget who she was or who she thought she was.

"Please make love to me?"

He grinned at her for the first time in days. "My pleasure."

Later she listened to his ragged snores and closed her eyes. The day rushed back: Bernie, thoughts of ending her life, her visit with Malia, loading the rug into Carin's car, the fight with Dan, the scene at dinner, France's accusations, Duncan's scared face, crying with her husband. A really long, really hard day. Tomorrow... but before her brain could go there, she slept.

Dan

With the tray of lasagna in his hands, Dan turned quickly and cracked his elbow against the corner of the refrigerator. Man, that hurt. He was exhausted. After he put this in the oven and made the salad, maybe he'd lie down in the guest room for a few minutes.

He frowned at life. The shame was the worst. Were the kids wondering, like he was, whether it wasn't the economy but was him? Was he losing his edge? He'd designed libraries and stores, houses and office buildings; didn't that prove a certain level of competency? Or had the weak economy exposed a lack of talent? Had he lost his feel for what was good, for what people wanted? Was he getting too old to be a contender?

But what else would he do? For the first time in his life, he felt completely defeated. It looked like they'd lose the house. Liz had thought about suicide. They'd gone from trying to get back to where they'd been to just trying to escape with the least damage.

Nothing was familiar. Not his wife. Not his belief in himself. Not their feeling of safety. Looking back, their life seemed so naive. They'd floated along on cushy assumptions of prosperity and security that had proven to be only illusions. How much longer could they hold out?

Putting the lasagna into the oven and opening the Chianti to breathe, he dismissed painting or running and headed upstairs to get his book. On the way, he noticed the bare floor in the den where the rug used to be.

Yeah, it was just a thing, an investment. But it symbolized when life had been an adventure. Sex still an exploration. Travel was going according to plan when they slept in train stations and went a week without a shower. A Friday afternoon invitation to a Maine ski house meant you threw your skis and toothbrush into the car and went. Life was spontaneous and wild, and afterward you still had the energy to bound out of bed the next day and go to work. With those days gone, it was nice, even essential, to be surrounded by tokens of your earlier self that reminded you to revisit that place in your spirit. Having to forfeit this touchstone was tangible proof that he was not who he thought he had become.

Having trudged upstairs, he picked up his book from the bedside shelf, and lay down on the bed. He opened to the dog-eared page but kept reading the same print over and over, the black letters not able to form words, let alone to become sentences with ideas. He tossed the book away and noticed the photograph above the bedroom's fireplace that he'd taken of the Himalayas. Looking at the photo, he tried to imagine himself back in Nepal snapping the shutter, but the recollection was too hazily remote and only made him think about the rug. Maybe it was better to forget how good it'd been. He rose and took the picture off the wall. He went into the closet and stashed it behind the bureau. As he left it behind, he noticed a man passing the full-length mirror who looked like no one he knew.

Chapter 15

"Mr. and Mrs. Burgess, the bank is very sorry, but your credit report shows a number of recent delinquencies. We cannot offer you the home equity loan you have requested."

Liz was so tired of sitting opposite people behind desks who callously told her, no. This one was a bland-faced paper pusher who probably got wedgies in high school, couldn't get laid in college, and whose own kids thought was a dork.

Surrounded by the bank's prints of sailing ships, Liz's ass was clenched so tight her butt cheeks were in danger of bruising. She wanted to reach across the desk and jam this guy's ballpoint up one of his nostrils.

Instead she said, "Yes, that's why we need the home equity loan. Our business has slowed with the economy, and we need a temporary cash infusion to cover expenses." The guy's face didn't move. She pressed on. "We have been customers of this bank for eighteen years, and our credit has been impeccable until very recently."

"When do you expect your business to turn around?"

"I don't know. The Chairman of the Federal Reserve doesn't even know. You are aware that we are in the middle of a protracted recession?"

Dan intervened, "Is there any way we could qualify for a smaller amount?"

"I'm afraid not; judging by your current credit situation, there is a strong likelihood that you won't be able to pay back even a small loan."

"I'm afraid..." Liz's voice was clipped by fury. "That if you don't loan us the money, it will pretty much ensure that we default on our mortgage. So, I guess what you're doing is making sure you can repossess our house."

"No, no. Not at all. We're in business to make money not own real estate."

"If that were true, you'd lend us the money so you could collect the interest we owed, and we'd have a fighting chance to stay in the home we built and love."

"Mrs. Burgess, we don't want your house. We want you to stay in your home."

"Really? You're not acting like it. I bet if we didn't have so much equity in the house, you'd be a lot more willing to work a deal."

"I am sorry. We would like to help you, but the bank has strict lending guidelines."

"I am sorry that the bank does not understand basic finance."

As Dan stood to shake the man's hand, she was already flying across the main lobby. Her eyes crackled at the opulent décor that she and a horde of other screwed customers helped buy. She slammed through the two sets of doors, causing a guy in construction clothes to lurch backwards. When Dan caught up to her, she spun and hissed, "How could you shake his hand?"

"It's not his fault."

"Then whose fault is it exactly? They could give us the money, but the only people they lend to are people who don't really need it." Why did he always walk slower when there was a reason to crank it up? He should have spit on that guy, not shaken his hand. And why didn't he have gloves on; it's colder than a witch's tit out here. She thrust out her wisely gloved hand. "Give me the car keys; I'll drive."

They were halfway home when Dan broached her silent storm. "Want to stop for coffee?"

"Are you kidding? Did you not hear the banker from hell? We are going bankrupt for God's sake, and you want to go buy a three dollar, paper cup of coffee? I don't think so."

Dan was understandably mute the rest of the way home while she ranted at offending traffic or muttered asides like: "I should have that prick's job." "Why didn't you say something?" or "Coffee! We can't afford bananas. Next thing you'll be wanting to add on a home gym." Even as she heard the words coming out of her mouth, she realized how out of control she was, but fear bitch-slapped her on.

When they got home, she slammed the van door shut like a steroid-crazed pro-wrestler. In the pantry/mud room, she threw a load of clothes in the washer while waiting for Dan to come in and walk past her so she could sigh or mutter at him. Where was he? Her anger slowly dissolved into shame. What a cliché to take out her frustrations on the person she cared the most about. She would apologize when he came in.

But he didn't come in. She heard the van start up and drive away.

Chapter 16

"I saw a great bumper sticker on the way over," Donna trumpeted across Malia's kitchen. "I'm still Hot but now it comes in Flashes." Laughing, she slapped a folded magazine on the edge of the kitchen table, sending the foil stalks sprouting from her skull trembling.

Malia chuckled and told Liz, "Okay, the water's warm; lean over."

"Ah, Malia, that feels great. I love how hard you massage my head."

"Can't tell you how many guys have told me that," Donna crowed. When they only groaned in response, she asked, "What are you girls doing the rest of the weekend?"

"I'm showing houses to a couple from Texas, which reminds me, Liz, don't leave without me giving you a copy of the brochure for your house."

"I still can't believe you're really putting it on the market," Donna yowled.

"Me, either. But it's better than losing it to the bank." Liz's voice faltered.

"Your scalp is really tight." Malia had earned money in college cutting hair, so she'd offered to color Liz's to help her save money. Donna came to make it a party.

Liz heard Donna say something, but her voice was quieter than usual and the spray rinsing her hair drowned it out. Malia stopped the water. There was an odd quiet. "What did you say?"

"Pete lost his job." The sound of their three boys cheering at something on the Xbox came from Steven's bedroom down the hall. Donna's voice became even more quiet, which was peculiar since she usually didn't hesitate to bellow about her vaginal itch in the CVS checkout line. "All these months I thought he was in the basement looking for work, but he's been logged onto porn sites. He's spent thousands of dollars on the filth. I'll cut his prick off if he lost his job because he was surfing porn at work."

Franco tried to take the blame when I found it in the browser history."

"I'm so sorry, Donna," Liz said.

Having wrapped Liz's head in a towel, Malia beckoned Donna to the chair by the sink. "Franco's a good kid." She patted Donna's substantial shoulder. "He takes after his mother."

"Thanks, Malia." Donna's voice was gentler, more vulnerable. Malia bent Donna over to remove the foils, so that Donna's voice rolled around the steel kitchen sink, reverberating back to its more typical sonic rumble as if clicked to a favorite channel. "I guess Pete prefers virtual sluts to a real woman. Nuns probably get laid more than I have. At Christmas, I tried to fire him up with a blow job, looked up to see if I should hop aboard, and there he was..." Donna stood up for dramatic effect, looking back and forth between her two-woman audience..."lying back on the pillows, casually rubbing lotion into his hands! Can you believe it? I said, 'Hell-ooo, I'm working down here.' Well, you can imagine, phfft. No action for moi that night either." The three friends' laughter was like water rushing over a dam.

"What kind of lotion?" Malia asked, and they laughed even harder.

"Donna, that is hilarious."

"Score for the Donnerator. Finally, a funny even Mrs. B. gets."

"What's so funny?" Steven had walked in the room. The women all froze, and then blasted off into hysterics again. Steven shook his head, "You guys are whacked." At this the women held onto their stomachs, bent over, tears coming to their eyes. Steven shrugged, "All right if I get some snacks for the guys?"

Malia roared, "Snacks? Donna, maybe you should have offered him snacks." She waved her assent to her bemused son and started to rinse Donna's hair.

Chuck and Franco stayed to sleep over Steven's. After a quick stop at the grocery store, Donna dropped Liz home to find an unfamiliar, orange cube SUV in the driveway. Liz carried in a peace offering to make up for being such a crab lately: steak tips and a bottle of port.

Bassa galloped across the snow-covered backyard to meet her at the back door, cold trumping the cat's desire to chase squirrels. Dan must have let him out when the unexpected visitor arrived. The knob didn't turn. Locked. She knocked on the door and waited. Bassa meowed impatiently. Where was Dan?

Had he and the cube's owner gone off with someone in another car? She took off a glove and began digging for her keys. The problem with big bags was the same as their purpose—they held a lot of stuff. Just as her fingers successfully closed around the jagged metal spurs, Dan opened the door; his face surprised and flushed. "Sorry, don't know how this got locked."

"No problem." Liz stuffed down her irritation, as well as a reflexively snotty remark. She stepped into the mudroom holding up the bag, "Here's some treats." She handed it to him, so she could take off her coat and hang it on a hook and realized this sounded more like something you'd say to your dog.

She turned to improve her comment, and a woman with long, straight blond hair was standing on the far side of the kitchen island her hands resting on the granite. "Oh! Hello," Liz said rather taken aback.

"Hello, Liz. I hope my car wasn't in your way."

Why was her name so familiar in this stranger's mouth?

"Liz, this is Pamela Moore from F. Scott Gallery."

"I love your husband's work. I usually only hang one piece from a new artist, but his work is so fresh I'm taking two." She flourished her arm in the air like a flamenco dancer. "And these chandeliers are extraordinary: fanciful and functional. Absolutely stunning. They will fly out of the gallery." The art expert sparkled at Liz's husband.

"I guess Dan can wear a headlamp when he makes dinner." Liz joked lamely in her discomfort at this surprise intrusion.

Pamela laughed gracefully. "And he cooks, too."

Liz winced at giving this woman another reason to adore her husband.

"When I met Dan, my affirmation for the day was discovery. Isn't that funny?"

Hilarious, Liz thought. "Crazy," she said.

Pamela and Dan beamed at each other as if they had each just discovered a long-sought treasure. Liz didn't like that look. Nor did she like how this woman said her husband's name, softly, deliciously, and possessively.

Still standing in the doorway between the mudroom and the kitchen Liz felt as if she were the visitor, so she pulled a mug from the cabinet to prove her residency. "How much do you think you can sell the chandeliers for?" In her peripheral vision, Liz saw Dan wince. Pamela must have seen it too, because she looked at Dan to assure him that she was fine with his wife's lack of tact. Liz still did not get what was so coarse about this question.

"Oh, at least fifteen hundred dollars. They are extraordinary. They'll be the exquisite jewels within the setting of our gallery's seventeenth-century house. And they'll be a great cross sell with his paintings." Pamela, probably in her late thirties, had a cultured bohemian look, impeccable manners, high-class grooming, and Liz noted, no ring on the fourth finger of her left hand.

"Congratulations, Dan." Liz stepped into the kitchen from the mudroom, hoping her movement would dislodge this interloper from their counter.

But the woman showed no sign of budging. Dan pushed off from the counter by the sink where he'd been standing between the two women. "Pamela, thank you so much for coming."

"My pleasure. It is always a thrill to discover a new talent." She walked around the island and placed her hand on Dan's arm. "I look forward to a long and profitable relationship."

Liz said, "I really like the sound of the profitable part." And began rattling around the kitchen, randomly taking pots out of cupboards since she had no idea which ones Dan would need.

"Liz, you are so lucky to be married to such a talented artist and live in this gorgeous home." She sighed. "A masterpiece." Again, Pamela focused her blue eyes on Dan and sighed very softly. Was he or the house the masterpiece? "Thank you for the tour. Do you think you could drop off a copy of your bio tomorrow? Be sure and mention Evergreen Designs."

"Sure."

Liz wondered why the bio couldn't be emailed.

"Shall I help you clean up?"

He smiled at the blond beauty. "No, that's okay. I'll load the paintings."

"That would be lovely." He went to get her coat and although he always did this for guests, when he did it for this one, Liz found it irritating.

"Good-bye, Liz. Nice to meet you."

Liz stood up from where she'd stooped down to get a frying pan, rising with the potential weapon in hand. "Good-bye, Pamela."

She watched them through the kitchen window as they walked out to the garage. Dan had converted their old office upstairs into his studio when they'd moved the business into the guest room to save money on heat. When the space heater wasn't enough, he'd come in to warm up his fingers in order to keep painting, and when he finished for the day, he'd bring his paints into the house, so they wouldn't solidify.

Liz studied every nuance of their body language. She hated suspecting a woman of man-hunting simply because she was single and very attractive. Maybe Pamela was just a habitual flirt, or this was how she charmed her artists to ensure loyalty. How stupid to spy on your husband out the kitchen window. Or perhaps, it would be stupid not to?

When they disappeared from sight for their next load, Liz put the meat she'd bought into the refrigerator, went into the library, and stuffed the real estate brochure into a drawer. Picking up their dirty wine glasses from the den, she hand-washed them as she watched out the window. When they reappeared, there was the muffled sound of over-enthusiastic voices, the hatch slammed shut, and the woman finally drove away in her motorized, neon box.

"Well, Dan that's great news. What a great idea about the chandeliers."

He grinned in a way she hadn't seen for a long time. She wanted to ask what percentage of the fifteen hundred the gallery was going to keep but refrained.

Dan spotted the bottle she'd placed on the island. "Port! Let's celebrate. You must have E.S.P. 'cuz I have even more good news."

"You do?"

"I got a job at Home Depot."

"You did?"

"Yeah, I went and applied right after the bank turned us down. They pay for health insurance if you work more than twenty hours a week." The radiance that had been on his face a minute ago was gone. "I'll train this week. I told them I needed the week after off for the kids' vacation. I was thinking, we could go to my folks. I can use Dad's workshop to knock off a couple chandeliers while we're there."

"That sounds super. We could all use a break." Especially from newly met, blond gallery owners who offered you your dreams. "I'll call Mom." Afterward, she'd get on the Internet and research properties that they could look at while up north just in case, since they should consider buying in a less expensive area after they sold this place. "Thanks for doing the Home Depot thing."

The lack of expression on his usually expressive face indicated that he'd rather discover he had a 16-foot-long tapeworm than work at a hardware superstore. After running his own company, putting on an orange apron and directing people to the doorknobs was not what her husband thought he'd be doing at 46. "Oh and I got you steak tips; they're in the fridge."

"You're the best, Lizzie." She hoped he really still thought so.

"And so are you, my famous-artist-Home-Depot-man."

Chapter 17

Dan's mother bustled around her linoleum-clad kitchen, as hearty and homey as the stalwart brown appliances she'd bought at Sears fifty years ago. Snow fell between the crisply white, Swiss dot curtains, looking as though some of the dots had leapt off to dance about the window panes.

Elaine pulled the Pyrex dish from the refrigerator. "I made the hotdog casserole yesterday, so all we have to do is cook it. Do you think people will want a salad with it?"

Knowing that Francine didn't really care for the casserole, Liz enthusiastically endorsed the greens and offered to help make this addition to the menu. She followed Elaine's instructions, getting out the cutting board and paring knife.

As Liz started dicing, Elaine chirped, "I'm so happy you're here. It's hard having you kids three hours away where we can't help."

Her mother-in-law had the same short, permed hairstyle she'd had in college in the 50's, although now it was steel metal gray, and her body had ripened into a classic pear shape to which menopause had added a round belly. Elaine had met Ken, Dan's dad, sixty years ago, at the town's agricultural fair. He'd been in the doodlebug pull with his souped-up Ford truck; she reminisced that he'd been James Dean without the wild streak. They'd married a year later and had three boys. Her only trip out of New England had been to touch their oldest son Ray's name on the Vietnam War Memorial Wall in D.C.

Liz and Elaine had met seven years after Ray was killed. Even though Liz's own mother wouldn't pass away for another year, Liz had instantly become the daughter Elaine had never had, and Elaine gave Liz the mothering she'd missed, so Liz felt safe here, free to be less than perfect. Ken, too, offered her what her father, who'd opted to be gone working instead of dealing with her Mom, hadn't been around to give.

"My friend Ruth Keene has some places to show you just in case; nothing up here is selling, it's a buyers' market, you remember Ruth had knee surgery four months ago, well, even though she's still using a cane, she wouldn't hear of not helping you and Dan; she's such a dear." Liz smiled at her mother-in-law's penchant for talking in run-on sentences when she was anxious.

Elaine wiped her hands on her apron and carried the finished salad into the dining room. Liz loved that Elaine wore an apron. It transplanted her snugly into the dependability of a 1950's sitcom, the re-runs she'd escaped into as a kid.

The next morning, Liz was roused by someone's squeaking tread on the stairs. The sound and scent of perking coffee carried down the short farmhouse hallway. She burrowed further down into the blankets and spooned her body around Dan's backside before falling back to sleep.

It was the bacon that woke her next. She lay there listening to it sizzle and to the hypnotically soft mumbling of kitchen conversations until she drifted back off.

When she opened her eyes again a muted morning light diffused across the lilac quilt covering the pine double bed and the wallpaper festooned with tiny sprays of violets. Dan's dented pillow was vacant. She felt heavy, pierced by the high-pitched whine of her exhausted central nervous system. The past months had worn her out. Now finally able to relax, her body collapsed into its need to rest.

The back door banged shut and her eyes flew open. Were they leaving to go somewhere? She stood up too fast. How long had she been back to sleep? Lightheadedness forced her back down on the edge of the bed. Stuffing her feet into her slippers and grabbing her robe from the coat tree by the door, she wrapped it around her on the way to the kitchen.

Duncan was at the table in his long johns, eating a Pop-Tart. Koko, his stuffed gorilla, sat in the chair next to him. "It snowed four inches last night! We wasted a snow day on vacation."

She went over and gave him a kiss on top of his tawny brown head. "We're pretty far north; it might not be snowing at home."

"So if we move here, we won't have to go to school as much!"

"Well..."

Elaine interrupted Liz so her grandson could hold onto his fortifying illusion. "Would you like some bacon and eggs, Liz?"

"Absolutely."

"We're going cross-country skiing. Wanna come, Mommy?"

"Of course."

Dan came down the hall laden with hats, mittens, and scarves. "Hey Babe, you're up! Didn't know whether to wake you."

"Do I have time for breakfast?"

"You bet."

"Dad, you told me I had to hustle or you'd feed me to a Swedish Shortsnout dragon."

"Your mother earned special privileges when she vowed to stay with me when I'm old and smelly." Dan dropped his woolen cache onto the floor by the back door. "How about while Mom's getting dressed, you go out and fill up the bird feeders for Gramma?"

"Sure, Dad." He gulped down the last of his milk, pushed back his chair, and ran over to pull on his snowsuit.

"I'd better throw it into high gear." Liz had a bite of eggs then quickly gulped some coffee.

"France and Chuck still have a ways to go shoveling the driveway. Take your time."

"By the way, I don't remember any reference in our wedding vows to your getting stinky as we age."

"No worries, humans are brilliantly designed so we simultaneously lose our sense of smell."

"Brilliant."

The storm had passed, towing a cold front in its wake. The morning's trailing gray clouds had streaked off to catch up with the storm's back bumper, leaving behind a brilliant blue sky. The air was so dry and brittle Liz cleaved a sharp rent through it as she skied.

The red-cheeked Burgess family swooshed between grey birch and oak. Saplings clustered along the woodland path as if to cheer the passing athletes. Dan led; Liz took the rear, with their children safely sandwiched in between.

They traversed alongside what had been a narrow stream but was now about ten feet wide and not frozen solid because of its current. A snow-covered beaver dam offered a place to cross, and Liz imagined the beaver family's surprise when they heard her clan carve across the snowcap overhead.

A few hundred feet further, the hardwood turned to pine. The branches dipped and jigged discordantly as the breeze rippled their boughs. Her family quietly slipped through the green-walled corridor.

Duncan suddenly stopped, and the skiers to his rear vectored off, their arms flailing to avoid a pile up. France's choice words earned a sharp rebuke from her mother.

"I saw a buck right there! Just standing watching us." Liz's head swiveled to where Duncan's mitten pointed. "See the tracks, Mommy?" Her heart quickened, remembering the buck she'd seen after girls' night.

"Good eyes, Duncan!"

Francine wailed, "Oh, for God's sake, get going. My face is freezing off."

When the woods ended, they all paused at the edge of a broad meadow; the snow glinting fiercely in the sharp sunlight. The blue sky dazzled against the brilliant white landscape. Scattered ski and animal tracks crisscrossed the field. A red-tailed hawk cried its hunt. Liz looked up to see it circling, scanning for small rodents to pop up from their tunnels under the snow.

She took a deep breath, filling her lungs, tightening her torso slightly to hold in the gathered air until it warmed inside her body, then exhaled slowly as she watched the hawk cruise the chill air currents. What was it like to soar high above the broad landscape and yet also see small details so keenly? Her focus was the detail—organizing and assigning categories. Life was more manageable when things were either right or wrong, good or bad, friend or foe, except that their current situation had shown her that things weren't so cleanly labeled.

She jumped when the hawk suddenly streaked to the ground, sending up a spray of snow before it lifted off with something dark clasped in its talon. Duncan yelped, "Wow! Did you see that?"

His father roared, "That was so cool. Isn't it great here?" No one answered. A year ago, they would have cheered heartily, but now, they didn't want to say anything that would sound like agreeing to move north. A benign rebellion, but her children's stoic silence was hard to bear.

Cold had begun to trickle in under her carefully layered clothing, the kind of cold that worked its way down your body, starting at your nose, eradicating the fingers, and then finally turning your toes into white stones. The open field beckoned—space, freedom, air. She pushed off to cut across, merging with some deer tracks. The cold burned her face as she flashed along. Push out, glide, push out, glide, push out, glide. Her breath timed with her stride. Her arms and legs stretched elegantly in opposition. Away she flew.

When she regained the woods, she halted to check back. Her family was racing to catch her, rosy cheeks and bright eyes. Their light spirits reminded her of how things could be if she hadn't screwed them up.

Chapter 18

Only a couple days until winter vacation was over. Dan's dad, Ken, still fit at 77 from clearing land and walking three miles to the post office every day, was wearing the vest Francine had knit him for Christmas. He plunked two decks of cards down on the round oak pedestal table. "Time for 'Up and Down the River.' Let's play teams."

"Daddy and Gramma; Chuck and Grandpa; Duncan, France and me."

"I want to be with Grandpa," Francine protested.

Dan called over from the fireplace, "I don't want to be with my mother; she's too competitive."

"I just play to have fun."

"Right, Attila," Ken joked.

"Traitor."

"Gram, you hear cards shuffling, and you come at a run with a battle axe," Chuck added.

"I love you, Grammie. I'll be on your team."

"Duncan, you always were my favorite." She hugged him around the shoulders and stuck her tongue out at everyone else around the table. "And for my darling son," she blew a raspberry at Dan, then turned to Ken. "Deal 'em up, Graybeard."

"Grandpa doesn't have a beard," Duncan puzzled.

A thud and commotion drew everyone's attention to where Dan was squatting in front of the fireplace. "Argh. Oh my God! A squirrel fell down the chimney. It's on fire!" Everyone stood up and either rushed toward the fireplace or scooted away. Dan jumped up and faced them, "April Fools!" Expletives and complaints about it only being the end of February were lobbed at him.

"Why are you scorching popcorn in the fire anyway, Dad? Let me introduce you to Orville and the microwave," France droned.

"Where's your romance, lass?" He strode toward them, brandishing the popper in front of him. "Watch out! Coming through."

Clam dip and chips were already on the table. Dan slid back the top of the rectangular, metal popper and poured the popcorn into the empty bowl. All of the kernels on the bottom of the popper were stuck, charred black. Chuck chugged the salt shaker over the popcorn bowl.

"Slow down there, Buckaroo. I can feel my arteries hardening just watching you." Ken winked and cut the deck. "Hearts are trump." He dealt eight cards to each person. "How many tricks do you think you'll get?"

"Two."

"Ah, Gramma, you're just up to your old tricks," Chuck punned.

Dan hit the table with both hands. Everyone jumped again. Dan's mouth was open in mock astonishment, "What was that?"

"What?"..."Another flaming squirrel?"..."Oh, come on, Dad."

"I can't believe it, your mother just laughed at a joke!"

"But it was funny," Liz claimed, which set off roars of laughter because it wasn't really.

The phone could barely be heard over their racket. Ken answered it and called Dan over. They quieted down so he could hear. Dan hemmed and hawed and hmmed, and after he hung up, he walked back to the table with a very serious expression.

"What was that all about," asked Liz.

"It was Malia." He stood behind his chair with his hands on the back of it as he slowly looked around at everyone, his voice level, not revealing any emotion. "She has an offer on the house." A deafening silence depressurized the room.

Then Chuck started laughing, "Good one, Dad, another February April Fool's joke, you loser."

"Dan, that's not funny." Liz looked like she could spit hot coals.

"I'm not joking."

"That was Malia on the phone," Ken confirmed.

Again silence, until a wail pierced the collective anguish. When Duncan jumped up and ran from the room, the howling left with him. Dan stood, "I'll go. Everyone else get on your coats. We're going for a walk."

"It's a blizzard out there," Francine groaned.

"Perfect," drawled Chuck.

They stood side by side in front of a light green ranch. Liz asked Dan, "What do you think?"

"It's cheap because it's so ugly, but if you blew out the kitchen so more than one person could be in there at a time, put in two large windows instead of that bay, added a garage and a second story over that part of the house..." His arms waved as if he was a sorcerer conjuring his words. "It could be charming. It's close enough to the mountains, so if we moved back near Boston, we could sell it or rent it to leaf peepers and skiers."

"I don't think this is the economy for a flip or a vacation rental." Liz scratched her wrist between her glove and jacket. She looked at the itchy patch and saw raised red bumps—hives. She'd never had them before. She pulled her jacket sleeve over them, so Dan wouldn't notice. "What will we do if we live here?"

"I don't know." Dan ticked off career ideas on his fingers. "We could renovate a big farm house for a Bed and Breakfast. Or, I could design ski houses for rich New Yorkers and Canadians. I could paint, and make chandeliers, and you could run a gallery. Or my favorite, we could work on the mountain and be ski bums."

"Dan, you're babbling. Be serious." It was all she could do not to screech.

"I am serious. Okay, maybe not about being ski bums but we'll figure it out. It could be exciting."

"Exciting? Leaving our friends. Losing our home. Having no jobs. Starting over."

"Liz, we may not have a choice."

His quick flip to pragmatics, to the bald truth, was unnerving, and she realized his optimism was just him trying to buoy her spirits again. She grimaced at the green heap in front of them, "This is such a nightmare."

"Character building."

"Ha, ha. Hilarious."

He took up her mittened hand and led her to rejoin Elaine and Ruth by the car.

"Do you want to see some more or have you had enough?" Ruth asked.

"I have a couple more in me. You, Liz?" She nodded numbly as they got into the back of Ruth's tan Lincoln.

"This next one has about thirteen acres and a small garage." Ruth turned onto a road so rural that no white line ran down the middle.

"We were just talking about what we could do up here, maybe we could have a horse farm."

"Dan, what do you know about horses except from John Wayne movies?" Ruth and Elaine giggled and shook their heads.

"I like the smell of manure."

"Well then, by all means, I think we should do it," Liz's voice lilted with teasing sarcasm, but the respondent laughter was only empty cascades of volume, speed, and pitch. Everyone was trying hard to keep this search within the bounds of doable.

Ruth waved her hand as if to diffuse her tittering, "Elaine, could you hand them the folder that says 13 Spofford Street on top?"

Dan and Liz studied the listing sheet together, and he commented on some of the dimensions and pointed out that there may be flooding issues from the pond, as well as that the rusting oil tank in a photo could be a problem.

"I always thought it'd be neat to have chickens and goats." Liz could at least pretend to be a possibilities person so that Dan didn't feel like he had to carry her.

He looked at her open-mouthed. "Before we got married you didn't want to have a house or a garden and now you're lusting after goats?"

"*Cold Mountain* made goats sound really practical," she tried to make her comment sound within the context of her personality.

"You may be onto something, Wife. We can have a goat herd and make Middle Eastern style yogurt, organic of course. Can you make yogurt from goat's milk?"

The ladies in the front seats started chuckling again. "Liz, how do you put up with all his silliness?"

She'd wondered this many times, but she patted his thigh and said, "Because tucked inside this goofball is brilliance beyond compare, plus he's easy on the eyes." He smiled and covered her mittened hand with his gloved one.

Elaine pulled down the visor's mirror, "Well, he got his looks from his mother." She flipped the visor back up and faced the back, "You are both handling this so well, it would break up so many other marriages, Ken and I were saying..."

Liz tuned out the rest of Elaine's run-on and looked at the paper in her lap with its photos of a strange building that they might have to call home. The squeezing ache in her throat returned. Dan gripped her hand a couple times as if to pull her back to him.

Liz passed the paper to him. "I am trying to stop feeling like the world's spinning out of control whenever things don't go exactly like I think they should."

Dan stared at his wife in amazement again as she took deep breaths and, as Malia suggested, imagined pulling in golden light and exhaling a grey mist of negativity.

"All right, who are you and what have you done with my wife?" He leaned over and kissed her cheek. She looked at him expecting a mocking expression, but his eyes were dead serious and admiring. In a grateful voice he whispered, "How did I ever find you?"

She wondered if he really still thought so or was this just another habitual phrase. Just him trying to placate the mother of his children for the sake of the family? She felt the ghost of Pamela sitting between them. Who would they have ended up with if they hadn't met? Maybe she'd be with a guy in the insurance industry with a 401-K. And he might be with someone like a gallery owner.

ஐ௸ஐ௸ஐ௸ஐ௸

"Francine, don't just bring in your own bag. Go back out and get another load." She took off her coat. "Ugh, I feel sick; the 'Happy Meal' is not living up to its name."

As she sprinted for the bathroom, she noticed the light blinking on the answering machine. Caving to the demands of modern technology, she pushed the button and placed her hands over the pressure in her abdomen as if to assure herself that it would be held in place. The voice was officious and abrupt. "This is Heather Stone from F.I.B. calling for Liz Burgess. We still don't have an appropriate full-time job; however, we do have a consulting project that would entail roughly three weeks of work. Please call and let us know if you're interested."

Chapter 19

Warm air lay atop the winter landscape, melting the snow into the night air in a silver fog. When Liz pulled up, Malia ran out to the car. "It's too warm for this coat, but it's force of habit to put it on." She slid into the passenger seat swathed in her burnt orange wrapping. "Your buyer probably thinks this is the Arctic. He's a professor from Duke moving up to teach at Wellesley, smart guy obviously, saw Dan's talent and the quality right away. They want to move before the school year starts, so you need to decide soon."

"Argh, I know, believe me, I know. I've worried a hole through my stomach. My house was the only stable thing when I was a kid, so I want to do that for mine, but a bird in the hand..."

"Liz, you and Dan are your kids' stability."

"Not lately. First, not making any money, and now with me away working in Boston and Dan working, too, they're on their own like I was."

"It is nothing like what you went through. And maybe this is making the kids stronger, independent, who knows?"

Liz squirmed in her seat, leaning toward the windshield. Malia's said this before, and it sounded too trite and new age-y, even a bit insensitive. "I can't talk about this right now; I need to concentrate on driving."

Malia went to the door when they got to Donna's. After some kind of commotion, Malia came back to the car alone. "She'll be out in a minute. I'm not sure what's going on." Liz reached behind to clear a space in the backseat.

Donna came dashing out, then turned and went back into the house, then reemerged struggling with her hat. She was puffing when she landed in the van. "Sorry I'm late. Nikki got some shots at the vet's today and puked on the living room rug. After I cleaned it up, there were two clean spots, so Franco and I were just rotating the rug to hide them under a chair."

"You are the only person I know who'd hide the clean spots," Malia chuckled.

Liz pointed at the floor by Malia's feet. "The directions are on that paper. No, not that one. The smaller one."

"I know how to get there. I've been over a couple times," Donna volunteered from the backseat. "Turn right here. Then take a right at Uplook Drive. Never met the husband, sounds like a primo prick; he's got the family wound up tighter than Anne of Green Gables twat."

The lights at Carin's split-level ranch were all on, inside and out so that the mist glowed incandescent. Carin met them at the door and took their coats, directing them upstairs and to the right.

Immediately, Liz saw her rug on the living room floor; it eclipsed everything else in the room as if she'd glimpsed an old crush at a high school reunion. It felt profane to have an emblem from her life lying under someone else's couch, and she wondered what other parts of herself she would have to sell?

She tried to look anywhere but at the rug. A gas fire was lit in the fireplace. The room, a combination dining and living area, was dominated by the immense blankness of a TV screen that was like a gaping black hole in the wall. Atop her Tibetan rug, as if marooned, was a semicircle of seats facing the fire: leather recliner, upholstered chair and sofa, three dining chairs and a giant beanbag colored to look like a basketball. The back of the sofa's muslin slipcover was covered with smudged crayon scribbles.

Carin came in from the kitchen carrying a platter of cheese, crackers, and fresh raspberries. "So, did you notice my couture couch? The little shit did that, like, two weeks ago. Hopefully, it's a sign of a budding artistic genius, not a juvie." She put down the platter and motioned toward the chairs. She looked utterly exhausted. When the doorbell rang, a crazed yipping flew up from the floor below. "That's Kipper, our new Labradoodle puppy. After the animal communication at your house, I decided it'd be nice to have someone here I could talk to. He's adorable but crazed."

Malia offered to get either the door or the wine and was assigned to the refrigerator. She returned with the bottle in one hand and a stack of cocktail napkins she'd discovered on the counter in the other.

Sarah appeared up the stairs. "Carin's waiting for Molly, who pulled in behind me."

With all present, the group settled into its rhythm; bantering and shuffling, seats chosen, snacks and drinks procured, initial observances exchanged. "Can you believe this weather?"..."The temp is supposed to drop thirty degrees tonight, another storm's coming."..."Only in New England."..."Your sweater is gorgeous."..."Molly, I love your haircut."..."I'll go shut up the damn dog."..."Is Chuck finding the geometry homework hard?"..."That teacher is an absolute witch."

"Carin, I showed your house a couple times before you bought it. You've done a lot of work. What a difference," Malia exclaimed.

"Oh, so you saw it in all its glory. A 70's time machine, reeked of cat piss. It had fruit wallpaper in the kitchen; I told Carl Jr. it was scratch and sniff, quietest ten minutes in three years." Her audience smirked. "I put in the lights over the fireplace, but I wish had even more lighting in here." She turned to Liz, "Too bad I didn't know Dan. Contractors don't like think of those little, really important details." She swept her hands around as if the surroundings furnished sufficient proof. "I'd do the kitchen differently, too, but after all the money we spent, we can't like do it again. Carl would kill me."

Liz felt sick over the lost business. A project like that would have covered a couple months of expenses. She'll have to brainstorm how to reach real estate agents and new home buyers with Malia and Dan.

Carin absently braided her hair as she spoke, combed it out with her fingers and then braided it again. "I'm still not used to all the nature out here. Last week, a loud scratching like the living dead in the attic woke me up. Now, I have three squirrels in Have-a-Heart traps, and animal control can't come until Friday, so I'm feeding the stupid things so they won't like die." She flipped her now loose, bright blond hair to her back as the women bounced with laughter.

Struggling to get out of the beanbag, Donna rolled onto her knees to scoop up a handful of raspberries from the bowl. "I'll come get them tomorrow."

"S'cuse me, s'cuse me, s'cuse me..." A little boy in footed jammies was standing in the hall after rapid firing his power phrase at increasing volume while Donna was talking. "You ladies—too noisy."

"Honey, come sit with Mommy for a little while until you get tired." The sullen, moon-faced toddler cautiously padded over to the recliner where his mother was sitting and stood leaning against the leather arm. Carin put her arm around him, which he bore for a few seconds and then shrugged off.

After studying the table, he demanded, "Where - the cookies?" Liz suspected this was the real reason for his appearance.

"Oh, I forgot! Good boy, reminding Mommy." Carin hopped up, and he climbed into her seat.

When Carin returned with the Oreos, she pulled over another dining room chair, abdicating the leather recliner. Molly shifted the attention from the enthroned child, saying, "Donna, I am so sorry about Pete losing his job."

Donna raised her glass of Fresca and cranberry juice. "That's the way the cookie crumbles."

Everyone involuntarily looked at Carl Jr., his mouth already ringed in chocolate crumbs, a cookie in both hands and two more in his lap. Noticing that everyone was looking at him, Carl Jr. crammed a whole cookie into his mouth and covered the others over with his little hands.

Carin reached to take them from him, but he burst into tears and threw the cookies at the table. "Carl, you know when your father gets home tomorrow night, he will be very, very mad if there are any crumbs in his chair. Time to go to bed, okay?" She carried the little darling, who was now so confused by his mother's mixed messages and possessed by his sugar overload that all he could do was scream and kick and pound her with his fists as they exited. There was a collective exhale as the screaming receded down the hall and behind a closed door.

Liz sat up a little straighter, "Well, I have some good news. When we got back from New Hampshire, First Insured Business offered me a three-week consulting job."

Ecstatic responses crackled around the room as her friends chorused, "Yea!"..."This is so exciting!" ..."Oh, I'm so relieved."..."Hot shit!"

Carin returned looking as if she'd wrestled a rogue elephant. Shifting her shoulders as if readjusting a load, she scooped up her glass, refilled it to the brim, and reclaimed the recliner vacated by the heir apparent.

"Did you have an activity planned?" Sarah asked.

"Oh! Right!" Carin bounded from the recliner as if she'd been spit out of it and went to get the dictionary, paper, and pencils sitting on the dining table. "I've never played this; got it from the Internet." She stood in front of them, spinning nervously to look at each person in rapid fire as she explained, "You pick a word from the dictionary that you think people won't know and write three definitions. The other people try to guess which one is real. If you're right, you get a point. For each wrong guess, the writer gets a point. Oh, I didn't explain that good. Do you get it?" Everyone assured her that they understood. Carin passed out the paper and sat back down.

"I did mine ahead: Garrote
1. A silk scarf tied around a man's neck, fashionable in the 18th century.
2. How I will strangle my husband with wire
3. Name for the metal gate in a water sluice."

Donna was the only one who guessed #2 correctly.

"Mommy!" This summons came screaming down the hallway then incarnated as a red-faced dwarf.

"Would you like me to try? I could sing him a song," Sarah offered.

"That'd be great." Carin dispatched a sigh that almost made her dissolve into the leather.

"Have you thought about giving Carl Jr. a nickname—his own name, a separate identity from his father?" Malia asked.

"Oh my God, I never thought of that. Do you think he'd be better if he had a different name?"

"I can testify to the power of having a name that didn't fit. I was named Lily." Donna tried to repress a satisfied grin at her friends' shock as she picked up the dictionary to start searching for her word. "My family sees ethnicity as pick-your-own. Mom was in an Oriental phase when I was born and thought Lily sounded Chinese. Her folks were Russian but Babushka changed her name to Martha after the first First Lady when they immigrated. Then in high school, I started going by Donna because I wanted to be Italian. I think I married Pete for his last name. Maybe there's a gene for giving kids bad names, after all, my son is Franco DiFranco."

"I like hadn't put that together!" Carin's laughter edged into hysteria, reminding Liz of a Jack Russell Terrier that'd wolfed down a package of chocolate chips and you didn't know whether to take it in your arms or make it throw up.

Chapter 20

On the way home from Carin's after they'd dropped Donna, Liz wriggled higher on the cushion to raise her view. "The fog's gone, but now it's black ice. Will this winter never end?" She turned the heater's fan up two notches.

Malia rubbed her arms. "I can't believe how cold it got while we were inside. I think it dropped the thirty degrees they forecast. Thank goodness, I wore my wool coat after all."

"Donna's so cute with Carin."

"I feel awful about what I said about Carl Jr.'s name." Malia let out an exasperated growl. "I've been trying not to be so sanctimonious, but tonight I was like a senile therapist with Tourette Syndrome. I couldn't shut up."

"Nature hates a vacuum, you just filled the void."

"I sounded like a trite, New Age blowhard."

Liz reached over to mockingly pat Malia's leg. "We're all on our journey. Just flow with what is."

Malia groaned, "Is that what I sound like? God, I am never saying anything but hello."

"Don't you dare. I need you to balance me."

"You are perfect without any help." Malia smiled and sincerely patted her friend's leg. "Okay, I'll keep talking as long as you tell me when to shut up."

Liz's eyes lit up as she came into their bedroom. "A fire! Cozy. We've hardly had any up here this year." Propped up in bed, Dan leaned against two pillows, his book open on his lap. She kicked off her shoes and bent down to pick them up. "The temperature really dropped. It started snowing pretty hard after I left Malia's." She went into the closet for her nightgown.

"It's not supposed to amount to anything."

"Carin had one of those piddly gas fires; this is so much better," she called from the closet.

"Did you have fun?"

"We played a word game." She emerged from the closet in blue flannel and headed into the bathroom. "It'd be fun to play with the kids." She raised her voice over the running water as she washed her face. "Carin told us that she left home and moved to Somerville when she was fifteen and worked at a Mexican restaurant while she got her GED." She stuck her face out of the bathroom door while brushing her hair, "I don't know why I didn't do something like that. My brother left when he was in high school." She disappeared into the bathroom again. "Why didn't I go?"

"That's not how you're wired. You're a rule follower. You probably subconsciously analyzed the risks and calculated a higher probability of more problems if you moved out."

"Well, following the rules sure hasn't worked for us lately." The toilet flushed. She wandered out, brushing her teeth, and leaned against the doorframe. "Wad ou ou ink we ould ou? Ed-ohm eh-winch?"

"Why don't you wait until you've finished brushing your teeth?" She grinned at him around the paste, went back in, spit, rinsed out the sink, and wiped it dry with a towel, then returned to the bedroom.

"What do you think we should do? Become Bedouins?" Her comment was obliquely teasing him about his often fanciful ideas.

He grinned back at her. "Nah, I don't like goat meat that much; let's do mutton, how about New Zealand." He ticked off on his fingers. "Already speak the language, traditional values, strong sense of community, sports nuts, beautiful country. You saw *Lord of the Rings*, how could we go wrong?"

She crawled into bed, picking up the novel Sarah had loaned her. "Nothing against New Zealand but let's stay with what we know even if it all may change."

"As long as we're good."

"Nothing else matters."

"We're a couple of saps."

"Always have been."

"Always will be." He leaned over for a kiss to close out their standard refrain and then rolled back.

"Carin made a comment tonight about never knowing what goes on behind closed doors. I was thinking about how people would probably drive by here and be green with envy not knowing what we're going through."

The waning fire sputtered. Liz plumped a hollow into her pillow and shimmied into it. They both read their books, cozied under the blankets. Hearth. Heart. Home. They really couldn't leave. This was the only place where she'd ever known this kind of contentment, this grounded rootedness, this sense of beloved belonging.

With the thought of selling having slipped in through some unguarded crack in her mind, her thoughts popped and sputtered like the fire but more like one that was leaping out of control. She placed her book face down on her belly and rubbed her palms around her face. What if this woman, Pamela, came into their house and stole Liz's happiness? What if this security she reminisced about had been a flimsy fiction, not the reality she'd assumed? "I don't think we should sell. You're right, let's get out of our comfort zone. This house is worth taking a risk for. Whadaya think?"

"What have we got to lose but everything? As we say, as long as we have each other..." A flash of light. Dan yelped, "Was that a blown transformer or lightning?" Liz was glad he'd seen it; she'd wondered if she was having a stroke.

A protracted rumbling trundled past the house, answering his question. They turned out their lights and both sprang to the window. Cupping their hands around their eyes, they pressed their faces against the glass. Two flashes in rapid succession lit up the backyard; the strobe momentarily freezing the falling snowflakes into a motionless curtain.

The strikes were so close together that the thunder claps overlapped to create a dramatic, rolling timpani. Dan and Liz squealed as if they'd spied Santa on Christmas Eve. Liz whispered in a rush, "Less than a mile away."

They had to wait minutes for the next flash. This one was so brilliant it shattered all ambient color, so that their retinas only registered gradations of white: bright and not so bright. Thunder instantaneously smacked against the house. The bolt must have hit the pond. "Wow!" "That was incredible!" They waited even longer this time. The next flash seemed like a flicker in comparison to its predecessor, the thunder more like someone's stomach after too much Indian food.

Liz gushed, "I've never seen lightning during a snowstorm before."

"That was so cool. Wish the kids could have seen it."

"I think that was a good omen. I'll call Malia tomorrow and tell her we're not selling."

Back in bed with the book in his hand Dan asked, "Where did Carin put the rug?" His question was so out of context that it must have been ready for a while.

"In the living room. There's already a stain on it. Her son ran by with chopsticks stuck up his nose when she was nursing the baby; when she tried to grab him so he wouldn't trip and impale his brain, she kicked over a bottle of baby vitamins. A black stain from the iron in it I guess. He's a handful and a half, that one."

It was obvious that "stain" was the only word Dan heard. She could feel the sinking in his chest from the look on his face.

"I'd hoped we could buy the rug back when we were flush again. Ruined, huh." Dan tossed his book on the floor and clicked off the light. "When Dick came over to see if he could think of any work connections for me, Duncan came down and emptied his pockets, which were stuffed with all his money. Said he wanted to pay Mr. Uppington for helping us. Dick graciously refused and praised Duncan's noble gesture, but that old Yank was wiping his eyes when Dunc went upstairs." Dan's voice was so rough it barely had any breath in it. "Me, too."

There was a long silence.

Liz quietly asked, "Was Dick able to think of anything?"

"Nope."

It was all she could do to force the words around the lump in her throat. "Well, it was nice of him to offer to help." She clicked off her light and turned to face the opposite wall, bending into a tight curl. Despair swelled but stayed inside to poison her mind. When you've cried so much that there are no tears left, the heart just cries away bits of your soul.

Donna

"Because I want you to help me with the squirrel traps."

Franco groaned. "Can't we do it later?"

"I want to pick them up before her husband gets back tonight."

"But the guys are all meeting at the library to work on our project."

"A project? Why didn't you tell me about this? What is wrong with you?" Her hands flew into the air. "You are such a loser." She turned her back on him and grabbed her fur coat. It crushed her when she heard her father's voice come out of her mouth like that. The bastard still controlled her even though they hadn't spoken in almost thirty years.

Franco's voice matched his steely face, "Steven's coming to get me."

She mirrored his tone, "Fine, I'm out of here." Donna picked up her keys and wallet and banged out the door, more upset than was warranted.

She turned the car key. Fleetwood Mac blasted out of the red Bronco's speakers, "And I still hear you sayin' you would never break the chain." Donna careened out of the driveway bellowing along with Stevie Nicks, momentarily taking her hands off the wheel to play the air drums. "Damn your love. Damn your lies."

Damn winter. At least, last night's snow layered some white over the dirty, old stuff. A menopausal hot flash mirrored her temper. She turned off the car's heater and couldn't wait to peel off her coat.

Stevie Nicks was silenced mid-rant when Donna pulled into Carin's driveway and killed the engine. Climbing down from the Bronco, she swung off her fur and launched it over onto the passenger seat, then scooped her cell phone into her jean's pocket.

She was careful to plant each foot along the snow-covered path and steps, so she wouldn't slip. At the top of the steps, she was struck motionless by a man's roar. The words were muffled, but his rage flew through the door, dislodging old memories, and her internal heat fled from an icy terror. The unknown man's fury was raw and predatory. She stared hard at the door as if trying to see through it.

A faint female whimpering prickled Donna's neck—Carin. A thud and a cry of pain. Donna's arm tore forward. The door was unlocked. Instinct drove her action and response. She was over the threshold. Her nose sensed a rich musk, her head swiveled right to register dog shit on the landing. The man's voice raged. "'Welcome home, Honey, here's a pile of shit.' How did I marry such a stupid cunt? I'll break this fucking bitch's neck so you learn respect, then I'm gonna stick your fucking face in that fucking pile and see how much you like it."

Donna was up the stairs and standing at the kitchen doorway in a couple of steps. Carin was arched backward over the counter, her husband's forearm pressed down across her sternum. He was shaking the wriggling puppy by the scruff of its neck, its teeth bared in terror next to her face.

They didn't notice her until she announced in a flat, commanding voice, "Put the dog down." Two faces, one small and pale, the other inflamed, snapped toward her. Carl was tall and thin. His dark hair was perfect; his face would look like an elf's except for being mottled and contorted at the moment. He was still in his suit, although his tie must have been torn off in a frenzy from the mass of wrinkles at his shirt's open collar.

He snapped upright still holding the dog. "Who the fuck are you?"

Every cell in her body stood tall and silently screamed, *I am Strong like Bull.* She wanted to plow across the space slamming this monster into the granite counter, smashing his skull against the cabinets—what she'd always dreamed of doing to her father or brother. But this was not about her or them. This was about keeping Carin and the kids safe. Her strength had to be of an altogether different kind.

"Your wife called the animal shelter, Sir. I've come for the dog and the squirrels." Donna watched his breath fly out in a fast exhale as his body clicked down from high alert. She continued, "She felt with small children, now was not the best time to have a puppy."

"Damn straight." His condescending tone conveyed his disbelief at the possibility that Carin could get something right. He moved toward Donna with the dog. It was all she could do not to smash her knee into his groin. Channeling all her self-control, she took Kipper from him. Their arms touched in the transfer. She couldn't have felt more revulsion than if she'd just brushed against a rotting corpse.

Donna said, "Ma'am, I'd be happy to help you clean up the mess on the stairs, then I'm afraid you need to come with me to the shelter to fill out some forms."

The look on Carin's face was a mixture of relief and desperation. "This isn't a good time. The children are here, and my husband just got home from a business trip."

"The kids can come. They'll love to see the animals. Your husband might like some quiet after traveling, such an ordeal nowadays." Donna had a different shelter in mind for Carin and the kids. She'd call the crisis center where Molly volunteered to find out where the closest one was.

Carl said, as sweet as pudding, "Thank you. I appreciate that." His tone insinuated that his wife would never consider his comfort as she had and that he and Donna were complicit in his disdain. He warned Carin, "Don't bring any other animals home with you." As he walked out to the living room, he said to Donna, "She's a pushover" as if making a witty pun about Carin's earlier position being bent back over the counter was appropriate. Donna recoiled.

As they were cleaning, Carin whispered so as not to be heard over the TV he'd switched on, "Thank you. But we're okay. You can go."

"Let's give him a little longer to cool down. We'll bring Kipper to my house, then swing by the animal shelter in case he asks the kids about it and bring back a meal from Let's Dish."

"Okay." Carin's voice sounded like a pre-schooler's after a long, exhausting day.

Donna would suggest the women's shelter when they were gone from here.

Chapter 21

As she scrubbed at the pots, the tension in Liz's submerged hands slowly dissolved into the hot water, her spirit warming with the sounds of home: running water, pots ponging together, the dishwasher humming. Francine scribbled away on homework at the table. The faint battle noises of Duncan playing with his Batman and Star Wars figures came from his secret space under the stairs.

Dan arrived home from his shift at Home Depot with a clutch of grocery bags in each hand, which he promptly dropped on the pantry floor. "I have some good news."

"You cannot tell me fast enough."

"I have more groceries to unload first," he teased.

"Dan, tell us!"

"I saw Malia at Market Basket. She has a client who needs some rooms painted, and she hooked me up."

"Dan, that's great." Her hands flew up, spraying sudsy water through the air.

"This Mary Dunn is flipping a house. She bought it for her son to live in, and then he moved to New York City, so she wants to sell it in order to raise cash for him."

"How old is this kid?"

"In his thirties."

"And Mommy is still paying the bills?"

"Nice gig if you can get, it I guess."

"Kind of pathetic. What does she want done?"

"What does Dunn want done?" Dan was silly with excitement. "Malia and I swung by the place. I suggested they could boost the resale for not a lot of money if they knocked out a couple of walls and put in some molding, but Malia said Mary just wants it sold fast without investing much. She had painters but they weren't doing any prep work, so she wants me to finish the bathroom and do the living room and kitchen. Malia quoted me at $35 an hour, ten dollars less than the other guys were charging but way more than I make at Home Depot."

"Can you do both?"

"Sure, it'll only take a week or so."

France piped in, "Dad, I can help when I'm not in school."

"That'd be great, Pixie."

Liz praised him warmly, "Dan, this is great."

"We have our good friend Malia to thank."

"I'll call her after I finish the dishes." She passed the frying pan to him and nodded at the dish towel.

"Mr. Parks is the meanest teacher ever. He doesn't listen to anything," Francine said more to her algebra textbook than to them.

"Maybe because you should be listening to him," Liz responded since the book wasn't likely to answer.

"I knew you'd side with the grownup," Francine snapped.

"France, I'm on your side. Just giving you a reality check. Would you like some help?"

"I'll do it myself, and you'll see he can't teach."

"Good idea. Fail the course to prove a teacher's incompetence. Brilliant, Pixie Girl." Dan was shot a nasty, betrayed look from their daughter.

The back door crashed open. Donna careened in through the mudroom. Dan drawled, "Don't you ever knock?"

"No, and it's a God Damn good thing!" Donna looked as though she'd been sucked up by a tornado and spit from the vortex, spinning into twice her usual size and frenzy in the process. "I need a cup of tea." She plowed over to the table; the chair skidded across the wood floor as she landed in it. Francine gathered her math materials in closer.

Liz put on water to boil and got down three of Francine's pottery mugs. "Donna, what's happened?"

"I went over Carin's to get the squirrels and heard trouble through the door, so I went in and that monster she's married to had her bent over backwards, stuffing the dog in her face."

"What?" Liz was aghast. She wondered if she should ask Francine to leave but decided it'd be a life lesson.

Donna detailed what had happened, during which Liz handed her a mug of tea. Afterwards, Liz suggested that she and Donna go into the den so Francine could finish her homework. When they closed the French doors behind them and were sitting together in the twilit turret, Liz said, "Carin complained about him, but she never said anything about physical abuse."

"They don't."

"Why don't they tell their friends? Or get help?"

"Kind of like how you didn't tell us about your problems for more than a year?"

"But this is dangerous."

"She's afraid of what he'd do if she left. Said it's better for the kids to have their father."

"Are you kidding? He's no father." Her own Daddy issues were triggered like Donna's. "Is she okay?"

"Her arm and back are bruised and she thinks a couple ribs might be broken, and the left side of her face is starting to swell."

"What? Oh, my God! What can we do? Should we call the police? Do you want Dan to go over with you and get them out of there?"

"She wouldn't even go to the hospital. I tried. I called the crisis center, and they said most shelters are for single men, not much for abused women or poor families; the closest one is in Cambridge. But they have a network of people who'd take them in. Carin freaked out and got all pissed off. I told her she could call any of us anytime day or night. Cried all the way here after I left them there with him." Donna's voice faltered, then her head fell into her hands and she started to sob.

Liz sprung for the box of tissues. Donna wiped her eyes and her anger returned, "I tell you, I wanted to kill the bastard." She was fidgeting around in her chair as she spoke, her hands chopping at the air. "All my anger at my father and brother was dying to come out of my fists, but right as I was about to charge at him, all of it just left, totally gone, quick as a pity fuck." The look on her face was utter amazement and disbelief. "I went from Mike Tyson to the Dali Lama in a flash. It was wild." She blew out a blast of air like a killer whale as she collapsed back into the chair.

"When I had every reason to take this asshole out, I didn't. I did what had to be done to keep Carin and the kids safe, instead of making it worse. I've never done that before." Donna raised her sizable paw and roughed up the back of her curly head. "It felt good to let go of all that shit. Fifty-two years of baggage gone. Like I was staring down the old man and just shrugged him off. As good as it would have felt to scramble this guy's face, I stepped around the prick and walked by."

Donna looked down at the floor, shook her head, then raised her eyes back up to Liz. "I stopped what was going on there, and what shocks the shit out of me is that now I don't give a flying fuck about my old man one way or the other."

She looked tired, confused, and kind of blank. With the rage that had driven her for so long gone, she seemed puzzled about how to go on.

Liz put her mug down on the plant stand and leaned toward her friend, her Alanon partner. Her expression was earnest. "Donna, we can't help Carin until she asks us to, but I think this is a very good thing...for you, I mean."

"I think so," a nascent hope dawning. "Yeah, Mrs. Burgess, it probably is."

Chapter 22

Liz laid out a Mexican wool blanket on top of the ratty carpeting that Mary Dunn was going to replace once Dan finished painting. "When can you stop for lunch?" Liz noticed her impatient tone and attempted to amend it by adding, "I miss you" in a smarmy coo. She was relieved when he good-naturedly answered that he was almost to a good stopping place.

She took the chicken Parmigiano subs he'd made last night out of the picnic basket they'd gotten for a wedding present. He'd been baking bread to save money; the thought of the soft sub rolls was making her mouth water. She opened the bottle of cheap Spanish wine and poured it into their plastic cups to breathe.

This house had been built after World War II when the primary words in construction were "speed" and "utilitarian." The walls were thin, the roof pitch steep, the doors flimsy, and the windows drafty. The layout reminded Liz of the forts she and her brother, Wayne, used to build out of the large appliance boxes their Dad brought home during the couple of years he drove a delivery truck for Maytag. Even new paint and carpeting wouldn't cover up the stubborn echo of dust and mildew and greasy residue. Liz shuddered. They may have to move somewhere like this.

In the bathroom, the house's odor was overwhelmed by the twang of the oil Dan had rubbed into the overhead wooden beam. She checked the cabinet under the bathroom sink for a new roll of toilet paper and instead discovered a homemade apple pie with a couple of pieces missing. "Dan, there's a pie under the bathroom sink."

"Ah, yeah." There was a pause. "Pamela stopped by with it earlier."

"She did?" She wanted to say more but couldn't come up with anything else she should say out loud. She sat down to use the toilet and think. Why would the owner of the art gallery come here for any reason other than the obvious: to seduce another woman's husband? And how did she happen to bring Dan's favorite dessert? Why did she even know he was working here? And worst of all, why would Dan hide the pie, in other words, the fact that Ms. Artsy Chic had been here? Liz felt sick. Damn, no toilet paper. "Dan? Could you bring me a napkin? There's no paper." When he came in, she said, "Why don't you take the pie out of here, and we can have it for dessert?"

"Sounds great. I'll be done in a couple seconds."

She heard the roller, trundling paint up and down on the opposite side of the wall. Finished, she wandered into the room he was painting. "Looks great. Want me to help?"

"After this section, I'll be done with this coat."

"I'll finish getting lunch ready."

Dan came in, wiping his washed hands on his shirt. "I'm starved." He sat on the blanket with the heavy weariness of an exhausted man. "Mary's making me nuts. She took four days and a million splotches on the wall to pick out a color." Dan stretched his back, took a sip of his wine out of the plastic glass and sighed.

"She's probably taking things out on you. Malia said the son she's supporting is a drug addict." Her voice was low as if the walls might report her gossiping back to their owner.

"Can't blame him, I'd self-medicate if she was my mother."

"Dan." She handed him his sub and a napkin, and he winked at her mock reprimand reminding her of how he'd flirted with her summers during college when she'd visited him at his job clearing trees. Now it seemed Pamela was stopping by with the same intent.

"Do you think we should buy this and move here?" He asked between bites.

"Couldn't even if we wanted to; Malia said Mary is asking six hundred grand for it."

"She's out of her mind; that's almost as much as we were offered for our place."

"Malia said four ten is more like it, but Mary is adamant."

"She's a force. Today I got scolded for taking too long on the beams. They kept soaking up oil, probably hadn't been done in sixty years, no sense in doing them unless it's done right. Plus, I did it while she was taking forever choosing colors."

"The beams came out great."

"What did you hear from F.I.B.?" He took a huge bite of his sub.

"It sounds pretty straightforward. $115 an hour." She grinned when he whistled. "Three days of meetings to start. They'll loan me a laptop and give me access to their intranet, so I can work from home. I'll probably only have to go in a couple times a week after the orientation. Three, forty-hour weeks would be $13,800."

"Sweet! Not that I'm trying to get rid of you or anything, but when do you start?" He grinned.

"Tomorrow."

"Can't come soon enough."

"Dan, can't you ever be serious? Or maybe be a little sad that I'll be gone?" Her tone came out more whiney than she wanted. She tried to recover by pretending to push her sub in his face. The way she'd been acting, probably tomorrow couldn't come soon enough for him. She was as good as throwing back the covers for Dan and a certain pie-toting gallery owner to roll into her bed.

Thankfully he laughed as he pushed her sub away. "Okay, okay."

"With both your jobs, are you going to be able to get Chuck to Drivers' Ed this week? And France wanted to invite Ashley and Brittany over."

"Sure." He wiped his mouth on the napkin and switched topics. "Between selling the car and the rug, F.I.B., this painting job, and Home Depot are things looking better?" He pointed at his fingers with his sub as he ticked off all their recent cash inflows.

She'd taken another bite so held a napkin in front of her mouth as she answered, "Well, with our spending cuts and paying off some debt, our basic monthly expenses are now about $4,200 a month, so we can probably keep going..." She paused for a few seconds calculating, "about three months."

"Man, you turn me on when you spin numbers like that." He lasciviously wriggled his eyebrows. "So since no one's here..."

"What if the witch shows up?"

"Mary's not coming back until tomorrow."

She was glad he thought of Mary and not her with her witch comment, but she'd been thinking of Pamela.

They tossed the remains of lunch into the basket and then tossed their clothes on top, taking care to place their naked bodies on their Mexican blanket and stay off the skuzzy carpeting. During their foreplay, while she could still think of something besides what they were doing, Liz said a silent prayer than she was the only woman Dan had made love to in this house today.

France

It is soooo boring. Nothing's on TV cuz we don't have cable anymore. Video games are stupid. No more pottery. No more anything. There's nothing to do. Homework's even done. Everyone else has things to do. Britty's at gymnastics; Ashley's horseback riding; Chuck's on the computer; Duncan's playing the piano...

France scattered the balls on the pool table with her hand then flopped down on the couch in the TV room. Argh. There is no money to do anything anymore. It totally sucks. It's so not fair. Only bad stuff happens to me. I get blamed for everything. I get left out. I can't do anything good. My life sucks.

She pulled apart her braid and then tugged her mass of red hair loosely through the elastic, so it was a russet pile on top of her head. Erica Bean was so mean today. Hey, that rhymes: Erica Bean was so mean. She rolled the chant around in her mind like a red-hot candy on her tongue.

France picked at her toenail polish. Erica's such spoiled snot. So what if her parents have a red Mercedes and a Hummer, she didn't do anything to get them besides being born. Everyone's heard nine million times how she's skiing at Verbier in the Swiss Alps for vacation. La-dee-dah, Poop Queen. Of course I told her to get over herself, so she crossed her arms and wagged her shoulders at me, "Where was I going?" I could have ripped her hair out, the Ho. I told her I was looking for a house far away, so I wouldn't have to smell her anymore. Then, she said it couldn't be soon enough or far enough. The worst part was Britty didn't say anything.

France's face flushed and her eyes teared up again at the memory of having to stalk off to the girls' room alone and rinse her swollen, red eyes with cold water.

Guess the FABs (France, Ashley, Britty) weren't so fabulous anymore. Ashley spent most of her time with her boyfriend Clayton, and Britty seemed to be hanging more and more with Becca and her gang. So what did it matter if she moved away?

No one would miss her. And she wouldn't miss them either. Her throat tightened. It was so not fair! She swung her legs up over the back of the couch; her head hung upside down off the edge. It helped keep the tears in.

After a few minutes, she decided that was boring, too. She heard her mother coming up the stairs. Mom's been such a freak lately. All sweet and what can I do for you, would you like to play a game one minute and then screaming about the milk being left out the next. Dad was getting the worst of it. Mom crabs at him all the time. France swung up to sitting.

"France? France?" Here she comes. "Oh, there you are. What are you doing?"

"Nothing." Duh.

"Want to play a board game?"

France wished her brother would look up from the computer so she could roll her eyes but instead she made her voice drag, "Which one?"

"I don't care."

"No thanks."

"Can I get you anything?"

"No."

"Have you done your laundry?"

Laundry. Now why hadn't she thought of that? Thrilling. She swung back upright and sat cross-legged. "Could you do it, Mummers?" For this request, she twirled her voice into a confection and made her eyes wide.

Her mother smiled at her, "Sure," then went back downstairs, and France could hear her loading the washing machine. That was too easy. The rest of them got sucked in by Mom's lovey-dovey moves and then got slammed when she went postal, but France knew how to evac before the shit hit the fan.

She flipped upside down again. Still boring. She slid further down; her hair cushioning the thud when her head hit the floor. Erica's taunting flooded back like motion sickness; France's mouth twisted in shame.

"Francine, get down here and do your own laundry." Oh, oh, Dad's pissed.

"Dan, leave her alone. I told her I'd do it," her Mom snapped.

"She's walking all over you. She can get down here and do it herself. Francine, now."

Her mother barked that she was going over to Donna's and then slammed the back door. Dad won that one. He'd pay later. Meanwhile she had to do laundry. She slithered her back all the way down to the floor and rolled to standing. Dirty clothes. More fun with the Burgess family. Stunning.

Chapter 23

The Burgess house was dark and quiet with only the hum of the refrigerator as Liz walked through the house clicking on lights. How had she done this for so many years? Bassa lapped the water in his ceramic bowl. The house's silence spun up this small sound into waves on a lakeshore. It made her think how she'd like to visit her rock by the pond for fortitude.

Showering in the guest bath, the warm water flowed over her body, calming her as if she was washing off one skin to don another. An initiation ritual.

She sat at the counter eating cereal in her new suit for her first day at F.I.B. when a high-pitched ringing pierced her left ear, the death throes of a tone—she'd read somewhere that it meant it was the last time she'd hear sound at that frequency. Perhaps it signaled the end of an era.

She pushed the generic Oat O's down into the milk with her spoon as she chewed. A tender sorrow seeped into the space that was usually filled with the sounds of her bustling family. She resisted putting her head down on her arms or rushing upstairs to bury her nose in the sweet earthiness of Duncan's hair and smooth the blankets over his curled body. She didn't have time.

She ate her breakfast, repeatedly checking the clock on the wall that Dan had crafted to match the chandeliers. Pamela would probably be tromping over here as soon as she left, wanting him to make a dozen of those, too. This thought forged a brotherhood with ancient knights errant, who left their castles unprotected as they galloped off to the Crusades. She frowned while pouring her tea from France's pottery mug into a silver thermal travel cup. 5:40. Time to go. She transferred the lunch Dan had made from the fridge into her Mary Poppins bag and headed out to the cold car.

As she hurried along the fieldstone path to the garage, the sky brightened from vague pastels into vividness; objects firmed up their outlines as dimension-lending shadows popped the landscape out into its daytime relief. Liz filled her lungs with the sweet morning air. It was one of the last breaths of fresh air she'd take until she turned off her headlights tonight and opened the minivan's door.

"Sign in, please, Ma'am. Who are you here to see?"

Liz was surprised by her pride as she answered, "I'm consulting for F.I.B." He checked a list on a screen and wrote out a temporary pass.

"You won't need to check in after you get an employee badge upstairs."

Liz read the *Wall Street Journal* in the 18th-floor reception area until H.R. Heather opened the glass doors. "Liz, thank you for coming. It's critical to have someone with your level of experience working on this project." They retraced their route of two months ago to Heather's office.

"Mr. Bowen, I am looking forward to working with you."

Mr. Bowen was lean and tightly sprung, as if he was waiting for a starting gun to go off. His eyeglasses and suit were more stylish than any other man's in the building, his office devoid of family photographs but decorated with museum quality art, leading Liz to deduce that Paul Bowen was probably gay and in this industry probably not very vocal about it.

"Please call me Paul." He had a firm, not overdone handshake. "You have a very impressive CV, Liz. We could not have found a better person to advise our team."

"Thank you."

"Everyone's in the conference room. If you're ready, why don't we go in and get started."

The morning was spent with introductions and becoming acquainted with the flow diagrams that illustrated how their risk-profiling data was currently gathered and analyzed. At lunchtime, two women grabbed their coats and headed out, while the others scurried back to their desks.

Liz stayed in the conference room to eat her sandwich, using the time to read F.I.B.'s marketing material. When they returned, the discussion moved onto what data needed to be harvested and how they thought that data could be manipulated by the new system they were designing. Liz guided the brainstorming toward detailing what they wanted the data to accomplish. How did they foresee it being used? Was other data relevant? At one point in the afternoon, they took another break.

Liz was having a ball. It was as if she'd never left; however, her fears of slipping back into being snippy and arrogant in this environment were unfounded. This morning she'd been a leader without being condescending. Her approach was more of a mentor than a dictator. The inspiring matriarch rather than the conquering warrior. This go round she was more comfortable in her skin as a woman and a person, and ironically, being relaxed was making her even more effective.

Before it was the adrenalin rush of recognition and acquiring power that drove her; now she was able to enjoy the process and the people. The opportunity to juxtapose who she was then with who she was now breathed a softer confidence into her.

Before she left, Chris Jenkins, an early-thirties, first-level manager, lead Liz to I.T. to get the laptop she'd use while on the project.

After using a pass to electronically open the door, she and Chris walked up a fairly steep ramp to the elevated flooring. Their steps echoed like flamenco dancers on the hollow subfloor that housed the labyrinth of cables and connectors that were the synapses that powered this financial giant and kept their secrets out of the pregnable wireless air. Chris introduced her to Raffi, a handsome young man from Jamaica with hundreds of tiny braids neatly tied back in a thick ponytail. He assigned her a computer and gave her some basic instructions. This very capable, Caribbean delight was undoubtedly a beautiful token of diversity whom this bastion of conservative financiers probably trotted out for visiting liberals.

Raffi showed her how to sign onto F.I.B.'s system, then handed her the carrying case, power cord and key to lock the laptop into the docking system. "Good Times, Mrs. Burgess."

"Good Times." She was beginning to feel like that could be true again.

Exiting, Chris flashed his badge in front of the security pad on the wall and opened the door. It was like leaving the brain of the Cyclops; the door, the behemoth's eye.

"Liz. Liz Burgess? Is that you?" She turned to see a broad man, no taller than Dan with salt-and-pepper hair and mustache, dark brown eyes, and a smile so open it amiably heartened everyone it found. He barreled towards her with open arms, crushing her in a hug marinated in Mediterranean sunshine, ouzo, and baklava. "It's been a long time! You just couldn't stay away from this mess, eh?"

"I was missing you too much, Kostas." Kostas Vosikas had been lured from the Greek isles by his vivacious future wife, Annie Gibson, thirty years ago. Liz had worked very closely with him at Mutual Benefit on a number of initiatives when they were both young enough to be wunderkinds. "When did you leave M-Ben?" she asked.

"About four years after you. These guys gave me the chance to run my own show. Are you working here?"

"I'm consulting with Chris and Paul's group."

He turned to Chris and thumped him on the back. "Good move, Chris. This lady is in a class all by herself. Whatever you're paying her, it should be double." He winked at Liz. "How long are you here?"

"Three weeks."

"Not long enough. You here tomorrow? Lunch?"

"That'd be great."

"Good. Call you in the morning." With that he thumped her on the arm, showed his pass to the pad and entered the Cyclops' eye.

When she pushed the mud room door open at 6:35 that night, her family jumped out from hiding behind chairs and the island. "Mommy! Surprise!" The table was set and the candles lit. Duncan rushed over to give her a hug. Dan parodied the classic homemaker inquiry, "How was your day, dear?" He looked exhausted.

"Fine. Actually, better than I thought. People were ogling over my ideas, quite an ego boost. And I ran into Kostas Vosikas from Mutual Benefit, he looked great. He's running their technology. We're going to have lunch tomorrow."

"Cool. Come sit and have an egg sandwich."

"Great." She smiled tiredly as Dan circled the table, pouring everyone a glass of sparkling cider in champagne flutes. "I'm completely wiped out."

"Bath by candlelight? Foot massage? Aspirin? Apple Martini?" Dan's fingers counted his offerings.

"A bath sounds nice. But right now I want to spend time with my family having this yummy dinner."

"I need to go back to Dunn's place after we eat. But first, a toast. Duncan are you ready?"

Duncan stood behind his chair, pulled a paper out of his pocket and read:

>Congratulations to Mummy on her first day,
>How proud of her words just can't say,
>She's so cool,
>She doesn't drool,
>And we can't wait to split her pay.

Everyone saluted with glasses lifted. "I wrote it on the computer today at school. It's a limerick."

Liz beamed at her family. "Thank you, Duncan; it's wonderful. Thank you, everyone."

Chapter 24

Figaro's was not like the salad place they used to go to for lunch with its tippy tables so close that you could reach over and spear a tomato from your neighbor's plastic bowl. Here, it was white linen napkins on polished wood tables and glass goblets of ice water with a wedge of lemon.

Kostas handed his menu to the waiter and asked Liz, "So, what have you been doing since M-Ben?"

"Running Dan's architecture company and raising three kids." This was a woefully insufficient description of everything she'd been doing but such was the bane of homemakers. She asked, "How old are your kids now?"

"Alexa is 23 and works in an art gallery on Newbury Street. Ari's a senior at Duke. Said he won't come north unless it snows at Christmas." Kostas gave a big laugh and shook his head at the wisdom of youth.

"I can't believe they're so old. What's Annie up to?"

"She's gone back to work now that the kids are gone; a curator of historical documents."

"Good for her." Liz noticed that her napkin had dropped to the floor. She leaned to scoop it up and put it back on her lap. Smoothing it out with her hands, she confessed, "I'm actually looking for full-time work. I interviewed with Heather Stone for the Assistant Actuarial Analyst position, but she thought I was overqualified."

"Argh, Human Resources. They should stick to explaining benefits and planning parties. I wouldn't hire their idea of a software designer for the mailroom. How can they know who'd be good in my department? They've never designed a computer system. They've never even spent fifteen minutes watching what we do. Liz, absolutely, yes, you were overqualified for the job; you're overqualified for 99% of all insurance jobs, but she should have grabbed you for whatever we had available."

"Thanks, Kostas." She realized she was mirroring him in tacit agreement: hands pressed on her thighs, elbows out, hunched slightly forward. She sat back. "It's so discouraging. I was told I was unqualified to manage a four-person auto parts place."

"Why the hell are you interviewing at auto parts? Are you out of your mind?"

"The truth is we haven't had any income for almost two years. I need to get a job doing anything, or we'll have to sell our house and move north. Dan's working part-time at Home Depot, painting houses, and selling paintings and chandeliers at a gallery in Sudbury, but it's nowhere near enough."

"He will have to call Alexa."

A gallery on Newbury Street; Dan would be to the moon. "Thanks, that'd be great!" The perfect distraction from any local gallery owners.

"These are scary times. So many good people out of work. The Federal Reserve keeps lowering interest rates, but it won't stimulate business, there's no confidence. Consumer spending is only up because people are using plastic; dining on their own hearts this spending money they don't have; it doesn't help the economy in the long run. We need businesses to think magnificently and invest in their own expansion." He flicked his hand in that enviable way people from the Mediterranean do that so beautifully expresses disgust and dismissal.

"Right now, we have a hiring freeze and hire consultants in a crunch so we don't have to pay benefits. Forty percent of the people working for me right now are consultants. It makes it impossible to administrate any long-term initiative. The person you need to ask about what's been done is gone. A really stupid way to run a business." Kostas slapped his hands on the table, leaving them there, his thick fingers spread wide. "But I didn't ask you to lunch to gripe about business."

"I love talking like this again."

He crossed his arms high across his broad chest. "Well, I'll talk to H.R. about you, and if you need a recommendation somewhere else just ask."

Liz uncrossed her legs, centered herself on her seat, and placed her feet together squarely in front of her chair. "American Guarantee called. I'm talking to them tomorrow."

Another hand flick. "You don't want to work there. The place is a hell hole. All they do is churn and burn their work force. They have to inflate their salaries in order to get anyone to work there."

"An inflated salary would be fine with me. Kostas, right now I would work for the devil himself."

He nodded his head repeatedly touching his chin to his chest as his index finger tapped his top lip, "You work for A.G., you might be."

Chapter 25

"Welcome to American Guarantee." From behind the reception desk, a woman Liz's age with ash blond hair smiled out of a soft, padded face.

"What job are you interviewing for?"

"I'm not sure. I applied for three jobs on your website, and the person who called about coming in to take the test didn't know which one it was." Liz dug around in the front section of her big bag. "Here are the printouts of the jobs I applied for."

"I'll see if I can find out why you're here." She rolled her eyes. "Sorry about that, the hiring's done out of New York. I'm Jackie, follow me." She lead Liz behind a large screen of frosted glass. "This is the kitchen. Would you like something to drink or eat?"

"I would love a bottle of water and cup of tea."

"Help yourself. Load your pockets." There were platters of antipasto and meats and cheeses and rolls. Huge plastic bowls of strawberries, edamame in the pod, and a three-bean salad. Below the counter were glass-fronted drawers filled with packages of cookies, crackers, nuts, candy, chips, and the like. Hot drinks were available in tall silver thermoses, as well as hot water to make tea, oatmeal, or instant soups. Mini boxes of cereal were stacked in a glassed cupboard above the counter. The refrigerator was stocked with bottles of water, fruit juices, milk, and cream.

Jackie warned, "It looks impressive, but the message is that you're supposed to work through lunch and probably stay through dinner." Jackie's nihilistic candor about her employer evidenced burnout laced with hopelessness and confirmed Kostas' description of the company.

Jackie led Liz out from behind the frosted glass that separated the kitchen from the rest of the floor. A cornice of televisions, each tuned to a different station, lined the top of one wall. Underneath were two large electronic tickers, one with stock prices, another scrolling news headlines. The cubicles had low walls, so the only way to procure even a modicum of privacy was to sit down at your desk. Liz noticed a man hunched over while he talked into his phone's headset so that his head wouldn't pop above the hive divisions. The only enclosed spaces on the floor were two glassed-in conference rooms.

Jackie indicated an empty cubicle near the center of the room. "You have 45 minutes for the test. They're general questions to show that you understand the insurance business. Then, you'll meet with Barbara Kane, the Boston manager. Good Luck!"

Barbara Kane was attractive in the way TV newscasters are attractive: feminine beneath a tough, well-engineered facade, although in her case the toughness did not seem natural. "A trainer's job is about 60% travel to visit trainees in the field for their evaluations and field training. Are you okay with that?"

"Yes."

"Our employees stay at the Ritz or Hilton. Only the best."

"If you only hire the best, then I'm your woman." Liz was in blatant b.s. marketing mode.

"I should warn you that we have a very involved hiring process. The next step is a psychological profile test, then an interview with the home office in New York that we do from here by videoconference." She said this as if she'd just informed Liz that they had the ability to eliminate pollution by wiggling their noses. "The next step would be a two-day paid trial employment in New York and then a trial day in a field office. It's very selective. We pay the highest salaries in the industry because our people work the hardest and are the best. The decision to work at American Guarantee is committing to a way of life."

Liz recognized the brainwashing tactic called cognitive dissonance; however, her situation forced a compliant response. "Sounds good. Is there anything else I can answer for you today?" Need trumped choice in employer prospects.

"I think we're all set. We will call you if we decide to go forward. Thank you for coming in."

"Any idea when I might hear?"

"No. As I mentioned..." her voice condescended..."We are very thorough, which takes time. We will call you."

Chapter 26

"Hi. I'm on the 6:40."

"Hey, congratulations on your first week!"

"Thanks."

"Duncan and I will be at the station with kisses." She heard Dan click the TV onto mute. "We're dropping Chuck at Steven's on the way; France is out babysitting."

"Sounds good. See ya."

Too tired to do anymore work on the train and too bored to just sit there, she decided to call Donna. "Hi. Sorry I haven't called."

"No worries."

"How are you?"

"Like a daisy."

"Oh, good." She hoped that was the right response; half the time Liz didn't quite understand what Donna or Malia were talking about. "Have you heard from Carin?" Liz heard the hum of the road in the background under the sound of her train.

"Nope." Donna sighed. "Like Malia says, you can't help someone until they want to be helped."

"I am so worried. I wish we could do something."

"The dogs and I walk by her house every day, borders on stalking. Hopin' the kids drag her to the curb to see their dog." A wry laugh. "I just hope she knows I'm around if she needs me. And I hope he knows I'm watching."

"You'd scare me."

"Thanks, Red."

"Want a ride to Molly's Monday night?"

"I'll drive so Dan can have your car."

"Thanks. Where are you?"

"Heading to a Tai Chi class, it's kinda martial arts meets meditation. Malia said I should check it out. You move energy around and shit. My Sifu can make people fly backward just poppin' his hand...Watch out, Asshole! Some prick on his cell phone almost ran me off the road."

"Good thing you're not on the phone."

"Ha, ha. OK, I've gotta go move some chi, Mrs. B."

When they got home from the station, Duncan ran upstairs to take a bath. It took almost everything she had to take off her coat and hang it in the mudroom. "I am so exhausted, and it was only three days."

Dan got her plate from the refrigerator, took off the plastic wrap, and warmed it in the microwave. She nodded, "It's so good to be home."

"How'd the interview go, as bad as Kostas said?"

She snorted. "You'd think from the hiring process that I was applying for the Secret Service. Their big qualification is highly rewarded presenteeism. You get paid a lot of money to work fourteen-hour days and weekends, nothing said about quality - or being smart - or creative - or profitable. It was like a fascist state. Their other big claim to fame is they take forever to hire you."

"Sounds like a nightmare." He lit the candles and then went to pour her some wine and a glass of cold water.

"And the sad thing is they could have me if all they offered was lunch and benefits."

"I love that you're easy. Always have." Her mouth was full of chicken enchilada, so she responded by scrunching her face at him.

She swallowed. "What's up with the kids?"

"France was screaming at Chuck about scratching her iPod. Then, she yelled at Duncan to get off the computer. Duncan whined because Chuck gets to go to sleepovers. I reminded him that Chuck didn't get to go until he was eleven, which made absolutely no impression on him. And Chuck left the house pissed off because the computer kept cutting out."

"Fun times at 43 Winding Path Drive. Dinner's delicious, Honey. Thank you."

The irregular hop of little feet plopped down the stairs. "Armick to the rescue!" A jammy-clad Duncan ran across the room: a black cape tied around his neck, black eye mask, orange ski hat, and underwear printed with cars and trucks on over his jammy bottoms. He waved a stick in the air. "Any bad guys at work you need me to fight."

"Not today." She took off the hat and rubbed his wet head, smelling the lavender shampoo. "Didn't you use a towel?"

"Joey farted in the middle of math."

"Well, that's exciting."

"It was wicked funny. He tried to do it again but messed his pants a little."

"Eew. Duncan, I am eating dinner."

"I'm Armick."

"Oh, right. Sorry." Armick was the superhero he'd invented playing in the woods that fall. 'Arm' was short for armor, and 'ick' stood for his stick weapon.

"Can we watch a movie tonight?" Armick asked.

"Go pick one out; I'll be done in a minute."

"Daddy made apple crisp."

"Our favorite!" As Armick scampered up the staircase she asked Dan, who was still speckled in caramel-colored paint from working at Mary Dunn's place, how the painting had gone. There was even some on his eyelashes. Liz happily joked, "Did you get any on the walls?"

He leaned back in the chair, hands behind his head, his elbows out akimbo. "Mary fired me. I wasn't finishing fast enough." He looked beaten down. He'd been acting upbeat for her sake. Sometimes he was too good to be believed. "I told her Chuck and I would work this weekend and be done by Monday, but she told me not to come back."

"That's ridiculous. She won't even be able to get a quote from anyone by then."

"Yep."

"Dan, I am so sorry."

"The worst part is she gave me a check for about half of what she owes us because I, quote, 'wasted time oiling the beams and choosing paint colors' even though she chose the paint. She complained that I painted the outlet covers and light switches to blend in with the walls."

"So, she's cheating us out of two grand because of $10 worth of light switches?"

"Yep."

"What a bitch! You did a way better job than the other crew and for less money." Liz was furious. Mary Dunn knew their financial situation. What kind of heartless scum stole from a struggling family? She'd like to scratch the woman's face off. "This is illegal."

"She knows taking her to court would cost us more than the two grand she's not paying. But, I took pictures on my phone before I left."

Even though this is painting, not architecture, and even though this woman was nuts, Liz knew Dan would take this as a hit on his ability. "She is sick. She had no intention of paying from the start."

"Nope."

Liz ate some more food for Dan's sake but barely tasted it.

They joined Duncan in the TV room with their bowls of apple crisp to watch *The Princess Bride* for the umpteenth time. They were all stacked together on the couch, leaning within one another's arms, cozied up under the afghans that Liz and Francine had knit a few summers ago. Bassa lay on Duncan's feet, anchoring their chain. Every time the pompously brilliant villain exclaimed, "Inconceivable!" Liz thought about the day and had to agree.

Chapter 27

During the past week and a half, Liz had worked at home. After four solid days of rain, the sun's running dive through the window vectored glaringly off the computer screen straight into her eyes.

Failed attempts to rig a shield out of books, pillows and a towel had resigned Liz to close the shades and turn on the lights, which was like working inside an oxymoron on such a sunny day. Pulling up her sleeves, she sat back, stretched, took a sip from her large plastic cup of iced tea, and put her fingers on the home row like when she was ten and learning touch typing on a manual typewriter from a 33rpm record.

Bassa kept trying to lie down on top of her papers next to the computer. After about ten minutes of intermittent bouts with the cat over territorial rights, she was up and out of her chair to refill her cup with more caffeine.

Breakfast dishes were still on the counter, but as she started to clean them up, Dan yelled in from the library where he was dusting that he'd take care of them later. She took the furniture polish in to him. "Here you go."

He looked up and smiled at her. "How's work going?"

"Fine. What time do you head in?" He tensed at her reference to Home Depot.

"3:00."

She held out the can to him.

He shook off her offer. "The stuff I sprayed on the dust rag is working fine."

"But it doesn't condition the wood."

"See ya." He shooed her away with the hand not holding the rag. She put the can down on a shelf in the bookcase and left, hoping he'd reconsider.

Back in the yellow and blue guest room, she sat atop her toile pillow booster. With the appearance of a new lap, Bassa jumped up, walked around in a couple circles, kneaded her thigh, and settled. When she paused to think, Liz scratched Bassa's neck as though mining for gems. A couple of hours later, she heard Dan rummaging around in the kitchen and headed to join him for her lunch. "What are you making?"

"Spaghetti and meatballs for supper."

"Yum." She peered into the bowl. "Was the hamburger on sale?"

"Jesus, Liz. Back off. If I come in to write, you'll probably snark about how I breathe."

"You were planning on breathing?" She was relieved when he laughed. Buttering two pieces of bread for a grilled cheese, she asked, "How did painting go this morning?"

"I finished *Anxiety*, the companion piece for *Fury*, but now I'm seeing it as a triptych, so I'll start *Despair* tomorrow."

"Just what people want hanging over their heads—Fury, Anxiety and Despair."

This joke fell flat. The look he flashed was extreme irritation. "Man, are you hostile! You getting your period or something?"

Her neck stiffened. "I am, but that has nothing to do with anything. God, I hate it when you say that." The toaster oven dinged for her to flip over her sandwich.

His latest idea to drum up business was writing a monthly article for the local paper about interior design: how to redo your kitchen, where to get supplies, et cetera. He'd gotten Home Depot to take out an ad on the page. The first one was scheduled to run in the Saturday real estate section two weeks from now.

After finishing the dinner prep, he threaded his way between the guest room's queen bed and the desks they'd moved in from the garage, so he could open the window to let in some fresh air, but his incursion made Liz feel more claustrophobic.

As he settled in to work, he was oblivious that she was studying him much as a cat studies a chipmunk. Listening to his iPod through a headset, his head bobbed to the Allman Brothers band; his rag wool socks padded out the invisible beat on the wood floor. In his UNH t-shirt, cardigan sweater, faded ripped jeans, reading glasses, and backwards baseball cap, he looked like a juvenile, aging, academic with rock and roll fantasies. Endearing. She wondered what she looked like in her stretch pants, headband and Patriots Super Bowl sweatshirt. At best, a middle-aged matron going to work out at the Fitness Factory. At worst, a hag having a bad hair day.

She glanced back at Dan. His head bounced so emphatically to the beat, it was surprising that his Boston Red Sox cap didn't fall onto the keyboard. Sporadically, there was a flurry across the keys, and then pauses during which he might add an air drumming riff into the mix while he thought. He was a million miles away from her, that is until he looked over and grinned, and in an overloud voice because of his inserted earbuds said, "This is like old times, working together like this. We're good, Babe."

As she responded with their usual refrain, "Always have been," she wondered if they still were "good" because they seemed to be pulling away from each other at the speed of light.

"Always will be."

An hour later, Dan announced that he was done with the first draft. He walked over to deposit a kiss on the top of her head. "I think I'll go out and get started on *Despair*."

"I could model for that one."

"Rough going?"

She just hummed an affirmative.

He said, "Maybe I'll hear from Kostas' daughter about the Boston gallery this week."

"Call."

It was his turn to hum a response. Bassa extricated himself from looking out the window behind the drawn curtains when he heard Dan pour dry cat food into his bowl. The back door thudded as he headed out to the second floor of the garage that was now his unheated studio.

He was still out painting when Chuck and France came home from school. Liz heard the kids come in and root around in the kitchen. A few minutes later, Francine appeared at the guest room door. "Mummers, can I go to the mall with Ashley and Britty?"

Pushing her hands down on her knees and flexing her back straight, Liz turned away from the computer screen toward her daughter, "Well, hello to you, too."

"Oh, yeah, hi. Can I go?"

"No."

"Why?"

"The mall is a magnet for trouble."

"Everyone else will be there."

"Francine, when have we ever done anything because of what everyone else is doing?"

France stormed off. "When do we ever do anything?" Liz heard the back door slam and decided to go to the kitchen for some water.

Chuck was sitting at the counter, eating the fried egg and cheese sandwich he'd made for himself. "You have to trust her sometime, Mom."

Liz sighed and plopped down into one of the chairs. "This is not the time."

He shrugged. "How'd your work go today?"

France flew in the back door, grabbed her coat and was almost back out, when Liz barked, "Where do you think you're going?"

"Dad's taking me to the mall on the way to work."

"What! No, he's not. I told you no, which does not mean go ask your father and see what he says."

France's glare could have blasted Liz's nose through the back of her head. "Next time I won't ask you; you never let us do anything."

"Go upstairs and cool down." Liz hissed through clenched teeth.

Francine responded to this suggestion by throwing her jacket on the floor and stomping through the kitchen, saying in that nasty teenage tone, "If you want to get rid of me so badly, then let me go to the mall."

Liz was firm. "I am not trying to get rid of you. This is called parenting, and I've decided the mall is not a place to hang out."

"Argh!" Francine continued her stomp up the stairs to her bedroom sputtering, "We never get to do ANYTHING." Her voice got louder the farther away she got, "We have to be soooo good because we don't have any money, and everyone is sooooo stressed. Well, I am sick of it."

Her comment about having to be so good was the poison dart that hit its mark. Liz was speechless until France had stormed to the top of the stairs, by which time Liz's shock had swung back to anger. "And don't slam that door." The door wasn't slammed, but the defiant force with which the doorknob was wrenched as the door was quickly, but quietly, closed clearly communicated Francine's point.

After Liz met Duncan at the bus, she went back to work in the guest room and listened to his distant piano practice as she banged away on the computer keys. When she took a break to get more iced tea from the fridge, she noticed that the music had been replaced by a muffled whimpering. She started up the bedroom stairs. "Duncan?"

"Mom?" The muffled response came from under her feet. She wheeled around and headed back down the stairs and into the library.

Pulling open the secret door, she saw a teary little boy sunken into the pillows. "What's the matter?"

"I wasted a sandwich."

"What?" She reached in to wipe his face with the blanket and then pushed his hair back from his forehead.

His lips shook, rippling his words. "I got hungry and didn't want to bother you, so I tried to make a sandwich, and I made jelly and fluff instead of peanut butter and fluff and now I wasted two pieces of bread—that costs money!" He flipped onto his side so his back was to her and pulled the blanket over his head, but it did little to dampen the impact his sobbing had on her heart.

She crawled in on all fours and enveloped him with her body, holding him, rocking him. "Duncan, it's okay. It was a mistake and not even a big one. It's okay. You're more important than two pieces of bread or any amount of money. Please don't cry.

I'm so proud of you for making your own sandwich. You're such a grownup, helpful boy."

"I'm bad."

"No, you just made a mistake; that isn't bad, that's part of learning. But, if you do it again then you'll have to sit in the yard next time it rains." There was a little giggle under the down-filled duvet. "But I doubt that will happen. Lesson learned. We'll scrape off the fluff and give the bread to the birds. They'll love the treat."

Duncan

"Duncan, that was the art gallery on the phone. They sold my two paintings! Let's go drop off the triptych and pick up the check. We can get some hotdogs and sparkling cider on the way home to celebrate."

Duncan looked up from under the piano. "Do I have to, Dad? I'm gonna have a battle when I'm done building my Lego city."

"Will you be okay here by yourself?"

"Yep. Put the alarm on, and I won't answer the door like Mummy says."

"I shouldn't be more than an hour."

"'K. That's really cool, Daddy."

"Don't tell Mom if she calls. I want to surprise her."

Duncan was under the piano, engrossed in acting out an imaginary battle with his superheroes.
"Get out of here. Leave and never come back.
- I will rule the world and you will be my slave.
- Never.
- Then fight and learn the meaning of defeat.
- That's where you're wrong, Muldar. You will be the one to know annihilation.
- Help, Batman. I'm trapped. Save me.
- So that is where you have taken her, Muldar. You'll never win. Good always triumphs over evil. Didn't you watch cartoons when you were a kid? Take this.
- Argh
- Ugh
- Patew
- Kkk
- Ugh
- Take that.
- Ugh
- Now maybe you'll..."

Whanh. Whanh.

Duncan's head shot up and the figures froze in his hands. Whanh. Whanh. The house alarm was blaring. He scrambled out from under the piano, shot a look at the kitchen to make sure no real-life bad guys were coming, and darted to his secret place under the stairs. He quickly and quietly closed the panel in the wall behind him but didn't dare turn on his flashlight.

Once hidden, he opened the peephole that looked out into the den; he didn't see anything, but the view was very small. He sat back. His heart was like war drums in his ears. The superheroes in his hands were shaking. If only they were real. The alarm was still blasting. When will Daddy get home? Whanh. Whanh. It was so loud he couldn't hear if someone was in the house. Will they find him? Did they see him come in here? Bassa was out there all by himself! Would they hurt a cat?

There was only the narrow stream of light from the peephole. He looked through it again then cowered back. Did he hear something? His ears strained for any noise buried under the alarm to tell him what was going on. Would a big, hairy hand with dirty fingernails open the panel of his hiding place? What would he do? If he screamed, no one would hear him. Repeated visits to the peephole—nothing. Should he make a run for the woods and hide there until Daddy came home? Wait! The drumming in his ears shot faster, booming. Heavy footsteps. Men's voices. Someone help! His breathing was fast and shallow. He had to stay very still. His skin pulled tight. Daddy, where are you? Please come home. No! Don't come. They'll kill you. Crying flooded his body but he tried to gulp it down so the men wouldn't hear him. One walked up the stairs above his head. He shrank lower with every heavy tread. Dear God, please help me. I'm a good boy. Please help me. Another pair of boots crossed the living room. He froze. He looked toward the peephole. Go look, then you can tell the police what the man looked like. But he couldn't make himself move. Quick, look before the man leaves the room! Duncan heaved himself at the peephole. The man was out of view. Here he comes. He's big. He has on all dark clothes and a big hat.

A policeman! Oh, thank you, God.

He crawled out of his hidey hole. He tried to call out to the officer, but his voice was only a scratch in his throat. Then some sound came stabbing out. "Help. I'm here." He tried to stand but his legs were so weak; they were going invisible under him. The sound of running boots.

"Son, are you okay?" Strong arms around him, helping him up. "Those are nice super heroes you have there."

Duncan looked at the toys still clutched in his hands. His withheld sobs suddenly loosened in gulps that stabbed through his whole body. He whispered to his superheroes, both plastic and human, "Where's Daddy?"

Chapter 28

Liz came flying into the house drenched and wild eyed. The sound of her shaky, sobbing son on the phone had sent her sprinting to the station through the torrential March storm that was smashing down on the sidewalks.

Sarah had picked her up at the train and dropped her home because no one had picked up her return phone calls. Her voice bounded ahead of her into the house. "Duncan! Where are you?"

"Mummy! You're home early!" By now fully recovered, he ran to her with Koko the gorilla in his arms and his smile lighting up his face.

"Duncan, Mummy has been so worried about you. Are you all right?"

"The policemen let me run their siren!"

"So, you're okay?"

"Yep. They said I was really smart to hide in my secret place. I showed them since they're the good guys." She kissed both his cheeks and hugged him again. "Mommy, you're getting me all wet."

"Sorry. Where's your father?" She refrained from saying *because I am going to kill him.*

"In the den. We're playing Yu-Gi-Oh!. I damaged two thousand of Dad's life points using a Yami enhanced Ga Jinn, the mystical genie of the lamp."

"Good for you." Liz took a chance that this was the right response since she had no idea what his last sentence meant. She looked up as Dan came in looking shamefaced and braced for an explosion. "Duncan, could you go get the mail?"

"In the rain?"

"Oh, right. Why don't you go play on the computer for a few minutes, so I can talk with Daddy?" He and Koko vanished almost before she could finish the sentence, thrilled with the offer of extra computer time beyond the usual hour-a-day limit.

Liz reeled on her husband, her tone souring instantly. "Where were you? I've been calling and calling."

"Sorry, I unplugged the phone; people kept calling when they heard what happened."

"But where were you when the alarm went off?"

"I ran to the gallery, and I guess I didn't shut the back door all the way so when the wind kicked up before the storm, it blew the back door open and set off the alarm. I got home ten minutes later."

"A lot can happen in ten minutes." Pamela's face flashed like a red warning light in her mind. "Why was seeing Pamela so important that you'd leave him like that?" She was breathless from having dashed into this mine field: reckless, daring, and terrified.

"He was fine. If it hadn't been for the wind..."

"He was not fine," her voice shrilled. "We are lucky DSS hasn't shown up to take him away!" Weeks of pent up anxiety and anger gushed up her throat. Her mind was jumbled. She wanted Pamela to disappear. She wanted her old life. They didn't seem to be missing her. Dan wasn't doing the housework right, and he wasn't vigilant enough with the kids. Her breathing raced. "Why couldn't you wait or take him with you?"

"I wasn't thinking."

"Not about him." He'd been thinking about Pamela. Liz's thoughts were flying, savage, frantic, and someone was going to pay for her confusion, her fear.

"Liz, that isn't fair."

She knew it wasn't, but this was not about being fair.

"What's not fair is you playing Yu-Gi-Oh! when there's laundry in the den waiting to be folded and dirty dishes on the counter, the cat hasn't been brushed, and the groceries weren't put away where they're supposed to be. It's like a frat house. How can I go off to work with the house falling apart?"

"I get it done eventually."

His voice was calm, but flat; he wasn't rising to her bait, so she threw more at him.

"What kind of example are you showing the kids? You need to grow up and take some responsibility."

"What! Screw you, Liz. I am responsible. I just have a different way of doing things."

"Responsible? Responsible! You call having the police show up at the house responsible? It's all about having a good time with you. You just want to be the fun guy, so the kids like you better."

Silence followed as they digested the words she'd just spiked over the net; then Duncan's voice came from the top of the stairs by the computer room. "Please don't fight. Don't be mad at Daddy. I'm okay." They heard his feet coming down the stairs. "I got scared for a little bit, but the police said I did a really good job. Everyone gets scared sometimes." He appeared at the bottom of the stairs still clutching Koko, his face more scared now than when she'd come home. "And Dad said real courage isn't doing something dangerous; it's facing your fear. Right, Dad? I was courageous." The house held its breath.

Liz exhaled then said, "Yes, you were. Mummy got scared too, and it made me yell. I guess I didn't handle my fear as well as you or Daddy. I'm sorry. How about we go in the den and I watch you guys finish your Yu-Gi-Oh! game?"

Dan waited for her to cross by him. "I am really sorry, Lizzie. I'll try harder. I won't leave him alone again."

"Being home is the hardest job in the world." He could take this as an olive branch or not. She wasn't even sure how she meant it. She liked being back at work, but she wasn't comfortable with his being the one at home. This just got messier and more ridiculously complicated. She was exhausted and aggravated. She'd go to bed as soon as she'd snuggled Duncan up. She needed to hold him close after today's scare, more for herself than for him.

Chapter 29

"Hi, Mom. Did I wake you up?"

"No." Elaine's voice was worried. "Where are you?"

"I'm driving into Boston; Dan didn't need the car today. One more week at F.I.B." Liz then answered the next question before it was asked. "The traffic's slow; I'm using the hands-free to call and confess how I laid into Dan last night." She took a sip of iced tea from her travel mug and told Elaine the alarm story, then admitted, "When Duncan said everyone gets afraid, it hit me that I was so upset because I'm afraid that the kids like being home with Dan more than with me. I would. And I'm afraid that if I get a full-time job, I'll be an even smaller part of their lives."

"Liz, don't be silly. You're their mother."

"Lots of people don't like their mothers, take it from me."

"So is this about your relationship with your kids or with your mother?"

"Wow. Umm, probably more about my mother. How stupid is that since the woman's been dead twenty-two years?"

"It's not stupid at all. You're trying to learn from her mistakes. That's smart. But Liz, you're a great mom and wife whether you work in Boston or not." Liz loved Elaine so much.

She nodded her head even though Elaine couldn't see, and then scratched at the budding itch on her forearm through her jacket. "I hate it when I call home, and they're having this jolly time. My heart just about breaks."

"Then don't call home."

"Oh!" Could it be that simple? "But what if they need me?"

"Then they'll call you."

"Right."

"So, how is Dan doing when he's not neglecting the kids?"

"A lot of what he does isn't bad really, just different. You know how men let kids take more risks. It scares me to death, but the kids are probably learning to be resilient and independent. Yesterday I would have treated Duncan like a baby, and he couldn't have felt proud about being brave." Liz sighed as the truth of what she was saying sunk in.

"What a wonderful thing to notice. See what a great mom you are?"

"Thanks." She changed lanes to one that might move faster. "I think Dan is really discouraged."

"Of course he is. I am, too. It's ridiculous someone as talented as he is can't get work. You either."

"No one's hiring. And no business is going to redo their office when they're laying people off."

"It's amazing the country can keep going with the bunch of ninnies that are running things."

"It's so frustrating being up against this faceless power that's driven by greed and self-interest, not common sense or compassion. Get ready, we may be moving in with you before you know it." The traffic inexplicably picked up speed.

"We'd be thrilled except that it'd be awful for you to leave your beautiful home. Dan's a very lucky man to have you, Liz. We've always thought so."

"Thanks, Mom."

"For what?"

"Listening."

"We love you."

"Thanks for that, too."

The sun was rising over Boston, its bright rays stabbing straight into commuters' eyes. Liz grabbed at the sunglasses in the well between the front seats even though they'd only tint her blindness. She clutched the steering wheel of her hurtling automobile. It felt as though she'd already been up for hours, and the day hadn't even begun.

Chapter 30

Elaine's words stayed with Liz like the vestiges of a vivid dream that tainted your morning, whispering promises that something would be resolved although it's not clear what exactly that something is.

"Liz?" Liz rolled back on the chair's casters to see Leesa Keller standing at her cubicle's opening, her tawny hair pulled back in a clip, emphasizing her stylishly framed hazel eyes, aristocratically long nose and small chin. Leesa adjusted her glasses snuggly against her face. "Caitlin and I were wondering if you'd like to walk with us?"

Liz surprised herself a bit when she responded with, "I'd love to."

"Meet you at the elevators in fifteen minutes."

Liz reached into her leather bag for a report and saw a greeting card envelope with her name in Dan's blueprint font across the front.

The card had a vase with bright flowers next to a teapot and cup of tea in which he'd written:

> *"A mother is not a person to lean on*
> *but a person to make leaning unnecessary."*
>   -*Dorothy Canfield Fisher*

> *Liz,*
> *I know it's hard not to be home and even harder to watch me do it so badly. You laid a super foundation that makes my job as stay-at-home parent so much easier. I see your work every day in their manners, their hard work, their thoughtfulness and their self-confidence to be themselves. You are still teaching them by being the incredible woman you are.*
>   *Love,*
>   *Dan*
>   *xoxoxox...*

How did she ever land him? He was cute and kind and smart, and she was awkward and withdrawn and moody. Even though she could spin numbers like a human calculator, she'd screwed up their finances. And now, she was so afraid of losing him that all she could do was push him away. She swallowed down the lump in her throat and called to thank him for the card and tell him how wonderful he was. When she asked what he was doing, he listed household chores, and she imagined him cradling the phone on his shoulder, ticking his tasks off on his fingers. In her effort to stop micromanaging him, she checked herself from asking whether he'd put the dishwasher on the Sanirinse cycle.

"By the way, congratulations. I heard Pamela's message this morning about selling your paintings!"

He graciously didn't point out that Liz hadn't given him a chance to tell her last night and instead answered the question she would invariably ask, "I only get 40% so my cut was..."

"$440." Argh, shut up. Why did she have to be such a stinking know-it-all?

"Nope, $402.84, after taxes." She could hear the grin in his voice.

"Okay, wise guy, see ya in 5.25 hours."

He chuckled. "Looking forward to it. We're a great team, Babe."

"Always have been."

"Always will be." As she hung up, she burrowed into the comfort of their traditional chorus. He sounded better. She hoped it was because of Pamela's news about his paintings and not because of the woman herself.

All Liz knew about Leesa and Caitlin was that they were both bright, in their early thirties, and married with children. Both women were taller than her but then so was almost everyone over the age of twelve. While Leesa's face jutted forward, Caitlin's was rounded with no prominent features except a lovely smile; when she took off her makeup, her face probably all but disappeared.

Leesa suggested a figure-eight loop around the Common and the Public Garden, so they headed west through the financial district's vertical cement and asphalt grid. It was hard to accommodate three abreast on the sidewalk at this time of day, so they kept jostling backwards and forwards while maintaining verbal contact, in order to weave around and through the oncoming or slower moving foot traffic.

"How old are your children?"

"I have Jack, who's 4 and Eden, who's 2. Caitlin has Claire, 5, and Dylan, who's 6 months."

"Dylan just weaned himself; a blissful end to furtive bathroom pumping and storing it in the fridge next to Paul's lobster ravioli."

As they chatted, they breezed by the Granary Burial Ground, where three signers of the Declaration of Independence as well as the victims of the Boston massacre lay, passed Park Street Church, and crossed into the Common, passing the sausage cart next to the subway entrance and headed up the hill toward the State House.

Liz was puffing a bit with exertion as she shared, "When I was nursing my daughter, I was working late and had to pump in a bathroom stall when a V.P. and an intern came in all over each other. They crashed against my stall door, the lock gave; I jumped up, the pump came off, milk sprayed everywhere; it was all over them, the stall, me." Caitlin and Leesa stopped walking, their mouths open; Liz had to circle back for them. "Mortifying, but it paid off. Four months later when I decided to stay home, somehow, magically, I got a ten-month severance package."

"Sweet."

They started walking again as Caitlin asked, "Why did you decide to stay home?"

Liz slowed partly because she was out of breath and partly because she knew this was dangerous territory given the audience. "My husband's business had grown, and he needed to hire someone part-time, so we decided it made sense for me to do it. Back then, the money we saved on the daycare covered the health insurance I gave up."

"I keep wondering whether to keep working. I love it, but I feel like I should be home."

Liz was struck by her candor. "A friend of mine says, don't 'should' on yourself. Do what's right for you, and by extension, best for your family."

"But it's so hard to know what's best. Did you like being home?"

"It was really, really hard at first. Endless Candyland, dirty diapers, and tantrums couldn't compete with a paycheck and an assistant." Liz decided they sincerely wanted to know how she felt. "It's such an individual thing, but I felt trapped at home. It got more interesting as the kids got older, and I made friends and got into the swing of it. Truthfully, if the whole economy hadn't crashed, I wouldn't be here. Thirteen years ago I felt I should be home but wanted to be working, then a couple months ago I totally dreaded going back to the whole corporate thing, and now I think I'd like a full-time job."

"But your kids are older," Leesa reasoned. "They're more self-sufficient."

"Kind of, although sometimes I think they need me even more as teenagers."

"I'm lucky to have the choice whether to stay home, but then I feel guilty about choosing work, like I'm being selfish," Caitlin said. "I'd lose my mind at those playgroups where they talk about 'lil sweetie pants' last poop."

They were at the bottom of Beacon Hill and turned left along the western edge of the Public Garden.

"Choosing what makes us whole isn't bad or selfish. Being in our kids' lives doesn't come from being there physically, it's about listening, being engaged emotionally, and them knowing that you really have them as your priority."

"But how can we know we aren't dooming them to years of therapy?"

They turned into the Garden and crossed the bridge spanning the drained lagoon with the swan boats still in dry dock. Liz sighed, "My friend Donna says that kids will blame you no matter what you do, so you may as well do what you want...actually, 'let your tits fly free' is what she says."

"What?!" They'd crossed Beacon Street back into the Common. "That's quite the philosophy."

"Think I'd like her."

Liz smiled at herself, surprised by what she was about to say, but knowing it was absolutely true, "I guess it just comes down to: do what makes sense until it doesn't anymore."

Dan

He should get up off the couch, but he couldn't make himself do it. This morning, he'd put chicken in a Ziploc plastic bag with Italian salad dressing to marinate, folded the clothes in front of the TV, and gotten sucked into *Die Hard* for the next hour and a half with the only interruption being Liz's phone call to thank him for the card he'd slipped into her bag. After lunch, it was like he'd collided with a wall of sludge, so he'd lain down on the couch with the library copy of *Architectural Digest*, but when his eyes kept closing and Bassa jumped up on his chest, he threw the magazine down and stretched his legs out under the afghan. He didn't have the strength to hoist the "it's a happy day" mantle anymore, so the last thing he was still providing his family was gone.

Both his and the cat's eyes flew open at the sound of the back door. "Daddy? Anybody home?"

Dan's head felt like cement; his tongue, mud. He garbled out some tonal response that didn't carry into the kitchen. His feet flailed, pedaling in the air, trying to get free of the blanket. His arms windmilled for some surface to push off. With coordinated motion still a bunch of heartbeats away and his breathing as rapid as if he'd just run a sprint instead of this ridiculous thrash with an afghan, he called out "Duncan, I'm in here."

"Can I have a Pop-Tart?"

"Sure." Liz would have told him to have a banana first. Sitting up, Dan pulled the comforter around himself and picked his magazine back up.

Duncan walked in with a milk mustache. "The fire's out, Dad. Want me to stoke it up for you?"

"Sure." Duncan was the age when fire held the spot that sex would have in a few years. "Do you have homework?"

"I did it on the bus." Duncan yanked a few leaves of newspaper from the wicker box next to the fireplace. The supply was getting low now that *The New York Times* and *Boston Globe* had been cancelled. "What are we going to do when we run out of paper?" He crumpled the pages up and tossed them onto the coals.

"Luckily, fire season is almost over."

"What about next year?"

Dan knew the question went beyond fires. Duncan was asking if they'd still be living here; if they'd be able to afford newspapers again. To reassure his son, Dan forced energy into his voice, "A lot happens in a year. By next year, we could have a garage full of newspapers or we might be reading the paper online. Anything's possible." He mussed his son's hair, who'd come to sit next to his dad.

"Yep." Duncan studied the fire.

"Besides, you guys empty enough cereal boxes to start bonfires all winter anyway."

"Yeah!" He jumped up and ran out to the recyclables bin in the pantry and came back triumphantly clutching flattened, store-brand oat O's and corn flakes boxes. Dan put down the magazine and watched him. Duncan held up the box of six-inch long matches. "Can I light these?"

"Sure." Duncan's smile spread wide at being granted this privilege. Happiness didn't have to cost a lot. Dan sat up. "Buddy, your energy's inspired me. After I check emails, I think I'll go out and paint a bit. You want to come?"

"Nah. I think I'll practice. Can I still light these?"

"While I'm in the office but no playing with the fire or matches when I go out back." Dan picked up Bassa and carried him to the computer in the guest room. He opened an email from Liz that she'd sent to him and her girlfriends an hour ago:

Hi Everybody,
After walking with a couple of co-workers at lunchtime, one of them sent me this. I thought it summed up our Monday nights, as well as Dan's outlook (though happily he's very much a man):

Today is International Very Good Looking, Damn Smart Woman's Day, so please send this message to someone you think fits this description. And remember this motto to live by:
Life should NOT be a journey to the grave with the intention of arriving safely in an attractive and well-preserved body, but rather to skid in sideways, chocolate in one hand, wine in the other, body thoroughly used up, totally worn out, and screaming, "WOO HOO, what a ride!
Yours, Liz

Dan typed his reply:
To my Very Good Looking, Damn Smart Wife,
What a ride!
Love,
Your Tired, Adoring, Damn Lonely Man

He clicked *send* and sat back in his chair, his eyes locked on her email. Taking a walk break at work, forwarding emails that a year ago she would have instantly deleted...intriguing. He collected the snoozing Bassa into his arms and headed out to the garage after telling Duncan to stop messing with the fire.

The studio wasn't as cold today. With the electric teapot filled and plugged in, he slid on his painting shirt.

He hoped Pamela would like this piece. Quite a woman, she balanced being a strong, successful businessperson with being really feminine. She had a great, light-handed sense of humor. Maybe it was her artistic side that softened her. When they talked about art, the creative process, or even cooking, there was that cool connection you have when someone really gets you and what you're talking about. Like her idea to paint houses and offering to be his first client. House painters get ten grand or more a job around here. She'd joked about a brilliant painter using his talent on her clapboards. How was a woman as bright and fun and hot as her still single? And what a body. His painting prep got jouncier as he thought about it. His chest expanded. He shook his head to release the adrenalin. He thought about last week when she had mentioned that she'd never been to the Arnold Arboretum in Jamaica Way. Liz was working in Boston, and he wasn't scheduled to go into Home Depot until that night, so they'd headed in on a whim.

It'd been one of those great, late April days. Warm, but the air had a cool edge around it. The leaf buds were still tiny, light green florets so that the crisscrossed branches tatted a fluttering lace edging along the skyline. Daffodils, tulips, grape hyacinth, and forsythia filled the gardens, while later plants were shooting up young stalks, putting in a bid to raise their colors next. He'd felt so energized. Younger than he had in a long time. They'd talked and joked. She'd struck a pose in front of a fountain as if she were a statue of some nubile goddess. She'd laughed and lightly touched his arm as she mentioned that she'd always wanted to pose for a nude. Eyes alight she'd asked, could he paint her? Caught up in her enthusiasm he'd said sure and had to put his hands in his pockets until his hard-on went away.

He picked out a brush from the can and squeezed his pigments out on a piece of plywood. Today he was working on a new piece, Unease. He loaded his brush with Ultramarine Violet and streaked it across the canvas.

Some people got knocked around under stress because they braced for the impact. Liz been like that since she was a kid, but this time, she was relaxing into the stress a little. It'd be nice if she could really let go. He was going through the same shit, and you didn't see him henpecking and bitching at everyone.

He stepped back from the canvas. There should be a sense of apprehensiveness to the piece he was painting: a tautness, some self-loathing. He put the brush handle he'd been using in his mouth and dipped another into Talens Red. He painted a large hollow circle then plopped the brush into a palette cup. Applying Brownish Madder to a third brush, he made an outer circle around the one he'd just drawn. Sometimes she made him nuts, but he admired how hard Liz worked to get it right, to do life well.

He took the brush out of his mouth and made downward slashes as if they were a driving crimson rain. Next, he chose Burnt Carmine and stood back to observe what he'd done so far.

He nodded to the canvas, stepped forward, and thought about what paints he'd need to paint a nude of Pamela.

Chapter 31

It was the second Monday in May. The interior of Molly's colonial looked like a Country Homes pop-up book: Shaker furniture, stenciled borders, a quilt folded over a pine rack, dried flowers hanging upside down in clumps; the walls graced with prints of Grandma Moses village scenes and cross-stitched homilies.

When Liz walked into the dining room, Donna jumped up from the table, "Come on in, Red!" She had a red grape juice seltzer in one hand, chocolate in the other, and was wearing a hot pink, long-sleeved tee-shirt with "What a Ride!" scrawled on it in black magic marker. "Here's to Mrs. Burgess sending funnies over the Internet. What a hoot." Liz shook her head at Donna's antics as she took a seat. Oh, how she'd love to jump into her friend's skin for an hour and feel what it was like to be so irreverent, loud, and free.

The table was covered with colored and printed papers, stickers, beads, sequins, lace, colored ink pens, scissors with blades that cut different patterns, and other razor tools for making geometric-shaped cut-outs to mat photos. Molly was teaching them how to scrapbook, an activity Liz saw as involving way more time than the task warranted and resulting in a product way too tacky to be displayed.

"The email was hilarious," Molly agreed. "But it made me think how somewhere between the peanut butter and jelly, I've lost my oomph."

"Midlife is a bitch, Miss Molly. I have to wear reading glasses in the shower to shave or I end up with hair-striped pits," Donna cackled.

"I had a better idea of who I was when I was eight. Now, I'm like the lost sock buried under everyone else's stuff," Molly moaned.

"Where's the passion in our lives?" The clutch of photos in Donna's hand arced through the air as she waved her arms with mock drama.

"Exactly!" Molly was cutting out red, white and blue stars. "It's not like I don't do things for me: the women's crisis center, yoga, scrapbooking. But there is still something...I don't know...something missing."

Sarah's melodic voice was earnest. "I think you're looking for what the French call your métier, the passion you have to do no matter what."

"But how do you find it?"

"The answer's inside us; it just gets buried like you said, Mol." Malia glanced to Liz to check if she should shut up. Not getting any signal, she continued. "When we get quiet enough, we can hear what our heart already knows." She picked up some paper and the circle cutter. "You can ask God or your inner wisdom what your passion is and then keep a look out. Clues will show up, but you have to keep really open because the answer can be very different from what you're expecting. Even from what you think you asked for. If you get too attached to a specific answer, you can miss the truth." When Liz touched her chin, their "stop talking" sign, Malia shut her mouth and gave Liz an appreciative wink.

Donna raised her glass with gusto, "Well, I'm all for getting a boatload of passion into my life...To indulging our métiers with wild abandon!"

"To our métiers! To wild abandon!"

Molly jumped up and went to the bookcase. "So, before we get started, I thought you might like to see a couple of my albums for ideas." Each page had a theme and coordinating color scheme.

"This is a work of art!"..."An heirloom, Molly."..."You put so much time into this."

"Thank you."

Even though Liz thought the scrapbooks schmaltzy, she noticed Molly's pride, something she would have missed a year ago. Another unfamiliar observation popped off her tongue in separate syllabic bubbles. "Molly, you light up about your scrapbooks. Could they be your métier?"

Molly considered it then shook her head, "It's just a stupid hobby."

Even more surprisingly, Liz went on, "Nothing that makes you happy is stupid."

"But it doesn't help anyone."

"It helps you recharge. You don't always have to do things for other people." Liz felt the surge that feeds inspiration course through her. "Couldn't you offer scrapbooking workshops to the women at the crisis center? Like art therapy. The scrapbooks could document their courage starting a new life, a creative support group. It could be really empowering."

There was a stunned pause; Molly was radiant. "What a cool idea! Liz, that's awesome."

"I just noticed what you were saying."

"Good noticing." Malia beamed at Liz.

Their talk moved onto some photos Malia had of Colombia, but Liz's thoughts stayed behind. What she'd just done was so new and felt so good that she wanted to let the hum of it soak into her skin, to acknowledge it so it could become her natural response.

Molly brightly interrupted, "So, Liz, how's your job in Boston going?"

"Friday's my last day. It's been a lot of fun having people say "good job" instead of France telling me I'm a moron all the time." She smiled.

"Anything from the other place?" Sarah asked.

"They've scheduled the next step in the interview process."

"Cool."

"A friend said it's a nasty place to work but beggars can't be choosers."

"Too true." Donna grumbled.

"Well, since I last worked in Boston, I've aged from wonder girl to crone. The young mothers ask my advice about balancing work and home, which is a riot because it's the last area I have any expertise." Liz voiced something that had been bothering her for awhile. "I've felt caught in between working and at-home moms. Why are women so judgmental of each other?" She put down her scissors. "I feel like I have to be so careful about what I say, which is so ridiculous because basically everyone's concerns are the same—money, family, getting it all done for everyone. Why don't women show compassion instead of being so competitive?"

"And we all need to find our métier." Molly added.

"And help each other."

"Ya, and let other people help us."

Liz blurted out another idea before she had a chance to think about it. "Why don't we organize a charity walk that brings women together, like for breast cancer or the school?" Her brain felt like a cool, sweet breeze had just moved through; this must be how Dan feels when he's designing. It was intoxicating. She noticed from her friends' postures that her charge had shot around the circle.

Donna boomed like a downshifting semi. "You're on fire tonight, Red!" She slapped her thighs. "We'll raise money to help women like Carin!"

"What a great idea!"..."Let's do it!"..."Finally, something we can do."

Molly yelped, "A shelter! After Donna couldn't find a place for Carin to go, we've been talking at the crisis center about how the closest shelter is all the way in Cambridge and how it's usually filled. I bet they'll be wild about the idea."

Donna stood up, "Great, now that we can cross that off the World's Troubles list, I've gotta piss."

Liz looked at the page she'd been working on. Frilly and sloppy. This was definitely not her métier. She looked up from the mess in front of her to mention, "Dan and Chuck are going to paint houses this summer, and France and Duncan are going to weed for people."

"Our house is way overdue. We will totally hire them," Sarah enthused.

"Speaking of painting, has Mary Dunn ever paid you? I feel awful about getting Dan involved with her."

"Don't. It kept him busy and gave him the house painting idea. I called her yesterday and said she was scheduled to appear in small claims court June 12, and she coughed up another twelve hundred dollars, which I deposited first thing this morning."

"Oh, thank goodness," Malia said with obvious relief. "I just sold her house, and it's only right that part of the commission should pay off the rest of what she owes you."

"Malia, that is ridiculous."

"Dan's work helped sell it."

"No. Malia, that's too much."

"I could give it to your kids, and they could split it between something fun and their favorite charity. It could give them a sense of empowerment to help someone else when they might be feeling kind of powerless."

Liz reflexively looked down at her hands as she squeezed the scissors in a vice grip.

"Please, Liz, then I won't have to feel so guilty about the whole mess."

Liz rolled her lips together. Her friends were so amazing. "That..." Her voice faltered, "That would be really nice." Such an inadequate statement. "Thank you."

Donna came bombing back into the room. "So today I told my no-job, no-sex, porn-trolling, piece-of-shit to move the fuck out."

Donna sat down casually as if she'd just announced tuna was on sale at Market Basket. Everyone else looked as though the cans of tuna had all just fallen off the shelves onto their heads.

"Is he gone for good or is it a break?" Sarah asked.

"Don't know. But right now, I'm feeling pretty much like, 'been there, done that'." She picked up her glass of grape juice. "So, here's to my métier: freedom from Pete the Pornster."

"Donna, I'm so sorry."

"Don't be, Molls. It's okay. Poverty will be a small price to pay for my freedom. Beth Black's my divorce lawyer. Total hot shit. Hey Red, how about I move to New Hampshire with ya? We could take Carin and the kids with us."

Sarah said, "Why don't we all move to New Hampshire? Love the license plate."

They raised their glasses for the third time that night. "Live Free or Die!"

Chapter 32

Paul Bowen hung up the phone and nodded to her. "That was Roy Smoyer, the Executive VP in yesterday's meeting. He's decided to adopt all your recommendations company-wide. Great job. You went beyond anyone's expectations with this project."

He handed her a piece of paper. "Have you turned in the laptop?"

"Yes."

He walked around his desk and extended his hand. "Liz, I hope we can work together again."

She stood up to shake his hand. "I do, too. Please keep me in mind when you have a full-time position."

"You bet. And if you dig up something else before we can grab you, I'd be happy to give you a strong recommendation."

"Thank you."

"So all that's left is Heather for the exit interview. She called about fifteen minutes ago."

Once again, Liz sat in the 18th-floor reception area. This time she didn't pick anything up to read.

The receptionist looked up. "Liz, you can go into Heather's office now." Liz used her badge to buzz through the large, swinging glass doors.

"Liz, come on in." Heather, in a pink and lime bouclé suit, fringed at collar, cuffs, and the pencil skirt's hem, stood to welcome Liz and then sat in her chair, whirling to get a form out of a file drawer. "I've had a number of very positive phone calls about your work, as I knew I would. You made me look brilliant for hiring you." She faced Liz with an Academy Award-winning smile. "Thank you."

"Hire me again, and I'll keep confirming your genius."

"We'd love to have you here full-time." Before Liz's heart could leap, Heather's voice confidentially dropped. "But today sixty more people get pink slips." She brightened.

"However, . . . as soon as things turn around, you will be one of my first phone calls."

Like a scavenging gull, Liz inquired, "Do you think there will be more consulting work because of the layoffs?"

"No one has mentioned anything yet, but you never know." Well, that level of commitment sure wasn't going to put Mark Wendell imported teas back in the teapot or keep their house off the market.

Liz stood up, putting her ID badge on Heather's desk, smiling. "Heather, thank you so much for this opportunity." They shook hands. "I can see myself out. Thank you again."

As Liz exited the elevator in the lobby, she addressed the regular security guard she'd exchanged bits with in passing during her tenure, "Well, I'm unemployed again." He shook his head in a "been there" kind of way. Smiling, she asked rhetorically, "Know of any jobs?" He shook his head again, this time with a chuckle that said *not one you'd want*. She added as she continued walking by, "Who needs health insurance or food anyway?"

"If it's really that bad, you can get health insurance from the state."

She was almost past him but stopped short. "Really?"

"Yeah, MassHealth. My sister's on it. You get it if you don't make much money." He nodded up wryly to indicate, *unlike the obscene amounts the people sitting on the floors above us make; the people who stream past me every day as if I were a potted plant.*

"That would help a lot. Thanks. I'll look into it as soon as I get home." This meant Dan could stop working at Home Depot and be able to make more money painting houses with Chuck. She and the security guard wished each other luck in a world that seemed to deal out good or hard fortune indiscriminately.

Spewed out of the revolving door, Liz reflexively pulled the delicious, early summertime deep into her lungs. She'd endured the severance process by tightening every muscle from her neck to her lower back, allowing only half breaths. Now, she could gather in the silken June breeze to soothe her frayed mind, and tonight she'd have a hot bath and let the jets pound out the kinks. Checking her watch, she saw that she had some time before her second interview at American Guarantee.

She sat down on a stone slab bench by the fountain in Post Office Square Park. White-collar employees sprinted by with efficient, gulping strides, probably not even aware of the sounds around them: birds twittering in the young trees; tires whirring along the asphalt roads; snips of conversations. A young woman in a suit with her shoes kicked off sprawled on the grass soaking up the sun. A couple who could be co-workers or lovers or both ate take-out on a nearby bench. All while she sat waiting to go to an interview with a company she would never consider working for if she weren't without choices. She sighed. Life had taught her that strength comes from not showing weakness. If you showed fear, they'd abandon you or devour you, so she would not feel afraid because she would not allow herself to feel anything.

So she struggled to stay calm before the interview. Last night she'd run her family's numbers and with the money they'd brought in recently, they could pay off about three-quarters of the credit card debt and some other bills, which would get the creditors to ease up for awhile, but the truth was clear, she had to get this American Guarantee job.

In this desperate frame of mind, Liz stepped into the building to sign in and take the elevator up to A.G., where Jackie greeted her. "This is a world record. Three weeks and you're already back for the phone interview." She beamed at Liz. "You must be really good."

Liz wondered whether they'd hired Jackie consciously as a front person to screen visitors from the nastiness inside, or did their hiring process have a glitch that allowed this heretic to slip through? If so, there was hope.

On the way by the canteen, Liz grabbed a banana, peanut butter crackers and water to save lunch money and followed

Jackie to one of the glassed-in conference rooms. Liz asked if the results of her psychological testing had come back.

"Yes, you passed; you're crazy enough to work here."

"Good." At this response, Jackie's eyes dilated in disappointment, not understanding that Liz's fledgling sense of humor fled when she was nervous. Jackie pointed where Liz should sit and then adjusted the camera and microphone.

On the monitor, three men appeared sitting behind a table, Inquisition style: one was pale, sharp featured, and balding (Liz anointed him Baldy); the one in the middle was swarthy and well-dressed with the look of someone who spent a lot of time at the gym (Gym Rat); on the other flank was a fat man with his collar so tight that his head looked like a pink peony blossom drooping heavily on its stem (Peony.) They introduced themselves, and Liz wrote each real name next to the nickname on her pad of lined paper in a scrawl only she could read.

Gym Rat began. "Liz, you have an impressive resumé, but your insurance experience is dated. That concerns me."

"I've stayed abreast of new products and legal changes, and I just finished a consulting job at First Insured Business. They will be happy to supply recommendations assuring you of my current proficiency."

Peony noted, "Your psychological profile indicated that you are a black-and-white thinker. That's fine for analysis, but we need people who can also think out-of-the-box, be creative."

"As you can see from my experience, I problem solve through analysis, which demands creativity. It takes flexible thinking to run a small business, and I will apply those skills here at American Guarantee. Whatever the environment, I am results-oriented and get the job done."

"What would you advise if a prospect wants to structure a guarantee into the contract for stop losses at..." For the next quarter of an hour, the inquisitors proposed a series of "what if" questions, followed by mad scribbling as she answered. It appeared that this was not only an interview, but also an opportunity for them to skim free advice.

The pumping was brought to an end when Baldy, who had been tipped backwards, listening until now, leaned forward landing his chair on all legs. "The business has changed radically in the last few years. I'm not sure you're up to the demands of today's marketplace."

Hadn't Gym Rat made this same point at the very beginning? Was this guy being dense or cagey? Never one to suffer fools, even those masquerading as shrewd, she answered, "With all due respect, I did not have a brain dump eleven years ago. My absence is irrelevant; my talent is not."

Baldy glanced at his two colleagues, who didn't return his querulous look, and he tilted his chair back again, a bit deflated.

Duncan

After dinner, Chuck had gone to a school play, and France was at Ashley's. Alone, Duncan went to his secret place under the stairs. He adjusted the cape France had made for him out of a throw blanket so that he wasn't sitting on it. He set aside his light saber and took off the visored plastic helmet. His hiding place, presently a cave where he could plan forays against evil villains, was filled with two down comforters, stained pillows, and an itchy, wool UNH blanket that he'd balled up against the wall. He leaned against this bolster with his journal to sketch a self-portrait of his superhero identity. The picture he drew was all chest and muscles with his arm and stick raised in defiance. Lines streamed out from the cape to show the speed of his attack. He was quite pleased with it. His friend Sammy was a better drawer, but Duncan had watched him draw at indoor recess last winter and learned a lot. He'd show the picture to Chuck tomorrow.

He turned the page in his journal and drew Bassa and a dragon both wearing capes; then, he put arrows, showing how one transformed into the other. Tomorrow he'd ask France to make a cape for Bassa out of a dishtowel or something.

The clanging and low rumblings from the dinner cleanup in the kitchen stopped, and he heard his parents move into the den. He set up his medieval figures: knights, bowmen, and jousters on the soft, undulating battlefield. It was hard to make them stand up on the blankets, and he got frustrated and stopped. Time to spy. He picked up his journal and pencil and opened the peephole into the den. His father and mother were on the love seat, and his Dad was giving his Mom a foot massage. Their voices were clearer now.

"... just incomprehensible," came his mother's voice. He didn't know how to spell that word and didn't know what they were talking about, so he'd keep listening.

"What are you going to do if they offer it to you?"

"After what I said today?"

Duncan wrote—*Woman said*

"Actually, it will probably convince them you'll fit right in. Combative, obnoxious, and rude has American Guarantee written all over it."

—*Something bad.*

"I'd prefer to think of it as sarcastic, smart, and sassy, but you're probably closer to the truth. Of course, I'd have to take the job."

"You don't have to do anything. Did you call Kostas and tell him what happened?"

"I didn't want to bother him."

—*Didn't call contact.*

She continued, "I was so drained when I left F.I.B.; it was like being sent into exile. I saw all those people who have jobs and don't appreciate how lucky they are. Then, I got mad thinking about the people who have abandoned us like our family has some kind of disease."

—*Xile. Sick.*

She went on, "It's so disheartening. You think you have all these friends and then 'poof' you're alone."

—*No allis.*

"Maybe it scares them. Your real friends have been awesome though. Herb's been great, taking me to the gym and buying a painting. Sarah, Pamela and the Uppingtons have hired us to paint their houses. The people who count are still with us big time." He counted off their support on his fingers.

—*Scaring people. Regruping suport trupes.*

"Of course, but other people act as if we've just had to cancel our vacation plans for all the compassion they show. Hellloooo, we're struggling to put food on the table."

—*No food.* Duncan closed the journal with a deep sigh. His head felt big and like it was being squeezed.

He heard his Dad say, "You've had a long day. You're just discouraged. Look, we didn't know you'd get the job at F.I.B.; who knows what else will pop up. Chuck and I will get more painting jobs. Whatever happens we have each other and a lot of great friends. Look at the guy today who told you about the insurance. You never know where help will come from. You'll feel better..." Duncan closed the peephole and furtively crept out of his cave while his Dad again ticked off points on his hand. Padding across the library, he put a CD in the player and fit the headset over his ears. He sat at the piano and played "Awake Sleepers" from Bach's *Goldberg Variations* along with Yo-Yo Ma.

Chapter 33

Liz was waiting for him with a full plastic grocery bag and a blanket under one arm. Bemused by her unusual request for a spontaneous outing, Dan commented, "All that's missing is a rose in your teeth."

Her eyebrows scrunched together mockingly. "A thornless rose, I hope."

"But of course, Scarlett," he drawled.

She batted her eyes and tried to mimic the southern accent, "Rhett, could you carry my blanket?"

"All you have to do is put your lips together and blow."

She grinned as she opened the refrigerator to get the chilled bottle. "I don't think you're supposed to mix movie classics. It's sacrilegious or un-American or something."

"Where are we off to?"

"A short walk to a secret." She winced at the phrase she'd worked so hard on, it sounded so silly and awkward hearing it blurted out in the kitchen. The whole outing had been conceived as a desperate bid to reconnect, to quiet her niggling Pamela fears; she'd hoped that doing something so totally out of character would show him that she could change, was changing, that she was desirable and beguiling, not just a bitchy mess. But now it just seemed dumb.

"A woman of mystery. I thought we agreed after your 'we can't spend any money' speech that you weren't going to keep things to yourself anymore."

"Ha, ha, Funny Boy, just follow me." It was his secrets that worried her. But, a nascent hope glimmered as he eagerly joined in the play.

He opened the back door and took the plastic bag and blanket from her as she passed. Liz tapped the storm door, "We should put the screens on this weekend."

"Woohoo, party at the Burgesses. At least no money for mulch means less yard chores."

"It's 'fewer' chores; 'less' work. If you can count whatever you are talking about on your fingers, use 'fewer'." She grinned because of mentioning his habit.

He grinned back. "Your math stunts are a turn on, the grammar thing though..."

"Such a burden being married to a woman of intellect."

She was delighted when he swung the plastic bag at her. She jogged away a couple steps with a teasing look. But his comment made her notice that she'd dipped back into her usual pragmatics. No, for this mission she needed to channel her inner goofball—glitter, jazz hands, elves; *think moonbeams, Liz, think silly.*

But he was still hooked into her sensible lead, "I can't believe tomorrow is the last day of school."

"Thanks for taking a break from house painting before our solitude ends."

"I wouldn't miss this mystery tour for anything; plus since you're coming to paint with me after, it's a double bonus."

"My pleasure." At the end of the driveway, they looked both ways and crossed Winding Path Drive into the woods. She took his hand and skipped a couple steps; that maybe was a bit much, but hopefully it nudged them back onto a path less traveled.

The sky was as brilliantly blue and white as any child's painting. Fresh leaves tousled in the breeze, opalescent in their eagerness. They heard a rustle on the forest floor and spied a towhee kicking up last year's dried leaves in search of a bug buffet.

Dan followed her around the three birches, and she put her hand on her granite boulder to make the introduction. "This is my rock." He nodded. "This is where I come."

He crossed his arms, studied the rock, scanned the pond, looked over his shoulder to the woods, and turned back to her. "It's a good place."

"It's been good for me."

"I'm glad we didn't sell the house in February. This would have been hard for you to leave."

"Ya." It felt really good that he got it, still got her. She spread the blanket beside the rock and pulled two glasses and the bottle of sparkling water from the bag. Peepers croaked their insatiable lust from the pond's edge. Facing him, she said, "Malia thinks our culture suffers from a lack of ritual. So I thought, we could celebrate paying off the credit cards, not having to sell the house, and you guys getting two more painting jobs. Then, we can 'state our intention,' as Malia says, for a windfall of money so our troubles are over for good."

"Sure. What do we do? Any chanting or hallucinogens involved?"

She felt really ridiculous. "I thought we could build a fire."

"Cool." He helped her put stones in a circle next to the pond and collected kindling and a few thicker branches to place in the center. She retrieved a box of wooden matches from the bag and handed them to Dan. "Here you go, Fire Starter."

When he had the sticks blazing, Liz pulled a folder from the bag. It had a picture of their house on it and contained the appraisal and offering sheet for their home; she also had a printout of the last credit card bill. "Let's burn these and let our wishes rise from the ashes like a phoenix." She shrugged rather sheepishly. "Sounded like ritual talk."

Dan didn't snicker like she thought he might at her charade. Instead, he added, "Thank you for your strength and determination. Liz, you are my rock."

"Thank you for being here with me." Clearing her throat with growing confidence that this might work, she took his hand and placed it on the folder with hers. They held it over the fire. "On three. 1,2,3..." The folder almost smothered the fire, then it smoked, glowed red around the edges and finally burst into flame.

They both exhaled, having held their breath while watching their troubles burn. She slid over to stand in front of Dan, and he looped his arms around her as she leaned back into his chest. When the folder was only memory and ash, she nodded. "Okay, let's celebrate with some bubbles." They sat on the blanket and toasted with the sparkling water. "Here's to new beginnings, old homes, and prosperity." They toasted.

"Nice ritual, Lizzie."

"Thanks."

She put down her glass and clenched her hands in her lap while pressing her lips together between her teeth. "Dan, I cannot imagine going through this with anyone but you."

"Well, don't worry. You're stuck with me." He patted her hands.

"And I am sorry about being so critical and crabby. Part of it was feeling replaced as Mom."

"No one could replace you. You're one of a kind, a real freak of nature. Oh sorry, I mean a real treasure. And another thing..." He grabbed her, pushing her back and burying his lips in her neck, he ceremoniously bestowed a sustained raspberry. Belly laughs rendered her gulping for air as he said, "I love you, Mrs. Burgess."

She gasped, "I love you, Mr. Burgess, even when you give me raspberries."

"Or quite possibly because I do." He made a move for her neck again.

She laughed, "No! NO! No!" and then pulled him over on top of her, seeding little kisses all over his face. He rolled off facing the sky, and she snuggled against him with her head on his shoulder. They lay still, curled together as they studied the clouds' myriad white volumes and textures, their breath quieting.

After a long ribbon of time had wound around them, Dan began, "We're a great team."

"Always have been."

"Always will be." He propped up on his elbow and tossed her shirt back to expose her stomach, and dove as if to plant another raspberry, then instead deposited a languorous kiss, which developed into much more.

A gaggle of returning Canada geese skidded, splashing across the pond's surface as they landed. Squirrels, peepers, and the towhee approvingly witnessed another springtime mating, this time a pair of pale, furless, feather-free bodies. Perhaps too, there was a great buck standing guard deep in the woodland shadows.

Tough luck, Pamela.

Chapter 34

It was probably crazy to head up to the North Shore to Gloucester's Good Harbor Beach on Fourth of July weekend, but they needed a break. Now that Dan and Chuck were painting houses ten hours a day, six days a week, family time was rare.

Dan had gotten everyone up at 6:30, allowing time for France's inevitable bathing suit drama, and as they'd walked out the door handed each of them an egg sandwich that he'd made at the crack of dawn.

Even though the traffic north on Route 128 hadn't been bad, the parking lot already had a couple rows of cars, and it wasn't even 8:30. Laden with chairs, towels, blanket, umbrella, cooler, books, as well as sundry beach toys and lotions, they set off for the haul to the beach. When their flip-flops hit the sand Dan announced, "Isn't it great getting here early? The sand isn't even hot yet," and instructed them to keep slogging around the bend where fewer people would join them later.

When they found a spot to set up camp, Chuck immediately dove into the food. He was burrowing through stacks of Pringles when France chided, "Slow down, Bloat Boy; you have the gut of a 40-year old."

"I'm growing."

"Growing tubular."

"Excuse me, I have to defend the 40-somethings," Dan protested.

"Daddy, I love you, but, Hell-ooo, you don't look like you did when you were a teenager."

"You want to go sit in the car with the windows closed?"

"Dan, that's not funny," Liz scolded loudly enough to drown out Chuck's snickering.

"What? You start understanding a few jokes and now you're the laugh police?" They all laughed at her expense, except for Duncan who was already down at the water.

"A lot of kids get a little chunky before they have a growth spurt," Liz explained to France.

"Well, Mr. Big Gut is going to have to be six foot five to churn through all that chunk."

"Enough, Francine. Speaking of growing up, Chuck, what do you want to do for your birthday?"

"I was thinking we could get my driver's permit and have carrot cake, then Friday night have some guys over to play pool and watch a movie."

Liz suspected Chuck would rather go to paint ball or throw up on roller coasters at Canobie Lake Park but was limiting his celebration because he knew money was tight. It was so hard not to be able to give your kids everything they wanted but in ways it was better. The look of pride on Chuck's face when he paid today's $25 parking fee from his painting earnings was priceless.

He stood up. "Man, it's getting hot. Dunc, race you to the water." Her boys sprinted to plunge into the ocean and resurfaced, sputtering in the frigid New England surf, quickly rebounding back to the beach to start construction on a sand city.

Never able to resist a castle in the making, her architect strode down to offer his design expertise. France and Liz began scouting the shoreline for sea treasures to adorn the guys' sand towers. It was a perfect kind of day.

When the sun was at its highest point, the family gathered on the blanket under the unfurled umbrella for the cranberry, walnut, and chicken salad wrap sandwiches that Dan and France had made last night. "These are really delicious," Liz enthused.

"Daddy, we should totally sell these and bottles of cold water on the beach. We'd make a fortune," exclaimed France.

"That we would, Pixie-girl."

"Your profit would be eaten up by gas and parking." Liz warned, but she marveled at the entrepreneurial spirit their situation had spawned in their kids. She inquired about France and Duncan's latest enterprises. "How much did you guys make weeding and selling bread last month?"

Duncan, who was in charge of the earnings spreadsheet Liz had helped him design, said, "$557.50."

"Was that revenue or profit?"

"Umm, revenue."

"So, what was your profit after you took out your costs?"

"Almost four hundred and twenty five."

"That's great. You can go to Water Country a few times with that."

Duncan said in a very business-like tone, "We decided to use it for school clothes and save the rest." Liz looked at Dan, and they exchanged a proud moment.

"That way we can buy what we want," said France, slightly dulling the shine of their motives.

"Within reason, Pixie. No see-through tops or jeans low enough to show your butt-crack."

"Oh Dad, thong underwear covers the crack," she grinned impishly.

"Well, you guys are awesome." Liz brushed some sand off Duncan's proud shoulders. "Have you decided what you're going to do with the charity money from Malia?"

"I'm donating to Colombianitos," Chuck said through a mouthful of chicken salad. "Steven told me how much it helps really poor kids in Colombia. The pictures on the website are a force. Nobody should have to live like that."

"Malia will love that."

Competing for approval, France quickly interjected, "Mine's going to your Walk for Women, Mummers. Is Mrs. Harris still with her douche-bag husband?"

"She is as far as we know."

"She should dump the asshole."

Dan mockingly schooled her, "Francine! Don't call him that. The prick is actually a fucking shit-head."

Chuck shot his mouthful of food out into the sand at his Dad's string of obscenities. "Dan!" Liz was the only one who could speak; everyone else was laughing too hard.

"I'm not giving it to a charity." Duncan grinned at Liz's confused expression. "Travis in my class lives in a trailer and his Dad's not around, so Dad and I got gift cards for the grocery store and Game Stop and left them in an envelope on the door. I did it anom-men-nom-men-osly, so he wouldn't feel bad."

"It's 'anonymously' and 'wouldn't feel badly'. But that was a great idea."

Duncan was already onto his next thought. "Daddy, could you set up the tent in the backyard, so I can sleep out?"

"Sure thing, Cowboy. It'll be too late tonight after the fireworks, but we can do it tomorrow."

Last week's storms had spawned body surfing waves, and the kids were having a ball. Liz was sitting in a chair under the umbrella while Dan lay on his stomach asleep in the sun. She watched her children tossed in the curling white, oblivious to anything but the rollers, then jumping up with fists victoriously raised after a ride all the way into the shallows, sand weighing down their bathing suits, the sun sprinkling congratulatory kisses on their salty skin. She was both envious and relieved by their joyous abandon into the moment while she sat with her mind roiling in anxious anticipation of her looming trip to American Guarantee's New York City office. AG was flying her in for the next step of their interminable hiring process: a two-day trial employment. If she worked it right, this could be the end of all their worries.

Dan inhaled a rasping snore. She dug for her book in the beach bag, changed her mind and hurled herself up from the chair and stumbled toward her children, hoping their energy was contagious. The scorching sand seared the bottoms of her feet, distracting her until she plunged into the mind numbing, icy clutch of the North Atlantic.

Dusk clung onto the horizon by its fingertips with the last of the day's failing strength. Five thousand faces watched, willing the light to abandon its struggle. Finally, the last glowing wisps hastily deepened from orange to red to purple to blue-black. A layer of anticipation hovered over the assembled crowd's collective impatience. Liz looked at her family on the blanket they'd relocated from the beach to Stage Fort Park's grass. With the remains of their picnic dinner strewn around them, all worry was held at bay by their expectation. Liz directed them, "Quick, let's pick up this mess before the fireworks start." BOOM. Too late.

Five thousand necks arched, pointing five thousand noses skyward. Red peonies. Orange chrysanthemums. Blue squiggles whistling downward in colossally elegant corkscrews. Green streaks vectoring in all directions pocked by white pops.

"The falling fairy dust ones are my favorite!"

"They can make squares now!"

"That one looked like the flag!"

Pink and green umbrellas. Blue discs that turned to green and then melted into falling orange sparkles. The crowd ahhed and cheered. The sky crashed with concussions that threatened to shake loose the stars. Boat horns blared, drawing Liz's attention to the display's muted reflection in the harbor. Gloucester had become a jubilant fusion of swirling color and sound.

The finale. Successive thundering explosions arrayed Technicolor smatters in a dome over the crowd. A deafening, brightness crescendo. Liz clapped and smiled, glancing at the intoxicating joy on her children's faces. This show was a celebration of freedom, liberation, and life. Duncan and France jumped up and down, clapping their hands over their heads. Dan stood behind her, his arms clasped around her ribs. He leaned down, giving her a squeeze and pressing his cheek against hers before looking back at the erupting sky. Happy Fourth of July.

France

Britty hollered down the drugstore's cosmetics aisle, "France, come look at this cool lip gloss; it stays on for twenty hours."

Ashley was in front of the nail color. "I love this one. Oh look, these stars and stripes nail decals are 70% off cuz it's after the Fourth." France was less interested than usual since she couldn't get any of this stuff. She'd spent her babysitting money on her yearbook and a new bathing suit. Britt and Ashley took forever deciding what they wanted. When they finished, France stayed studying the polish. That orange one would look great with her swimsuit; she took the bottle out of the dispenser and jogged to catch up with her friends in front of the magazines.

"Look at Kim Kardashian. She's such a freak."

France stood close behind Britty, looking over her shoulder as her friend flipped through a tabloid. "Miley Cyrus is a freak, too. Look how skinny she is, she doesn't even look like a girl. At least the Kardashians have booty." France put her hands in her pockets. Britty flipped some more pages, "That guy from Get Rich is so gorge. I'm going to get this for my wall. You guys ready to go?"

France took her hands out of her pockets and followed them to the checkout line. Britty got the magazine and lip gloss. Ashley got gum, soda, and eye shadow. France shifted from foot to foot. Her skin felt hot and tingly. She tickled Ashley. Her head snapped up when Britty whispered, "There's Hunter with his Mom. He's so cute."

"He's weird. He helped Mrs. O'Brien carry stuff to her car."

"He's probably gay."

"No, he's not."

"Come on, you guys, let's get out of here." France bumped into Ashley to push her along. Her heart was pumping. Her hands tingled; her breath was shallow. They jumbled out of the store, almost stepping on each other's feet. They were out, the humid air thick after the store's AC.

"Let's walk over to the pizza place. I'll pay for you, France."

"I'll pay you back after I babysit for the Kanes." When they were halfway to the Pizza Factory, France put her hands in her pockets and wrapped her fingers around the fingernail polish. She'd done it. She hadn't really thought about what she was doing. But she did it. The fingernail polish was hers. Her breath deepened. Thrilling! The most thrilling thing that had happened in her boring, stupid life for ages. "Come on you guys, beat you there."

Chapter 35

The cab pounded over the Williamsburg Bridge from JFK airport towards Manhattan. It'd been years since she'd done this. She used to come for business, even had meetings in the World Trade Center, but she hadn't been here since before the 9/11 terrorist attack. Today, when her plane circled to land, her reaction at seeing the maimed skyline was as if a dear friend had come home from war disfigured, a body part missing. The sight of it stirred anger, sorrow, revulsion. Such heartless destruction.

But in proud resilience, the city stood tall; the Freedom Tower, ascendant, speared the sky. Healing. Hope. Possibilities. Liz pulled in the energy pulsing across the East River. She drew inspiration from the magnitude of New York's spiritual recovery. This could be the turning point. She rested her head back against the taxi's seat, then popped it upright, thinking of the thousand greasy, hair-sprayed, or lice-infested scalps that had paused there.

After hanging her clothes up in the hotel closet and putting the rest in drawers, she pressed Home in her mobile directory and left a message. "Hi Dan, I'm here safe and sound. It's exciting to be back in New York. The hotel is gorgeous. Once we're working again, we'll have to bring the kids. I'm going out for something to eat and then I'll read my book and go to sleep early. My love to everyone. Hope painting went well. Talk to you all soon."

Next she called Donna, who told her, "Malia's listed my house. She said we could stay with her when it sells, but I've found a condo in Marlboro that looks out over a horse farm. Franco's gonna live in Pete's apartment during the school year. Scares the shit out of me, there'll be no supervision. I'll stalk the kid on the Internet and texting; maybe I'll implant a GPS in his arm while he's sleeping."

"Is Pete being reasonable about the divorce?"

"He just sits there and nods like always, which in this case is a good thing. Beth says one of the easiest splits ever."

"I'm so sorry you have to go through this."

"You know what, Red? It's okay. Heard the 99 Restaurant in Concord is hiring. Haven't waited tables in decades but I think it'd be a hoot. I feel like a freaking twenty-year old. My own place, my own scratch. I'm actually looking forward to it. How are things shakin' in New York?"

"Kind of weird being back, but I'm feeling like you are; it's kind of exciting. I know what you mean about feeling younger."

"You think you're going to land this baby?"

"I have a really good feeling about it. There's still the field office visit after this."

"In the bag. Make them wine and dine your ass. My girl doesn't come cheap."

"Absolutely right. Have you heard anything from Carin?"

"Nope. Nikki, Kipper and I still walk by every day. Hey, the newspaper printed your article about the walk, and Molly's pumped up the PTA and her church, said the Crisis Center is stoked. She's got a platoon of folks working on this. Art Compton, you know, who owns the alarm company in town, said he'll match pledges up to fifteen grand! Guess his mom got it real bad when he was a kid—well, till he could pound the old man. Sucks how many people had to put up with this shit as kids."

"You guys are doing great. I'll see if F.I.B., M-Ben, and these guys want to sponsor the event or match pledges."

"Chow the Big Apple, Red."

Liz brushed her hair, put on Chapstick, grabbed two twenties and then, remembering New York City prices, slipped in another, as well as her phone and room key card and headed out.

The hallway, with its rich medallion carpet and hanging alabaster chandeliers, had that expensive hotel smell. It smelled clean but not of cleaning products. Even the air was luxurious, as if all the well-heeled patrons passing through had left behind an aura of success and refinement.

Outside the glorious summer day was still bright; the trapped city heat bordered on stifling, but the air sparkled with the sensation that a festival could break out at any moment, and in New York City it might. Liz sauntered along, looking up to admire architectural details, soaking in window displays, and watching the wild characters native to this metropolis. The whole city was so much cleaner than it'd been twenty-five years ago when she'd come so often for business. Like Donna had said, being here bridged her back to that time and made her feel younger, more full of hope. Her shoulders settled, her ribcage filled, her chin lifted, her spirit crackled with possibility and adventure.

She wandered a few blocks surveying her dining options and decided on a Vietnamese restaurant with the sparkling décor of a 1950's luncheonette, the unlikely pairing too intriguing to resist. She sat at the counter and curiously surveyed her fellow diners over the top of her menu. Her attention was drawn to a woman seated where the counter rounded the corner. Roughly Liz's age, she was dressed in a suit, her hair perfectly coiffed, her jewelry spare but expensive, her briefcase propped at her feet. The woman chicly picked up her bowl of chilled soup and sipped it. She could be the president of a company, a lawyer, or perhaps an economist.

As if gazing through the looking glass, Liz saw herself as she could have been. Even though she had no regrets about her choices, she experienced the mild zing of what life would feel like if she'd been sitting at the power table all these years instead of the one in 43 Winding Path Drive's kitchen.

Since having kids, Liz had judged these career women with pity, pinched with disdain, dismissing their business accomplishments as coming at too high a sacrifice: unrelenting stress; shallow viewpoint; often no children. However, this chance encounter at this particular moment gave her the opportunity to slip into another skin and remember that there were also compensations: cerebral challenges that exercised you to top form, titillating social networks, autonomy, prestige, wealth, power. It was just a choice.

Liz's eyes flitted back to her menu with more uncomfortable grays introduced into her black and white world. She scratched her forearm. She used to know what was good or bad, easily dispatching judgments about people, absolutely certain about what was right and what should be. But how often had she really been wrong? A dawning clarity born out of ambiguity spun her mind around like a nebula before the birth of a star.

The career woman's perfume wafted over as she bent for her briefcase and stood to leave. Next to her vacated stool perched a shabby young man, probably a student, actor, or impoverished writer eating a bowl of plain noodles with a glass of water. She pictured Chuck sitting there in a few short years, so when she ordered, Liz anonymously sent over Vietnamese mint chicken, a side of vegetables, tea, and dessert. Surprised and pleased by her impulsive gesture, she thought how absurd it was to spend money on a stranger when she'd been agonizing over every dime, but this spontaneous empathy felt full and luxuriant even though it was illogical.

Liz paid her bill, acknowledging with a smile the complicit nod from the cashier, and left before the young man received the unexpected white Styrofoam box from his mystery patron.

While she'd been inside eating, the shadows of the buildings on the west side of Lexington Avenue had almost crawled up to the rooftops across the street. The air on this July evening had cooled to the point where there was no discernible temperature. Pedestrians were split between those rushing home late from work and those sauntering out to get a meal; Liz's pace fell somewhere in between.

She smiled and slid her hands into her pants' pockets as her adrenalin gently dissolved into calm. Her steps slowed. American Guarantee was spending more than a thousand dollars to bring her to New York, which they wouldn't have done if they weren't very serious about hiring her. Possibilities crackled in her brain. Excitement about the prospect of working for a big company and making a substantial income whirled into the space created by her relinquished beliefs. She didn't worry about making this move back into the corporate world anymore, and if this company was as horrible as her friend Kostas warned, when the economy turned around she could find something else.

The fingertips of her left hand brushed against a small, folded piece of paper in her pocket. She pulled it out and unfolded it as she walked. It'd been folded many times and when opened she discovered it had been creased around a penny. She stopped walking. The handwriting was Duncan's.

Dear Mommy,
This is the first penny I ever fond when I was litel. I saved it for speshill good luck. I want you to have it. Good luck in New York.
Love, Duncan

Liz pressed the paper and penny to her heart and looked up to the dusky sky. Her hands rapidly rose and fell with her suddenly shallow breaths. She moved to the side of the sidewalk, stopping in front of a narrow one-room store selling cheap, imported clothes to use what light spilled out into the darkening night to re-read the note and then press Home on her cell phone.

As the phone rang at 43 Winding Path Drive, she looked at the note again.

At the Vietnamese diner, she'd done something novel and spontaneous, and her world hadn't spiraled out of control. Her breath slowed again with a sigh. Maybe she did deserve all the love and blessings she had in her life. Maybe she could accept it with grace and not fear. She squeezed the penny inside her fist and felt some magic wrap itself around her heart. An auspicious time for good fortune and new beginnings.

Chapter 36

Surprisingly, there was no receptionist. Liz had checked in at lobby security and then was met by more guards when she exited the elevators on the seventh floor. She wondered if they were more afraid of terrorists or disgruntled former employees as she seated herself on the bench recessed into the wall by the coat alcove.

This morning, while waiting for the hotel's elevator, she'd checked her reflection in the mirror above the maple sideboard festooned with fresh flowers, a bowl of oranges, and a Terracotta Warrior statue. She'd been pleased with the smart-looking professional gazing back at her. While the black suit she'd bought for F.I.B. had the feel of a costume, it also gave her the confidence to fill the role.

Poised for her cue to enter onto the stage, she studied the set. American Guarantee's New York floor plan was sophisticated chrome and frosted glass. Dark wood was used only sparingly as an accent, as if anything authentically organic were an intrusion. The décor struck her as efficient, clinical, and sterile, like a hospital but without the aura of healing.

Unlike Boston, the cubicle partitions were constructed of three inch thick, opaque glass; like Boston, they were very low. Employees shimmered as blurred shadows at their desks. When not hunched over their computers, their heads poked up like pins stuck in a pin cushion. Even at her modest height, Liz could see over the tops of the work stations and out the windows to the neighboring building.

In the center of the room was an immense, opaque glass slab wall more than a foot thick securing floating stairs so that silhouettes hurried between floors on the other side of the frosted wall. On her side of this wall, an imbedded electronic ticker scrolled headlines, and rows of digital clocks displayed various time zones around the world above a flat-screen tuned to a 24-hour news channel. If she wanted to monitor the picture's accompanying babble, headsets hung from pegs above her.

The canteen area off to her left was the size of her great room, servicing a constant flow of patrons. A rare mumble was the only verbal intrusion into the area's muffled rustle of activity, nods usually sufficing when any acknowledgement was required. The ethos at A.G. reminded her of a tractor trailer truck versus F.I.B.'s feel of a luxury car; both were powerful, but A.G. lacked the class and polish.

Liz watched the television until Baldy, a.k.a. Bradley, shifted from shadow to man by coming around the glass wall from the stairs. He got a cup of coffee and muffin before coming toward her.

"This is American Guarantee New York." He announced the obvious fact as if bestowing a benediction. Since his hands were full of food and drink, he couldn't shake hers, and given how she'd thrown him to the wolves during the videoconference call a month ago, she figured this was no oversight. His next pronouncement was even more unnerving. "I am Head of Training."

His indolent eyes never left hers as they watched her reaction to the news that he'd be her boss if she was hired. She worked to keep her face impassive, hoping to obscure the alarm ringing in her ears, as he ordered, " Follow me."

So her calculated thrust during the interview had turned out to be a self-inflicted slash. It'd been amateurish, selfish, and a foolish gamble. She knew better, so why had she done it? Frustration? Desperation? Pride? She winced behind Bradley's back at another possibility. Could she have been unconsciously sabotaging herself, so she wouldn't get the job? At the time, she'd been so conflicted; jealous, and worried about Dan staying home instead of her, as well as concerned about what it'd be like to work for this company. Heat swept over her; her palms began to get damp. She had to get control of her impulses; her family was counting on her getting this job. She clacked down the stairs behind her prospective boss.

"Nice office," was all she could croak out.

"Mmmm." His stride had the confidence of a man who never stumbled. "When everyone slows down after the Fourth, we're nuts." Dan would have quipped that wasn't the only time.

The training floor was different from the one above in that it had walls and rooms instead of blurred cubicles. He lead her through this bulwark maze to an open corner of the building, where desks were arranged like the work groups in Duncan's classroom and possessed the same level of chaotic bustle. Shouted conversations, ringing phones, and the whirs and clunks of printers, fax, and two huge copiers, felt like an assault after the previous shush.

Thank goodness Jackie, the dissident receptionist in Boston, had told her that if you made it to the trial employment stage you were as good as hired; otherwise Liz would have been a basket case.

Only two people glanced in her direction; Liz waited for Bradley to introduce her to the group, but he only pointed to an unoccupied desk. "Clark's in Texas this week; you can sit there. I've got a meeting in a couple minutes." He logged her onto the computer, then handed her a piece of paper with two handwritten questions. "Answer these and drop it on my desk by 4:00."

Was this all she was supposed to do today? No explanation of how they approached training? No current training materials to read? Weren't they going to have her shadow a trainer? Why hadn't he introduced her to the people she'd be sitting with all day? This was really weird.

She typed her name, as well as July 8, at the top of her document, followed by the two questions:
1. What is the best way to train someone?
2. How would you design the curriculum for American Guarantee's new Iconic Century products?

Pretty broad. She thought about the first one and made some notes. When the gray-headed man next to her got off the phone, she asked him if there was any Iconic Century literature she could read.

"Not really. I got an email last week with a proof copy attached: would you like me to print it?" She nodded. He extended his hand to shake hers. "I'm Charlie. You here for a trial employment?"

"Yes. I'm Liz Burgess from Boston."

"Great. We need all the help we can get. We're swamped. They're hiring a lot of people who don't know much about insurance, makes training a haul. Can't figure out why they're hiring so many non-industry people when so many qualified people are out of work. Probably everyone in insurance has heard what a hell hole this is. How come you haven't?"

"I've been working with my husband in a different line of work for about fifteen years."

"That explains it." He smiled. "How long have you been interviewing with us?"

"Almost three months so far."

"Took me seven months, and I'd already worked with our Executive VP of Marketing over at Life Benefit."

Her shoulders tightened sharply backwards; she couldn't wait four more months.

Charlie's phone rang, so he pointed her toward the printer where the information she'd asked for would appear.

Periodically throughout the day, someone stood up and yelled that he or she hated their job. The first time Liz was shocked and looked at Charlie, who just smiled and shrugged. From then on, when someone threw their headset with a shriek or slammed a filing cabinet, she attempted not to register a reaction.

She waited to see if Bradley or someone would show up to take her to lunch but no one had by 1:30, so she went down to the corporate food bank, a.k.a. canteen, for something to eat at her desk. At four, she put her answers on Bradley's desk and watched people working or throwing fits until he showed up at 4:30 and waved her over.

She sat watching him while he read her five-page response. Finished, he thumped the papers down on his desk. "That isn't how we do things here. You totally neglected our marketing strategy. You have to show how our products offer affordability with the segment buy-in and time discounts."

"I'm sorry; those aspects weren't mentioned in the literature I found." He didn't seem to catch her insinuation about not having been given the necessary information.

"I thought it would be obvious to someone with your vast experience." Okay, nothing insinuated there, pretty clear that he resented her being forced on him and was probably threatened by her experience.

"I look forward to learning about your products and approach."

"This line here..." His pen stabbed her paper. "'Demonstrate to the prospect our superior client services by listening to their objections, writing them down, and repeating them back, so they know they have been heard before you counter with a rebuttal.' What kind of time-wasting, touchy-feely crap is that?" The Pez-headed autocrat in auto parts flashed in Liz's mind. Baldy then proceeded to verbally shred her responses for about an hour until he announced that he had other things to do before he could leave and that he hoped she'd do better tomorrow. Liz doubted he hoped that at all.

That evening she walked briskly down the Manhattan sidewalk. She had to get this job. Time was running out and there was nothing else in the pipeline. She had to keep her family in their home. Her fears about going back to work seemed so small and ridiculous now. If this loser kept her from getting this job...her stomach clenched. The taxi horns, the whir and clanking of the garbage truck, a car alarm all assaulted her; fear was making her hearing super acute while her vision had nearly shut down. She walked on using her spatial sense more than actually seeing her surroundings.

Since no corporate wooing was scheduled for dinner as she would have expected, Liz decided to scoot over to TKTS, the discount Broadway ticket dealer in Times Square for some diversion. She detoured into a Korean grocer's for a sandwich. Then, munching her dinner as she walked, she called home.

Duncan answered the phone and his enthusiasm at the sound of her voice winched her along.

A woman wearing a business suit carrying a briefcase and a plastic bag with containers of food from a restaurant smiled at Liz's joyful conversation with her son, probably a mother who'd shared such moments herself. Liz ended with, "Yes, I think the penny helped....I cannot wait to see your drawing of Armick...Is Daddy there? I love you, too."

"Dad, Mom wants to talk to you!"

"Lizzie, how's it going?"

"I have no idea. The whole process just gets more and more bizarre. I had to introduce myself to this Charlie, who was the only guy I talked to all day besides security guards and my boss. Everyone kept screaming about how much they hated their job. Oh, and my boss turns out to be the guy I trashed in the video-interview."

Dan groaned. "You're kidding?"

"Nope. He gave me two questions to answer and then I didn't see him all day until he ripped apart what I'd written. Nothing was planned for tonight, so I'm off to see if I can get a ticket for a show. How's everything there?" Dan caught her up on the news and then had to dash off to get France at Brittany's.

She was able to get a ticket to an off-Broadway show about two guys who scheme to embezzle money from a large corporation and then end up helping a single mother in desperate straits instead of escaping to the Bahamas with the loot. Liz exited the theater in the swirl of stage magic, almost believing that her family might find a couple of corporate fairy-god guys like the ones in the play who'd turn her family's life around.

The next day the security guard told her to return to the training department, which she did after getting a bagel, tea, and bottle of water at the canteen. Charlie said that Bradley was going to be at the New Jersey facility all day but that she was supposed to read the training manual and try to answer yesterday's questions again.

Why hadn't she been given this manual yesterday? Unless she was being set up to fail. Although, maybe this was a deliberate hazing into their dysfunctional management style. Something along the lines of: they treat you as if they don't like your work, so when they hire you, you will work like a maniac to win their approval. Her stomach hurt; the stress was taking its toll. For all the interactions she'd had with the people here, she could have done this in Boston.

Liz cracked open the inch-thick manual. A little after one o'clock, some leftover lunch from a training session was dropped off, and Charlie invited her to lasagna. So, new employees were treated to a catered lunch, but seasoned employees were only provided cold, repetitive food at the canteen. It had become clear to Liz that the bountiful kitchen offered only the illusion of generosity. In truth, it was a cheaper alternative to ordering in real meals for all of the employees who worked through their lunch and dinner hours as expected.

Back at their desks, she and Charlie exchanged backgrounds while forking down their scavengings. She said she was surprised how people just yelled out how much they hated their jobs. He said everyone knew it sucked there. The management style was bullying. They fired people over the littlest mistakes, so everyone hid any mistakes or pinned blame on everyone else.

"So, why do you all stay here?"

"The money and benefits." Charlie explained that he was divorced and supporting two households, college bills, braces… just living in New York could bankrupt you.

"How long have you worked here?"

"Six very long years. Ever see Pinocchio, Liz?"

"Sure."

"Remember the donkey island? Boys lured there with sweets only to become beasts of burden. Take it as a cautionary tale and run."

"Do you think it would be better working in Boston?"

"Doubt it."

At three o'clock, Charlie hung up his phone and said H.R. wanted to see her on the 21st floor.

Human Resources had glass enclosures shaped like floor-to-ceiling tubes. Probably so that if they decided not to hire her, she'd be sucked up like the container in the bank drive-thru. A hefty girl named Sophia lead Liz into one of the cylindrical cells and then asked the same questions as the other two interviews, as well as repeating that the hiring process took five to nine months and was very tough. "What are your reservations about this job?"

Liz, desperate to avoid giving any more excuses not to hire her, was very careful that nothing she said could be interpreted as negative in any way, which of course was what this supercilious, young woman was intent on flushing out. "You have a very intense, exciting environment here. I guess I would have to say that the only potential drawback would be if the amount of travel was more than 70%." Her real ceiling would be more like 25%.

Sophia wrote something down. The only time she looked at Liz was when she was asking her a question or was barking proclamations like, "We're tough; lots of hours."

"That's fine. I'm a tough old broad."

A scowl. "That can learn new tricks? I am concerned that you don't work in our style." She pushed yesterday's answers toward Liz, bloodied to mutilation by Bradley's red pen.

"I'm confident that I will after your comprehensive training classes. As evidence of my quick study, I have recently worked with First Insured Business and within three weeks presented a business model that was so on target that it's being adopted company-wide." Liz had rehearsed this in her bath after the theater last night and could kiss this young Miss for giving her the opportunity to use it.

"I see." Sophia didn't seem as enthusiastic. "One last question, Mrs. Burgess. What would your friends say is your most annoying attribute?"

Here was an interview question Liz had never heard before. She was flummoxed. It was a good one. Her mind whirred to arrive at an answer that wouldn't damage her image too much but which didn't appear flip or self-promoting. "Well, they are always complaining that I don't get jokes."

"That is the most annoying thing?" Sophia was skeptically scathing.

"With my friends, probably yes. They work very hard trying to get me to lighten up, so yes, I guess they find it very frustrating." Liz waited to be sucked up the tube.

Chapter 37

"Mommy! I see her! Mommy! Over here." Duncan shot forward as far as airport security would let him go, jumping up and down waving both his arms. The rest of them followed just as eagerly. After all the hugs and kisses, Liz said, "I know it's only been two and a half days, but it's so good to be back with my family."

Duncan, his eyes full of pride, asked, "Did you get the job, Mommy?"

"I don't know, Duncan. They take a long time to decide."

"I thought they were going to give it to you. You had the penny. Don't they know we need it bad?"

Liz avoided his question, "Badly, 'need it badly'." She saw her pain at having to disappoint Duncan mirrored in Dan's face.

Dan swooped in. "Even if they offer it, Dunc, we may decide it's not the right one. If they're going to treat Mommy badly..." He winked at Liz for using 'badly' instead of 'bad.' "...we don't want her to work there, do we?"

"No way!" Duncan agreed with great earnestness which quickly dissolved into fear again. "Were they mean, Mommy?"

On the off chance that they offered her the job, Liz didn't want him to worry that she'd be working with mean people so answered, "No, everyone was busy, and I was left on my own a lot. But if I worked there, I would be busy, too."

"We have a lot of options, and we'll decide what's best," said Dan.

Duncan looked momentarily confused. "But if you don't get a job, won't we have to sell the house and move away from our friends?"

The parents' eyes connected, and Liz wondered if Dan felt like throwing up, too. Chuck came to the rescue, "Yo little Dude, don' mada where yo crib be cuz you're one coo jacko an' you be havin' homies where-evah." The boys arced their hands downward with thumb and pinkie splayed, shrugging their shoulders doing some homeboy hoppy thing. After the bro's had slapped hands every which way and twinkled their fingers together high in the air, Duncan spotted the Dunkin' Donuts cart. "Can I have a doughnut?" If solace could be had via sugar and deep-fat frying, why not?

In the car after Liz had shared an edited, humorous version of the A.G. saga and the kids started listening to the familiar audio recording of the second Harry Potter book, Liz lowered her voice to Dan, "What did you mean we might not take the job? We have to if they offer it."

"We don't have to do anything. Liz, this place sounds like a nightmare. Kostas said not to work there, and what you saw totally confirmed it. The money wouldn't be worth it." He took her hand firmly in his, anchoring her to his resolve.

"We don't have a choice." Her voice sounded smaller than it ever had.

"In two days that company completely crushed my rock of a wife." He puffed up his chest in mock machismo. "I'm going to New York and head butt this Bradley guy." She laughed a nervous twitter. "Liz there is always a choice. This one is pretty clear. For God's sake, people working there were throwing their headsets and screaming about how much they hated it. How is coming home every night from that going to be good for you, or for us?"

Her hand trembled in his. "It would be hell."

"And they said that the whole family signs on. 'It's a lifestyle.'"

Her head snapped toward him. "That's right. They did!" She may be willing to sacrifice herself, but not her family. She pressed her lips together, clenching them between her teeth and looked out the side window. "I just thought it would get us out of this mess."

"I would miss you." He stroked her hand with his thumb. She looked at their clasped hands. "Liz, you're doing great stuff. F.I.B. let us take the house off the market for awhile. You found this opportunity and checked it out; you can be really proud of that. You've proven how marketable you are. Even these people who are totally threatened by you still know they should hire you, so something else will come along. Just keep doing what you're doing." He raised her hand to his lips and kissed it. "You're doing great."

She glanced back to make sure the kids were still hooked into Harry Potter, oblivious to their discussion. "If something doesn't happen soon, we'll have to try to sell the house before next winter."

"So, we sell it."

"Just like that?"

"Yeah, just like that. Lizzie, I can't have my best girl be a basket case. We took a gamble. Gave it our best shot. But if you're like this after two days, there's no way you should work there."

"I was getting excited about going back to work."

"You can, just not there."

She turned her head to look out her window again. Her stomach began to soften and uncoil, her lungs loosened to allow more air in, but her eyes were filled with tears. A couple minutes later, she quietly wiped her eyes and shifted to lay her head on Dan's shoulder. A few exits passed by. Suddenly, Dan abruptly hit the brakes, narrowly avoiding a blue Toyota that had swerved in front of them. Liz jounced away from resting against him, then leaned back over to kiss his shoulder and sat upright. "I just wanted to get us out of this."

"I do, too. And we will. One way or another."

Her voice set. "Given how Mary cheated us, I don't think I'll tell A.G. 'no' until they pay me."

"Getting my girl back; her pragmatics are on line again." He glanced at her with a grin and gave her hand a squeeze.

"Okay, so I'll talk to Malia, and we'll put the house back on the market; we don't want to take the chance the bank forecloses."

"Sounds good. No, it doesn't sound good, but it sounds like a plan." She noticed his shoulders relax; he arched his spine, circling his head to stretch out the kinks.

The town of Newton sped by. They merged onto 128 North for a couple of exits and then got off at Route 20, a country roadway with only one lane in each direction. Here, cars were no longer traffic and speed limits were halved. Everything started to spread out, except the trees, which gathered in larger numbers to become woods. Liz let loose a mighty sigh. She continued winding down from the week's fiasco as the kids listened to a story about the bravery of an unlikely hero, and their parents held hands.

Chapter 38

Malia absentmindedly hummed as she rinsed Liz's hair with the handheld sprayer. "You know, I have a book you might like. Remind me to get it after I blow dry your hair. Okay, you can go over to the chair."

Malia frisked the towel briskly over Liz's head. "Oh, I like how the color came out." The scissors clipped as Liz's hair wisped to the floor in a red shower. "So, you've decided to put the house back on the market?"

"Yes, but I'm so conflicted. I hope it won't sell right away because I'm not ready to leave it, but I'm also terrified that it won't sell and the bank will take it."

"We won't let that happen; if for some reason it doesn't sell, I'm sure I could rent it for enough to cover the mortgage."

"Maybe we should do that!" Liz perked up at the possibility of having found a way to escape losing the house, then crumpled. "No, then we'd have nothing to live on. But if we need to, renting would be better than foreclosure. Ugh, I cannot believe these choices."

Her life had become all about the lesser of evils. She looked forward to when she'd be able to take a friend out to lunch or buy something frivolous on impulse, like bottled water or candles. She also looked forward to when they no longer qualified for the safety-net programs that had saved them: gas and electric subsidies, the school lunch and activities fees program, the state health insurance. She swore to the gods that she would never grumble about paying taxes again.

And even though her insides tightened and rolled every time she thought about selling their house, it was also beginning to feel like a bit of a relief.

She sighed. "I have a better chance of getting laid by Johnny Depp than getting a job now that we're in the summer doldrums."

The shear's snips became more like snaps. "I can't believe you might be moving away." Malia slapped the scissors down on the table.

"You're done?" Liz was surprised.

"No, but it's not a good idea to cut someone's hair when you're upset; they end up looking like a troll." Malia leaned over to hug Liz around the shoulders and mumbled into the top of her head, "My love, I am going to miss you soooo much. My heart is so full of you." She held Liz for a long time, and Liz didn't feel at all uncomfortable. Malia planted a kiss on the top of Liz's wet hair. "I'll go get the blow dryer." She came back with a forced glint in her eye, wagging the nozzle at Liz. "I'll only try to sell the house, if you promise to back out of it again."

"A couple weeks ago we put a 'Support the Library' sign on the lawn for the funding campaign, and Duncan freaked before he realized it wasn't a For Sale sign. It breaks my heart to do this to them."

"Oh Liz. Poor Dunc. I won't put up a sign."

Their heads turned at the sound of the door opening. "Hey, *Chicas*. Sorry I'm late. Had to iron my shirt for work." Donna plowed in, followed by Nikki and Kipper, their claws clicking on Malia's tile floor. She had on the standard waitress white shirt and black slacks. "What'd I miss?" She saw the looks on their faces. "Oh, shit. What's happened?"

"We have to sell the house unless bags of money start falling from the sky. We haven't earned enough to keep us going through next winter."

Donna looked confused. "What happened to that nasty job?"

Liz shrugged, trying not to move her head since Malia had begun cutting her hair again. "Not a good fit. They deposited the money for my New York stint yesterday, so I called them to say no thanks."

Donna picked up a kitchen chair, spun it in the air, and slammed it down on the floor, so she could sit a couple feet away facing Liz. "Well, Red. That just plain sucks." She wrung her hands and then sat back, crossing her arms. "The Change is supposed to mean hot flashes and bitchiness, not divorce, bankruptcy, and friends moving away." She jumped up from the chair and stormed back and forth. Malia stopped cutting as they waited for Donna's rant.

But instead, she plopped back down in the chair and locked eyes with Liz, her voice shockingly soft. "I'm gonna miss the shit out of ya, Lizzie." She'd never called Liz that before. Liz felt the tears begin again. "It will totally suck not being able to bomb in on you and Dan screwing in the kitchen." Donna blinked rapidly and then winked at Liz. "I'll have Franco set me up on Skype." Donna lunged up out of the chair at Liz and engulfed her seated BFF in a bear hug. Malia covered their bodies with her own embrace until Donna griped, "Enough of the group hug shit. Malia, let me up, your boobs are smothering me."

Malia returned to trimming Liz's hair, and Donna sat back in her chair, saying, "At least some good came out of our dramas: my sad sack of a husband's gone; I'm finally okay with what happened when I was a kid; Liz worked in Boston and found out she won't turn into Godzilla, hell, you almost have a sense of humor now; and Dan's selling paintings and chandeliers at a gallery. Slick shit."

"Two galleries. My friend Kostas' daughter got him into one on Newbury Street."

"Fuck, yeah! See! Good karma, right, Ms. Gandini? And we're organizing a 20-mile Women's Walk to build a shelter for abused women and their kids. Pree-tty coo-ol." She sighed. "I just wish we could help Carin. They were getting in their car when the dogs and I walked by today. I yelled over and told her I'd left Pete, hoping it'd give her the idea. She just said good luck, hopped in, and took off."

"You're a good friend," Malia said as she brushed Liz's wet bangs off her forehead. "Oh Liz, the book." She held up a finger then disappeared into the living room and came back with a paperback in hand which she passed to Liz before firing up the blow dryer. Liz looked at the title, *When Things Fall Apart: Heart Advice for Difficult Times*. Yep, that fit.

Chuck

Chuck slammed the table beside the keyboard. He was just teleported to an arctic tundra by a witch wielding a loaf of bread as a wand. Time to take a break. At least they were still connected to the Internet, but that was only in case anyone ever wanted to hire Evergreen. Runescape was a good game and free, which was key, but it wasn't Skyrim. He slumped back in the chair, watching little figures run around the fantasy medieval village.

This whole thing blows. This time they were really going to sell the house. Sell. Don't sell. Sell. It's totally fucked up, such a bruise. When his folks told them it was really going to happen this time, France started bawling and ran up to her room; Duncan ran outside, and it was almost dark when he'd found him perched in the branches above the tree house.

No one had any idea, or asked, how pissed off he was about this whole cluster fuck.

Not their fault that the economy sucks, but now, they were moving to New Hampshire to live with Grammie and Gramp until they got a place. Dad tries to play it off like some great adventure. But it isn't. It so sucks. His last two years of high school and he has to leave all his friends and go off to the boonies, where they probably don't even know what Skyrim is. Or Dub Step. Or Eckhart Tolle or Ayn Rand or Sartre. He'll be different; they'll think he's weird. This is so not fair.

Malia would let him stay here with them if he asked, but he couldn't leave his family. Although it would be like he was leaving for college early and a lot of kids younger than him go off to prep school. Nah, Mom would flip.

Guilt settled on his shoulders. He shouldn't whine. It's not like he was sold into the sex trade or had to run through gang warfare to get to school or had an alcoholic parent like Mom did.

Tired of looking at Runescape's tiny, scuttling characters, he tapped the keyboard, messaging Steven that he was getting off and exited the program. He plodded into the TV room, rolled onto the couch, picked the clicker up off the floor, and then he remembered that they didn't have cable anymore and threw the clicker onto the rug. He dragged the afghan down from the back of the couch and spread it over himself even though it was 93 degrees out, and they weren't running the AC this year.

    He was sick of everything. All of it. Money. No money. Life. Work. Not moving. Moving. He was exhausted from painting so much. His shoulders and back ached. He'd just close his eyes until Dad came up to get him to go back to the job. He felt like a lion in a poacher's cage, or like a wild horse swept away in a flash flood. Powerful but powerless

Chapter 39

"Where have you been? I've been sitting there for three hours! How could you leave me there? They wouldn't even let me go to the bathroom by myself! Where were you?"

"Dad had the car. He had to leave his job, bring me the car, and then I had to drop him back." The fact that she'd inconvenienced everyone else was lost on Francine.

"There are groceries in the back. You ran errands and left me sitting there!"

"Yes. So?" A car Liz hadn't noticed in her escalating frustration backed out in front of them. She slammed on the brakes, throwing them forward from their seat backs.

"Jesus, Mom. Watch where you're going!"

Liz tensed every muscle to keep from lunging over at her daughter. Sarcasm was her handiest, least lethal barb. "I'm sorry. I was distracted by a felon screaming at me about being late to pick her up."

"I wasn't in jail. I was just waiting for a ride home."

When the other car cleared away, Liz swung into the vacated spot and threw the gear into park. "Are you for real? You were being detained until your guardian showed up because you were caught shoplifting. You weren't waiting for a ride home after the movies. Do you not get how lucky you are that they aren't pressing charges? That you're not headed to juvie?"

France waved her off with a beleaguered sigh. Liz's eyes popped. "What is that?" Liz imitated the wave with an exaggerated and snotty flourish. Then wailed, "Who raised you? Because I sure didn't raise my kids to be selfish, entitled kleptomaniacs. What were you thinking? Who do you think you are? Why would you think stealing from hardworking people is okay?"

"Mom, they're insured. It doesn't matter." Francine patiently informed her naive mother.

"What! Are you kidding? It does matter, Francine." She struggled not to let fly the swear and insult barrage that was careening through her mind. "It matters a lot. I suggest that you sit there and think about why what you did is wrong without saying another word." Liz backed up the car from the parking spot and swung it out of the mall exit. "And if I decide to screech a lecture at you all the way home, you will sit there and take it, and then head up to your room until your father and I call you down after we've decided what to do about this. Am I clear?"

"Crystal."

Dazed and feeling impotent, Liz gripped the wheel till she got a cramp in the palm of her hand, and decided to stuff down her reaction to this insolence by fiercely concentrating so that she wouldn't get going too fast as they headed for Winding Path Drive. Fury, confusion, and fear crackled through her mind in mocking rebuke. She felt like she didn't know, or even want to know, this adolescent manifestation of her daughter. There didn't seem to be a clod of common ground for them to stand on together. Where, no, when had this fissure begun to crack? Hormones? Unemployment? What warnings hadn't she noticed? Had she failed somehow as a parent? Was this because of the "gotta have it all now" culture that the media spat at these kids from their births?

Was France trying to tell her something? If so, she was missing it. She could kind of understand her trying alcohol or even drugs out of curiosity or peer pressure. But stealing? For her to think that taking something that wasn't hers was okay was completely beyond Liz's comprehension.

She glanced over at the stranger next to her whom she could touch but not reach. If she hadn't been able to communicate in twelve years that this was wrong, how could she hope to get through to her now?

France sat pressed against the door, arms crossed, head turned looking out the window. Frozen. No movement. No remorse.

What were they going to do? Where could this go?

Without taking her eyes off the road, she asked, "So, where have you been, France?"

Francine rolled her head in disbelief and aggravation, tossing her hands up, "At the mall, Mom. You just picked me up there. What? Yes, you were right. The mall is evil. I shouldn't have been there. You happy?"

"No. Are you?"

"Gawd."

"Okay, I'm not sure what that means, but what I was asking was, where has the girl I used to have so much fun with gone? The one who used to talk with me about everything. Who smiled."

"Motherrrr, I'm right here."

They drove on in silence for a few minutes. The sadness about what she'd lost with her daughter gathered like a dark mist across an empty field. She cleared her throat before she could quietly say, "I miss her...so much."

"How can we get through to her? We've been telling her this stuff her whole life." They were turning on every light in the den as if that would reveal the answer.

"Maybe she can tell us."

"But she doesn't talk. You call her down. Just my voice sets her off."

"Francine, please come down here." Dan's using her formal name would tell France how serious this was.

Her descent was slow. She came in and sat in a chair. No one knew where to begin or even wanted to. Finally, Dan sat down, straight backed with his hands on his knees. "Your mother and I don't understand what's going on...but we're here for you, Pixie, and we'd like to understand. Can you explain it to us?"

France shifted in her seat, never taking her eyes off the turret windows as though if she willed it she could sprout wings and fly through the glass. "I dunno." She put a strand of hair in her mouth and started sucking on it. Liz, shocked by the reappearance of this old habit, sank into a chair as invisibly as she could, not wanting to tip their situation's precarious perch. This child was such a puzzle. Potential for such creativity but choosing to steal. Sometimes so sweet and then so cruel. Talking a thousand miles an hour then becoming as communicative as a stone.

"Why did you do it?"

Gnawing on her hair, she just shrugged.

"We want to help, but we can't if we don't know what's happening."

She spit out the wet strand. "It was just something to do."

"You stole for a thrill? It hurts people. It's an assault, a violation. It raises prices for everyone. It is totally selfish."

"Geez, Mom. It's not that big a deal. It was just a pair of earrings. Relax."

"What! Don't you tell me to relax. It's not 'just' anything. It's wrong, France. Really, really wrong. Don't you get it?"

"We never do anything except chores. We never have any fun. It's sooooo boring."

"Life isn't just a lifelong hoot parade. You are so not going to play the victim card. We do plenty that's fun. You need to realize it's wrong and take responsibility for your actions."

Dan interrupted, "What is it you'd like to do?"

"I dunno."

This was getting them nowhere. "Would you like to go talk to someone about this, other than us?"

"No way."

Dan tried, "What's a punishment that will keep you from doing it again?"

"I dunno. Ummm, maybe not going to the mall?"

"That's a start. Mom called Mrs. Andersen, and you'll be helping at the Crisis Center three hours a day while you're grounded for the next three weeks. You'll help me hang my show and keep baking bread to sell with Dunc."

She slunk low in the chair. "Anything else?"

"You're basically our slave while you're grounded. Any grief about it adds another day."

Liz reminded him, "And the note?"

"Oh, and you need to write an apology explaining why what you did was wrong and deliver it to the store manager."

"Ugh."

"That attitude is the grief I'm talking about that'll earn you another day. Service with a smile, my friend. Go set the table outside for dinner, please."

Francine shuffled out, shoulders bowed, hands shoved into the pockets of her shorts. Liz got up and moved over to Dan, offering her hand to help him out of his seat. "Good job."

"We'll see...Why'd we have kids?"

"It was your idea."

"Right. Well, let's not listen to me anymore."

"Sounds good." She grinned wearily at him. They moved into each other's arms and after a long embrace headed out for supper.

The sun was heading down but still strong enough that the day's heat loitered around. Liz put the last plate into the dishwasher as France ferried the final load of napkins and condiments in from the patio. She stood up, wiping her hands off on the terry hand towel. "France, there's something I'd like to show you. It'll only take a few minutes."

"Okay." Her voice strained to be compliant but clearly communicated, *ugh, do I have to?*

Liz continued the pretense, which required her to force a lilt into her voice. "Great! Let's go."

"Are we going in the car?"

"No, just across the street." The respondent silence around her daughter was as jagged and sharp as a shattered glass; its threat pushed Liz ahead, so she led France across the street and down the path instead of walking next to her. She tried not to feel like she was dragging a sack of hedgehogs but didn't dare to turn around to check. She'd love to abandon this idea, but she was committed now so trudged on, pretending that this was a delightful excursion.

She had hoped that since her place by the pond always worked such magic for her when she was feeling down and had helped when she'd shown it to Dan that maybe it would help her reconnect with Francine. But she and Dan had been open to change, not this implacable blockade of teen omnipotence.

"Mom, where are we going?"

Overwhelmed by the glowering presence behind her, Liz didn't look back. "We're almost there." Nothing on the planet was more judgmental than a teenage girl. This was so not a good idea. They rounded the bend beneath the three birches leaning over the path, and Liz climbed up on her rock. "Come on up."

"Do I have to?"

"No." Liz's heart twisted into an iron Gordian knot, which fell out of her body and rolled away out of sight.

She looked out over the pond. The mosquitoes had already found them. All she could hear was their high-pitched whine, the slap of hands on skin, and France's exasperated groans. She couldn't think of anything except *let's head home*, but she couldn't say that.

The gloaming began to settle in, suffocating shadow and color. They'd have to go back soon, since there'd only be a sliver of waning moon tonight.

"Well, I guess this wasn't one of my more brilliant ideas."

"Nope."

"I'm just desperate, I don't know how to talk to you anymore and then I get all awkward, like everything I do is wrong and dumb, and I'm some kind of stupid cow, and then I get so nervous I can't think of what to say and end up acting like some kind of drip, whom even I can't stand." Thankfully, she finally found a place to end her run-on sentence and breathe, but at least it perfectly illustrated her point about being awkward around France.

France looked up from leaning against the rock with her arms crossed and laid her body along the side of the boulder. "Really?"

"Yeah."

"Hunh. That's weird." More mosquito slapping.

"I miss how easy it was before, but even so, I don't want to go back; I'd just like to go forward to when I can talk about stuff with you like I do with my friends." She smacked at a bug in order to cut short another never-ending sentence.

"Mmm."

"I'll always be your Mom, and I love you so much it hurts a lot of the time, but I'm still going to have rules and try to help you get ready for when you're on your own. But there's not a lot of time left for me to do that and sometimes I panic because the fact is, I can't force you to do anything, the choices are really yours and so are the consequences, so I guess what I'm saying is the time's come for you to step up and take responsibility for what you decide to do, and if you make mistakes you can decide to learn from the consequences—or not. It's your choice. It's all your choice." Sitting cross-legged on top of the boulder, she tapped her thumb against the sole of her sneaker in an unconscious rhythm. France traced cracks in the rock with her index finger; her lips twisting under knitted brows.

"It's really up to you, France. How do you want to live your life? Who do you want to be? And when you decide that, have what you do line up with who you are and what you believe in. Like Malia says, 'Live Awake.' Be mindful of your choices so that the consequences don't blindside you and end up closing doors before you even get to the hallway."

"Mmm."

"Okay. Well. Shall we head back? These bugs are really brutal." Francine had probably stopped listening to her five minutes ago anyway.

"Yeah."

"Thanks for listening."

"Sure."

Liz scrambled down; landing with a muffled thud on the weedy earth beside France, she patted the rock. "Just thought I'd introduce you to my old friend. I've been coming here since before you were a baby when I need to sort things out. My secret spot."

"That's cool." Hmm, finally a spark.

They walked for a ways, side by side. More relaxed, Liz now heard the mockingbird singing vespers with the frogs adding their bass.

They set a pace faster than the biting bugs could fly and land. France's flip-flops snapped with each step. The air had shifted, thinner but not yet cool.

"I hang upside down."

"Excuse me?"

"When I need to think, I hang upside down."

Liz processed this golden offering. "Well, that'd sure help see things differently," she said grinning.

"Yep." After they passed the place teenagers came to party, France said, "But I think I'll find a secret place, like you and Dunc have. Although yours isn't a secret anymore I guess."

"I've only shown you and Daddy."

"Really?" France smiled and then stepped in front of Liz to push a branch out of the way.

When they got back to the house, Liz opened the screen for France, who said, "Thanks, Mum" as she walked by. Liz was startled. Was that for holding the door open or for what she'd just shared? She knew better than to ask.

Chapter 40

"Liz, could I come over?"

"Carin?" Liz raised her eyebrows to Dan. No one had heard from her since the incident with her husband five months ago.

"Would it be all right if I came over now?"

"Of course."

"I'll be right there. I'm only a couple of miles away."

"I'll be here." Liz hung up, mild panic gripping her as she handed the car keys to Dan. Even though she'd been developing her empathic skills, Liz wasn't sure she was the best one for first contact. "You go ahead with the kids." They'd been about to leave to hike Wellesley's Elm Bank Reservation in an effort to keep their minds off the ache of having the house back on the market.

"We'll wait. I'll work in the studio; I need at least six more paintings. I still can't believe Pamela invited me to have my own show."

"I can." Conniving, predatory gallery owner. "Do you have a date yet?"

"The opening is August 15."

"Your birthday. That's neat."

"That's what Pamela thought."

"How did she know it was your birthday?"

His brows shot up and his expression froze like a fritzed computer screen. He recovered to say, "From the W-9 form." His relief at his explanation was palpable and made Liz want to die.

With forced enthusiasm, she chirped, "I'd be happy to help you set up for the Opening party."

"No, that's okay. Pamela and I can handle it. I know it's not your thing. Plus, I want you to be surprised when you walk in."

"All this secrecy." She labored to keep the conversation light, even though her fears about his infidelity were a glacier slowly scraping its destructive tonnage across her spirit.

"What secrecy? You're the one who keeps things from her spouse, remember?" His abrupt defensiveness cemented the resin of her suspicions. It felt like she was being dismissed. She turned her head away. Rejection. Self-protection. Avoidance of what she saw in his eyes, his posture. They were losing the house. Had she already lost her husband?

That afternoon by the pond last month when she'd shown Dan her rock, had their lovemaking been a second ritual of his letting go, of letting go of each other? Had his hand trailing down her spine to the dimple between her buttocks only been a rote response? That afternoon, the sun had felt so warm on her skin. She'd felt so safe lying there with him. Her eyes filled. She can't do this now.

As Dan pulled on his hiking boots, she headed to the sink. Her fist moved to cover her mouth as she cleared her throat. Carin would be here any minute. She had to talk to him but not now. She wet a washcloth and vigorously scoured the already clean counter.

"Good luck with Carin." The screen door banged shut behind him as he left. She stopped wiping and stood to watch him tell the kids the change in plans; then he moved beyond her sightline, exiting her frame. She felt as though her breath had been stolen by a cold gust—a premonition?

She heard a car pull up the driveway. Then, as they passed on the walkway, Dan offered to take Carin's kids to the pond. She sounded relieved and tired as she handed them over. Liz's kids tumbled out of the hammock to go along.

Carin came up the walkway like a stray kitten. Liz opened the screen to welcome her, "Come on in. Everyone's missed you at girls' night. Can you believe this weather? It's supposed to be getting really humid." She understood Dan's mother's penchant for babbling when she was anxious, she'd done it with France and was doing it now. "Would you like to go in the den? Some iced tea? Dan makes sun tea. It's fantastic."

Carin stopped short, watching while Liz got the drinks. Liz could tell Carin was focusing hard to stay on track as though any deviation in her narrow course would derail her. Liz led her into the den, cubes clinking against the glasses. Carin sat clutching her tea with both hands, her eyes stuck on Liz's face. The depth of suffering Liz saw there was what finally cut off her verbal spigot.

Carin inhaled, then exhaled in a punch of air followed by an interminable cessation, then suddenly inhaled again as if she'd just remembered that she should. Her words rushed out in a tangle of anxious, tumbling syllables, "You worked in insurance, so I thought maybe you could help me." An inhale, followed by another frantically exhaled cluster of sentences. "Carl has taken a life insurance policy out on me. I found a bill in a locked drawer in his desk that I jimmied open. I called the company, and he'll get a million and a half dollars if I die. How could he do that without my knowing?"

"I'd have to read the policy." Her left hand rubbed her chin as she considered the possibilities of how he could have arranged this. "Do you have any idea when he did this?"

"The start date was right after the thing with Donna."

"Are you afraid for your life?"

"Yes."

"What are you going to do?"

"What can I do?" Carin's expression was hopeless bewilderment.

"Do you have a copy of the policy?"

"No, but I can call them." Carin put her glass down and began pawing through her purse for the number. Her movements accelerated. She tossed crumpled papers and receipts on the floor like confetti, but without the flourish of celebration. When the paper flurry stalled, Carin covered her face with both hands and collapsed over the bag in her lap.

Liz kneeled next to Carin's chair and rubbed her back, offering a tissue she'd grabbed. At this contact, Carin threw her arms around Liz's neck and hung on. Liz, a bit staggered, braced but kept rubbing Carin's back. "We can find the number on the

Internet. We will take care of this." Carin nodded into Liz's shoulder. "If you're this afraid, should you stay there?" Liz restrained herself from screaming the obvious.

Even so, Liz's words pushed Carin against the back of the chair. "I can't leave my kids, and if I took them away from him, he'd find us and kill me." Liz noticed that the word 'like' had fallen out of Carin's vernacular.

"No. That is not going to happen. You think Donna would let him do that? Your Monday night gang would 'garrote' him first." Carin giggled in nervous release at this reference to her word game, bolstering Liz's confidence. "First, we should call the police. And I hope you don't mind but after what happened, we went ahead and lined up safe houses with friends and family just in case, since there's no shelter yet. Also, Donna mentioned your situation without saying your name to her divorce lawyer, who's offered to advise you for free. And Molly said the crisis center has a fund to help women get re-situated."

Carin's face was pure shock. Liz rushed to mend her faux pas. "We weren't assuming anything; we wanted to be ready, just in case." Carin's mouth hung open; she crossed her arms, clutching her shoulders. Liz was devastated; she'd screwed this up so badly. "I'm so sorry, Carin. We were just trying to be good friends. We had good intentions. Forget I mentioned it. I'm way out of line."

"No! No, you're not. You're all so wonderful." Carin blew her nose. "I read in the paper about how you guys are organizing a walk to open a domestic abuse shelter." She hesitated. "Am I the woman who inspired you?"

"Of course."

A sob escaped the scrunched tissue Carin held to her face. Liz softened her voice further, "Would you like to go with the kids to a safe house?" They both held their breath.

Liz continued, "It could just be for a couple days while you figure things out. The crisis center safely helps people through this all the time. We all really care about you and the kids, Carin. We won't let anything happen to you."

Carin peeked from behind her tissue and nodded. Liz needed to be clear, "Is that 'Yes, you know we care,' or 'Yes, you want to go somewhere safe?'"

"If we can really be safe, where he can't get to us, then yes, we've got to go."

"Okay, let's call the insurance company, and then the police and the crisis center."

The tension, which had been the only thing holding Carin together, snapped, and she began sobbing so fiercely that Liz could barely understand her when she asked, "Can Donna come over?"

"Here? Yes, let's call her right now. She'll be so relieved."

Liz made the phone calls at the desk in the guest room and took notes. Donna was on her way. The insurance company and Beth Black, who was Donna's lawyer, began the process of canceling the life insurance policy and getting discreet legal wheels moving.

Since they'd sold the second desk on Craig's List a few weeks ago, Carin sat in the guest room's reinstalled club chair while Liz made the arrangements. While she was on the phone with the crisis center, a car pulled up. Carin asked in a voice usually heard from an excited six-year old, "Is it Donna?"

Or was it Carl?

A blue sedan—Malia.

Liz, very relieved it wasn't Carl, turned and mouthed Malia's name to Carin who, to Liz's surprise, stiffened. Liz quickly concluded the phone conversation and asked Carin, "Do you not want Malia involved?'

"No, no. I mean it's okay. She's just so good. She's likewise, you know, like a wizard, she makes me feel like such an idiot." Liz noticed that 'like' was back, a good sign that Carin had calmed down a bit.

"Why don't you stay in here and rest; I'll go see what she wants. Shall I not tell Malia you're here?"

"You can tell her."

"Donna's on her way. Why don't you crawl under the comforter and take advantage of Dan having the kids, and rest. Here you go. We call this comforter, The Puff."

After nestling Carin in the guest bed, she went to meet Malia at the back door. "Carin's here."

"What?! I wondered whose Navigator that was."

"The police and Donna are on their way. She's decided to leave her husband."

"We're ready."

"I'm so glad you're here."

"You don't need me or the police if Donna's on her way."

Liz smiled and felt a great sense of relief at now sharing this responsibility. Malia said, "The reason I stopped was because there's an offer for the house."

"Really? How much?"

"It's a little complicated; this probably isn't a good time."

"Pour yourself some iced tea. I'll run across the street and get Dan. Chuck and France can watch the kids while we talk and wait for the troops to get here."

Liz jogged down the path to the pond. Warm air brushed her bare skin; she heard a frog splash into the water as she passed. Being able to help someone else with their problems was empowering. For the first time in ages, a smile that didn't feel like it was being crunched into dried Play-Doh softened her face.

Carin was getting free. And so were they.

A crow cawed its annoyance at being disturbed as it took off from the reeds. She cruised past his protest, excitement goosing her pace. After almost a year and a half of uncertainty and stress, selling the house offered them their chance. Closure. Moving on. And an end to the anxiety, to being so exhausted that she couldn't see straight. A chance to write checks for bills owed without her blood vessels pinching.

Up ahead she heard the animated babble of the tribe she sought. A few more strides and they came into view. France was holding the baby. Dan and Chuck were deep in conversation. Duncan and Ronnie (Carl Jr. now went by his middle name) brandished stick swords as they ducked in and out of the trees along the path. Her youngest was the first to spot her as she slowed to a brisk walk, no doubt because he'd been on the lookout for orcs or mountain trolls and the like.

"Mommy! What are you doing here?" He sprinted to span the distance between them, with Ronnie doing his best to keep pace with his commander. Duncan's hug landed just above her hips and then he stepped back brandishing his sword. "I am Armick and this is my companion, Gladin, the rogue dwarf. We are protecting this band of travelers from a pack of marauding goblins. Identify yourself."

"I am only a poor crone sent to invite your band to cool shelter and a sugary repast at the inn hither." Duncan grinned broadly at her entering his play, then took off to dash back to the others. Gladin, who had not quite caught up, reeled around to follow.

She waited, at peace. The sunlight rich and full lay in pools along the woodland floor. The hum of summer insects curled through the woody aroma of dirt, sap, and leaves. Liz inhaled the green as she steadied her breath. She waved, greeting the others, and smiled. A band of travelers—Duncan was right, they were all travelers, and theirs had been quite a journey of late. What mattered wasn't getting to the destination. What counted was how they helped each other towards it.

Donna had arrived in a flurry with the dogs barking madly and scooped Carin, who had fallen asleep, into her arms, stroking her hair.

The police were now taking Carin's statement in the library, and afterward, the cruiser would follow Dan, Carin, and Donna's cars to Carin's house, just in case Carl came back unexpectedly from his business trip to San Diego while they were loading things into the cars.

Birdsong floated in the open windows as Malia lay a manila folder on the kitchen table. "Two buyers have bid on the house: $635,000 and $650,000. It's a little tricky, though. The higher bid is from the people who bid that amount in June. The problem is that when you decided not to sell they contracted for another house, and in order to get out of that they will have to forfeit $25 grand. They'd like to subtract that from their offer, putting them ten thousand below the other offer on your house. However, they are also interested in purchasing some of your furnishings, which may put your total take higher than the other offer."

The kids all came to the door. Liz asked them to stay outside for a few more minutes with a bribe of popsicles. Duncan suggested a game of statue tag, and she turned back to Dan. "Which one do you think sounds better?"

He focused on his hands as he massaged his thumbnail with the pad of his other thumb. A minute passed; he interlaced his fingers and inverted them, stretching his arms out in front of him and then placed his hands on his thighs. "Liz, I'd like to sell to the professor and his family because we messed them up. Plus, I'd like to think of the house going to someone who loves it as much as we do."

Liz considered his face, trying to read everything written there, as well as the things beneath, but his deeper sentiments eluded her. Was his voice heavy with regret about leaving the house he'd designed or at leaving Pamela? She considered only what he'd said out loud and agreed. "I think that's a really good idea. Plus if they buy some of the furniture, we won't have to move as much stuff." Moving in with his folks meant they'd have to get rid of almost all of it anyway.

Dan nodded, "Okay, Malia. Tell them we accept."

"There's one more thing." They both tensed. "They want to be sure that you won't back out again, so they want you to sign an agreement that you will pay them $25,000 if you renege."

Liz sighed, "We can't change our minds this time."

Dan squeezed his baby finger, now that there were no other possibilities to tick off on his hand. "That's fine."

Liz, however, had her own tally. They would be leaving behind their friends. They would be leaving Pamela. They would be leaving the only house where Liz had ever felt at home and the only home her kids had ever known. The imbalance of these factors weighed with immense heaviness on the side of sorrow, and a flood of grief flashed a concussive shudder through her spirit.

Then she thought of how Carin had chosen to come to her, and how she'd been able to listen, comfort, and guide her and her kids to safety, and a dawning warmth much like the earlier woodland sunlight washed through her.

Chapter 41

The midsummer night's temperature was forecast to barely drop below sweltering. In the candlelight, Liz squinted at the pages of tattoo designs. The flames ducked and darted in the murky air's turbid twirl beneath the bamboo ceiling fan. Donna was cross-legged atop Malia's floral cushion on the screened porch floor, regaling them with tales from waitressing at the 99, interjecting, "Molly, I want the blue dragon. How long do these tattoos last?"

"About four weeks."

"So, is drawing on other people's bodies your métier, Ms. Moll?"

Molly giggled. "Yep, it's part of the art therapy at the crisis center along with scrapbooking. My other selfie is working on the Walk for Women."

Sarah pointed to the image of a crescent moon. "Could you add a music note to it for my tat?"

"Sure. Liz, here's the stag you asked for."

"He's perfect."

Malia selected a lotus flower.

"There are so many I could pick." Since leaving Carl, 'like' had completely fallen out of Carin's vocabulary. Right now, she was staying in North Reading with Sarah's college roommate.

Molly suggested, "The oak leaf could symbolize strength; or the phoenix for rebirth; or the two stars with the heart in between for your kids."

"That is so sweet! No, I'll have a dragon, too, only a red one." Carin winked at Donna.

"Okay. Malia, you're first." Molly took the lotus flower design and a piece of carbon paper and began tracing it above Malia's ankle.

Carin asked, "How's the Walk going?

"Liz's F.I.B. groupies got the company to sponsor the walk for ten thousand buckaroos," Donna crowed.

"Wow!"

"Molls got the PTA in six towns networking like mad to get the word out."

Sarah reported, "The Diamond Store is matching 25% of all pledges. I've written an article for the paper, and the banner will be ready Wednesday for the Fire Department to hang over Route 20."

"Chobani Yogurt and Market Basket are donating food for the walkers and for us to sell to spectators."

"Anyone else want some more of this gorgeous sangria?" Malia and Liz raised their glasses.

Molly sat up from bending over Malia's ankle. "The walk was a brilliant idea, Liz. Everyone at the crisis center is thrilled out of their minds."

"Donna thought of the shelter idea," Liz protested.

"It was your idea to do something big that'd bring women together. And it totally has."

"Learn how to take a compliment, Red."

Malia held onto the glass she was passing back to Liz, forcing Liz to look her in the eye. Malia's voice jittered as she said, "We are so blessed to have you for our friend." This wasn't just about the walk; they were trying to communicate their feelings about her moving away while still honoring her request for them not mention that this was her last girls' night.

Malia released Liz's glass and raised her own, "To an amazing friend."

"A great inspiration."

"A smart lady."

Donna bellowed, "Here's to that giant pain in the ass you miss when it's gone."

Sarah threw a grape at her as she sat down, but Donna's crack was perfect, and the emotional scene Liz had feared passed without incident. Malia asked Molly about her upcoming course work at Lesley University, counseling victims of abuse.

While Liz hadn't wanted a big goodbye tonight, she appreciated the toast and sentiment behind it. Quickly taking another sip to dissolve the swell in her chest, she wondered what her life would be like without her friends nearby.

"I'd like to make another toast." Carin raised her glass, "Emma, Ronnie and I thank you all so much. To five of the most amazing women and best friends I'll ever have. You are the angels of my heart."

Liz reflected that these words could have come out of her own mouth. Sitting in this candlelit room on this steamy summer night, without question, were the angels of her heart.

Chapter 42

It was one of those perfect summer days. Liz was relieved to see Donna and the boys pull back into the makeshift grass parking area with the Walk's start only a half hour away.

Donna slammed her SUV's hatch and turned to display the motto emblazoned on her tee shirt, WELL-BEHAVED WOMEN RARELY MAKE HISTORY. Chuck lugged two Dunkin' Donuts' Boxes O' Joe® out to the field where the walkers were gathering. Franco carried bags of donuts, muffins, and bagels. Duncan had the cups, napkins, creams, and sugars. They sluiced their way between the assembling, stretching, bantering groups. White tarps mushroomed the field where walkers lined up to sign in, get a 10-minute massage, or receive bags filled with sponsors' products. Occasional bursts of laughter tumbled across the field.

Liz addressed their group: Malia, Molly, Sarah, Donna, Donna's daughter Angela and her two college roommates, France, her friends Ashley and Brittany with their moms, and Liz's F.I.B. colleagues, Leesa and Caitlin. "I did a final tally last night; you raised $19,790, not counting the corporate sponsorships we brought in." A big whoop went up from the group. "With The Diamond Stores 25% match, our contribution is $25,737.50!"

"Hey Liz, what's the average we raised per person?"

Liz calculated, "Sixteen in our group so that would be..." After a very short pause, "$1,546.09."

Donna exclaimed, "Yep, I fell in love with her the first time we split the lunch bill."

"Try to stay together during the walk; if we straggle out, meet by the red balloon at the rest stops. I remind the type-A's in the group, this is not a race. France will have the first aid kit. Any questions?"

"Any chance I could get a rub down from the hottie in the jeans and cowboy boots when we're done?"

Sarah started singing "Lean on Me." The song swelled as others joined in. Groups nearby turned to look, many adding their voices. A cheer went up when the song finished. A voice over the loudspeaker called all walkers to the starting line.

Speakers shared heartbreaking, personal stories of abuse and expressed their gratitude to the more than 1,000 participants for the more than $325,000 raised, enough to launch the project and qualify for government grants.

The walk started with Steven blowing his trumpet. Everyone moved forward in silence. Liz got goose bumps; the walkers' collective intent palpably swirled around her, a shared spirit of purpose galvanizing legions of sneakered feet. Pride welled in Liz at having been a part of creating this. Anything could be accomplished when we worked together.

As they walked, their group shared serious talks, joking outbursts, private thoughts, and boisterous teasing. Liz's two camps of mothers, corporate employee and homemaker, melded into a seamless support group, the camaraderie of a Monday girls' night on foot.

Every few miles, members of their families met them with bananas, sports drinks, and energy bars, waving signs, like "Go Ladies!" "These sneaks are meant for walking," and they yelled chants, like:

"All for one and one for all,
Pick up your feet so you won't fall."
And Liz's favorite belted out by Dan and their boys:
"1, 2, 3...We Love France and Mummy."

But an unexpected sight at the fourth stop made Liz lurch. Sarah whispered to Liz, "If the babe with Dan is the object of our inspiration, that's some disguise." The blond head didn't need to turn around for Liz to know it wasn't Carin.

The walk's magic evaporated at the sight of Pamela laughing with Dan. Liz withdrew from the surrounding chatter, moving ahead as they neared each subsequent stop to blend in with other groups, so she could spy on the happy couple before they knew she was there to witness their teasing; Pamela bumping into Dan, her hands fluttering to his back too easily. Nothing brazenly wrong, after all they were with Carin and Liz's boys, but it didn't feel right either.

Back in their den Liz moaned, "I never knew I had so many muscles. Even my teeth ache."

"Advil? AC? What is your desire, memsahib?"

"Keep going on that foot while I consider your offer." Dan paused while she stretched and then resumed kneading the ball of her foot. Her other foot was in a plastic tub of hot water and Epsom salts. Bassa curled asleep on their Tibetan rug, his paw over his face. Carin had told Dan to take the rug back as her gift when they'd gone to get things from her house; today when she'd stopped by after the Walk, she'd grinned ear-to-ear at this symbol of her courage, liberty, and revenge.

"That was so great to be a part of. I can't believe how much money was raised."

"Pamela wants to run an art auction to benefit the shelter."

She shifted her sitting position and watched Dan out of the corner of her eye. She needed to savor the success of the walk, and she was way too exhausted to confront Dan with her fears about Pamela right now.

"That's nice." She slipped her foot back into the bath. "Did you talk about your solo show?"

"Yeah. Ylva and Alain Callewaert did an awesome job framing. She said the pieces look great, really pop. All of the guys in Sarah's band have confirmed. We've figured out where each piece will hang, and the chandeliers are already up. France is coming Thursday to help get the food set up. I can't wait for you to see the new chandelier."

His face was charged with mischief. "And there will be some surprises. Oh! Kostas and Anne are coming with Alexa and Audi, the Boston gallery owner. I'm so excited, Liz. Can you believe this is really happening? My first solo show. I feel like I'm starting a new chapter in my life."

"It's really cool, Dan. I'm so happy for you." And thrilled that after this weekend he'll be spending way less time with

Pamela. She prayed that the next chapter of his life will be included in the book of Liz and Dan.

So to help get him engaged with their storyline, she said, "I can't believe the closing is next week. I hate this limbo. Everything I do, I think, 'this is the last time I'll do this here'."

"Yeah, it'll be good to have it behind us—I guess." He reached over to pat her thigh. She shifted away from his touch, just slightly and involuntarily; the fear of losing him pushing her off her center. He didn't seem to notice. "We're a great team."

She pulled her feet from the bath to towel them dry and stared hard at her toes as she wiped them with the terrycloth. "Always have been."

"Always will be."

Chapter 43

In the flurry to open her umbrella while still seated in the car, Liz managed to get her arm, leg, and lap pretty well soaked, indicating she'd made the wrong decision in the wet head, hat hair or umbrella debate. She dashed across the parking lot towards F. Scott Gallery's eighteenth-century saltbox.

Dan had asked that she come a half hour after the party started for some reason. Another mystery added to the mile-long list of why she'd been dreading this event. She should have been thrilled about the opening for his first solo show, but the anxiety tossing around her insides testified otherwise. She'd tried on five different outfits, very unusual behavior, but finally gave up, having to admit that no effort could preclude her being eclipsed behind Pamela.

The parking lot was packed so it looked as if the rain wasn't keeping people away. A flash of lightning in the gray evening sky again challenged her wisdom in choosing to carry a metal rod pointed toward the sky.

When she opened the door, a sound bubble burst out with such volume and speed, she felt toppled. Trying to regain her emotional balance, she turned to close the umbrella, still holding the door open as if to let some of the noise escape. To no avail. Inside, loud laughter, music, and shouted conversations pummeled her fragile confidence. She was hailed immediately by a number of people while a young person took her coat and umbrella.

Kostas and Anne approached her first, and she was chatting with them when their daughter Alexa came up with her boss Audi in tow, who gushed about starting to sell the chandeliers with a solo show in January.

"Mummy, you're here! Come see! Come see!" Francine earnestly plowed toward her through the crowded room.

Liz excused herself and followed France's beckoning hand. She looked around for the first time since she'd arrived. In this front room were a painting between the front windows and two others flanking the side window. The triptych, *Anxiety, Fury, and Despair*, hung on the back wall, already with a red "sold" sticker. To her right were two more paintings. In the two corners without doorways hung the chandeliers and below them on pedestals were two pottery vases, beautifully glazed with flowing colors. France skipped over to the one that was sort of crumpled in design with an oblique opening for the vibrant, cascading tulip blooms it held.

France was beaming. Liz was confused and pointed to the vase. "I thought this was a solo show."

"Look at the artist."

Liz took her glasses out of her pocket to read the tag. "France! These are yours! They're gorgeous. When did you start doing pottery again? How?"

France was dancing, she was so excited. "When I volunteered at the Crisis Center, I asked Molly, I mean Mrs. Andersen, if pottery could be another art therapy, so I've been doing it with kids once a week after school. As a thank you, she let me do these pieces. She kept it secret, so I could surprise you."

"That is so awesome, France! I don't know which is cooler—that you're teaching art therapy or these amazing vases. Honey, I am so proud of you!"

"Thanks Mom. But I do the pottery part, and Mrs. Andersen slides in the therapy. Dad's in the back room. Come see my other one." As she took Liz's hand to pull her into the other room, France quickly scanned the patrons. "Dad must be in the food room on the other side. Whadaya think of Dad's multicolor chandelier? He wanted to surprise you. Come see." She tugged Liz to the opposite corner.

"Wow, so many surprises." Under the colorful glass chandelier, atop another pedestal, was a pottery lamp with a tree painted on it and a silhouette of a person hanging upside down from a branch. "Very nice, France."

"Do you get it?"

"Umm..." Liz rubbed her lips as she puzzled it out.

France turned the lamp around. On the other side was a pond with a woman's silhouette seated atop a boulder. She looked up at her mother expectantly.

"Oh, France!" Liz pulled in a slug of air equal to the depth of her feeling, filling her beyond capacity and leaving her breathless and without speech. She shivered and gripped her daughter's forearm, staring at the masterpiece. She let go to turn the lamp back and forth, studying the vignettes. Then she coughed away some of her overwhelm to say, "France! This is us...in our secret places." She sighed. "Oh France, I've never seen anything so wonderful. Thank you for making this. It's a masterpiece." But then her heart fell at the sight of the red sticker. "But it's sold. Oh, no! It can't be."

"Oh no, Mummy. It's not. I made it for you. It's a demo. See the sign? 'Order your own customized lamp'."

"Oh France, thank you! This is the most wonderful gift anyone has ever given me. Thank you, my love."

"You're welcome, Mummy."

Liz turned to hug her daughter, hoping this didn't cross some line of protocol in the teen code and was delighted when it was returned in earnest.

Due to her lower height, whenever in a crowd like this Liz usually felt like she was standing in a well. But this time the power of their love pushed back their human surround to a wider circumference and dimmed the nearby conversations to more of a murmur. Some heads were respectfully averted; a couple of faces mirrored their glow. Liz knew this would be a memory she would cherish for the rest of her life. Her arms pulled France a bit tighter. As they stepped apart, so too did some bodies in the crowd and she glimpsed the distinct lines and colors of the paintings on the opposite wall. Instead of abstracts, they were realistic forms, flesh and curves. As people shifted, different slivers pierced the throng, and as her mind pieced together the shards, her joy detonated as if the storm outside had blown apart the wooden shelter.

As though faraway she heard Dan's voice behind her, "Hey Babe. Whadaya think?"

Think? Think?

Here in this mob, so public and exposed, there was no space or shelter to process what she'd seen. Obscene. Scene-ick. Her mind ratcheted through streaming nonsense as it flailed for a handhold.

She pushed her way through the crowd, away from Dan towards the paintings. Forced to the front, she was too close to really take it all in. Thank God. Because it was too much. She wondered if this was the other surprise Dan had for her. What did it mean? One was of a nude lying down looking up at the sky, painted from a bird's eye view, literally from above as though the viewer was in a tree; one of the limbs of the branch lattice benignly covered the subject's thatch so the question remained whether Pamela was a true blond.

"Hey Babe. Whadaya think?" Can't he think of anything else to say? Did he really think she didn't hear him the first time? Pamela, who was camped out in front of her twin exposés, smiled at Liz and then returned to her conversation with a group of fawning admirers.

Did Dan really do these? Yes, his name was on the card entitled *Beauty in Repose*. She felt like vomiting on the reposing slut. She had to get out of here. But she must not make a scene. Well, she could, but she was not going to.

"Liz?" Dan was still at her side. She could see Pamela trying to appear as if she was unaware of them. Right, as if she wasn't totally focused on their exchange.

"Umm. These are really different for you. I've never seen you do anything like this." Would he understand all that she was saying? That she'd never known him to paint a figure. Paint in any style other than abstract. Or, hang out with another woman when she was naked.

What else had she never known him to do that he'd done? What did this mean about what he wanted to do? She scratched her head and looked at the other framed monstrosity.

Oh no. Not that.

It was Pamela in profile from the knees up in all her naked, seductive glory, handing a glass of wine to a man's hand reaching in from the left frame. Liz knew that hand. It was the hand that had massaged her foot the other night when they sat in front of the same fireplace that the yellow-haired whore stood in front of in this painting. In Liz's house. Their den. The mantle had none of their decorations or family tchotchkes. Here it was graced with the unfamiliar trimmings of another woman's taste.

There was no floor beneath her feet. She floated, suspended in noise. A grisly, vacuous, personal assault. She sensed a warmth beside her and addressed it with her eyes bound to the paintings, "France, have you heard from your brothers?"

"Nah, but they should be here soon."

"I'd better go check." She turned to Dan. "Congratulations."

She turned and moved away at a controlled speed back to the front room.

Her linebacker and her witch doctor had just walked in the front door. They were about to hand off their coats. Liz grabbed their arms. "Get me out of here." She let go and flew into the rain. Donna and Malia pulled their coats back on as they followed her to Donna's Bronco.

"Drive."

Her driver complied. In the backseat, Liz focused on her legs, so she couldn't see if her husband had come after her or not. Malia twisted back to her, reaching for her hand. Liz could barely tell them between sobs, "Dan painted her naked. Twice. Once in our den. Oh, my God. Oh, my God."

Donna peeled out of the parking lot.

Chapter 44

Her eyes burned from lack of sleep and the acid rain that had fallen from them. It'd been a girls' night convened for an emergency tribunal. Donna and Malia had taken her to Malia's and stripped her shaking body for a warm bath immersion in lavender scent, their company, and candlelight. They'd talked through the steam and then through the rest of the night about what might have happened and what might happen next. What Dan might have done and might do. What she should do in response to any possible scenario. She was armed with plans, contingencies, retorts, witticisms, and her friends' strength.

This morning, fortified with much Colombian coffee and a shower, she was dressed in one of Malia's shirts that hung on her and a belted cotton skirt. It helped to be wearing unfamiliar clothes that had no associations with her past, with Dan.

Donna drove her to Winding Path Drive, which had become an address she was loath to enter.

Last night Malia had left a message on the Burgess' machine saying that Liz was safely with them and would be in touch. Dan had called back and been told he'd have to wait.

Now, it was time.

As soon as Donna backed down the driveway, he was out the back door, walking fast towards her. "Liz, I am so sorry."

She stopped as if she'd slammed into a wall and stared at him with vacant eyes. "Are the kids here?"

"Duncan's under the stairs playing, and the other two are still asleep."

She stood for a moment considering. "Let's go to the garage."

Their former, upstairs office held the memory of yesterday's heat and their past collaborations. She opened the windows to let both escape and turned to face him.

"Please bear with me as I've not had any sleep, but I am curious and terrified to hear what exactly you are sorry for."

He nodded, acknowledging her request and communicating that he hadn't slept either, as she continued, "I feel like everything I thought was true about you and us and our life was a lie. I'm scared to death for the kids and for me. But I want to live in the truth and move on from there, whatever it is."

"It's not what you think."

"Have I lost you?" Her mouth was so dry, it was hard to get her tongue to move. "We've been under a lot of stress. And I've been a perfect bitch." Her voice shook. "I know I shut you out. I didn't mean to; I was just trying to fix the mess I'd made, so I didn't tell you what was going on. I can understand why you'd want to be out of this whole mess. Before we move, I think we need to really think about what's going to happen from here. I need to know what you want to do."

She turned away so that he was left to stare at the back of her head. She wiped her nose and eyes with Malia's sleeve, her friend's scent bringing some comfort. Her voice squeaked, "I've been such a witch. You deserve better. I just want everyone to be happy. Even if it means we won't be together. Everything's changing anyways..."

She walked to the window and leaned against it, looking out at their backyard. The lawn, the hammock, the grill and table, the trees. If they moved to New Hampshire without resolving this, her doubts and fears would just be packed up and lugged along; a black trunk of unsaid things sitting in a new living room. She'd finally begun to lift the lid, and she had to go on. "After last night, I am too exhausted to pretend that I don't see any more. Especially since you decided to declare your intentions pretty publicly. I've never known you to be cruel before this. I guess...I guess I don't know what I thought I knew."

Her heart hollowed as if it were a lump of clay spinning on a potter's wheel. She took a deep breath and looked over at him, wringing her hands as her eyes burrowed into his, hoping and not hoping to see the truth.

And so, she whispered what her heart had been howling for months, "Are you involved with Pamela? I mean are you having an affair? Do you love her?" She didn't recognize her own voice. Her hushed entreaty was the loudest that words had ever sounded in her ears, amplified by the fearful pounding of her heart. The space between her and Dan seemed to skid apart. Why didn't he say something? Not even a twitch. His eyes appeared twice their normal size.

And then he spoke. "Liz, I am so sorry." His answer was slow and emphatic, his features drained by remorse. She became ash from which nothing would rise. He ground on, "I don't know what I've done to make you think that...Well I guess, the paintings could have..." His voice sounded tiny at first, but it rolled repetitively in her mind, getting louder and closer. His words overlapped each other in her ears, creating a cacophony of babble that she desperately clawed at to make sense of. "You guys are my life. This is all so fucked up. I mean, we're moving out of our house, and you think I'm screwing around with the person who's selling my work just because she posed for a couple paintings? I painted nudes in college for class and you didn't mind."

She shrugged as if to say, *yeah, so?*

He answered her shrug with, "This year's been tough, but this? Do you want to split?"

She looked back out the window. She needed space to sort this out. She heard him move towards her and put up her hand and heard him stop. She started crying and kept crying for a long time.

Finally, she moved over to a chair, holding him away from her with her lifted palm. She folded herself into the chair, hugging her shins with the soles of her feet pressed down into the cushion. They studied each other from a distance like two unfamiliar dogs.

Finally he said, "Even how you're sitting, you never sit like that. When you're upset you always sit on the edge of the chair with your feet square on the floor."

"Everything's changing."

"Well, yeah. But I always thought that the one thing I could count on was you...and us."

"It's like we're on separate planets spinning away from each other."

"Why?"

Then it all came catapulting out her mouth. She gasped to talk at speed through the sobs. "You spend so much time with her. And you wanted to be alone with her on your birthday to set up the show. And she makes you apple pies and you hide them in the bathroom." Liz rubbed her face as she continued. "She's so artsy, and beautiful, and sophisticated, and young, and new, and nice. And I'm a stiff, crabby, old bitch, who scares pre-teens and doesn't know when to laugh..."

"Liz, Liz, take a breath, Honey!" His face was full of concern with a hint of a smile in the crinkles around his eyes. "Yeah, you're all that." She sagged further. "You're also brilliant and kind and sexy and strong. And you've lightened up a ton with this mess. You're going with the flow; you have people running to you for help. You not only got work in Boston, but you were mentoring young moms, heck, you're holding rituals out by your rock and talking with animals for God's sake. You are the smartest, most loyal, most loving, surprising, and inspiring person, I've ever met." He'd run out of fingers and had to reuse a few to make his points.

"Mmm." She wanted to believe him about Pamela, about herself. But it was hard. She got up to get a tissue from the bookcase then returned to fold herself back into the seat. "But I made this whole mess."

"No, you didn't. It's the economy, Liz. And I could have done more, instead of just babbling out every lame idea that popped into my head. It is what it is, Lizzie. Like you said before, you can't control everything, and you're learning to be okay with that, which is great."

He had a point, several actually, but she wasn't quite ready to let go of the other woman yet. "But you and Pamela have so much in common. She's so feminine—and gorgeous."

"Yeah and she gave my ego a boost when I was feeling like crap about myself, but I'm not interested in her. I mean, sure, having this young, attractive woman like my art was cool. But that doesn't mean I want to screw her. You're the one I want to be with. We have a family together and a history. A great one. I thought losing the house proved we are each other's home." She let go of her legs so they could dangle, her feet barely grazing the floor.

He noticed, his body relaxing at her more familiar posture, "Liz, I love you so much."

She half grimaced, half grinned. "Even though?"

"More like, just because. I'd always thought it'd be great if you were a little softer, but then when you got that way, it threw me. It felt like you'd left me when I really needed you."

"I'm sorry."

"Don't be. I think I depended too much on your being my rock and on your being so sure that you were right all the time. It gave me something solid to either lean on or push against." His face was so earnest. "But that wasn't fair. I wasn't letting you change. Maybe because I wasn't ready to step up my own game."

Liz looked down at Bassa, who had scooted in with them and had come over to rub against her legs. She scooped him up and held him. His purring was like a warm bath. She didn't take her eyes from the kitty as Dan said, "You are amazing. But Liz, I can take a turn at being the strong one." She looked up at him and nodded. "From the moment I saw you calling out for cows, I've never loved anyone else. I never will."

Relief poured out of her in such a rush that Bassa squirmed out of her arms. Dan tentatively phrased the beginning of their chorus as a question, "We're good, Babe?"

Skipping a line, she answered with two, slightly modified refrains, "We will be, as long as we have each other—because we have each other."

"Oh, Lizzie, thank you." And her true rock, the one she'd always gone to, took her in his arms.

Dan

His runs had always helped him slot things out in his mind. A moving meditation, a time when his body relaxed, his muscles stretched, his mind quieted so that he was able to hear what was really going on. But today he didn't want to process the fact that this was the last time he'd ever run the route he'd run so many hundreds, maybe thousands of times. Today would be the last time he ran back to the house he'd built at 43 Winding Path Drive.

He'd gotten through this by marking as he did during a tough run, looking ahead a short distance and picking a tree or a mailbox as his goal and once there, finding the next goal ahead to reach.

And now, thank God, the end was in sight. They'd had the tag sale yesterday (mark), next was the closing (mark), and then the move to his folks' (mark). It will be a relief to have it over. His step quickened; he felt lighter, more mobile than he had in a long time.

It was weird when they hauled a load of stuff to his folks' last week, knowing that now they were moving there, not just visiting. Driving through his childhood landscape, he'd recognized people and houses. He wasn't returning as the swaggering conqueror with his spoils or as a vanquished failure scuttling back to burrow into obscurity and regret; he was simply a man returning with his loved ones to a beloved place.

The cost of living was so much cheaper there. Liz said that if they're careful, with what they'll clear from selling the house, they'll be able be able to buy a small place and get along for at least a couple of years. He'll come up with something way before then. Or, she will.

His lope pulled away from the suburban roar of the lawn mower brigade and headed for the fields north of town. He pulled the hem of his t-shirt up to wipe his face.

The kids had been champs through all this, but as it was getting closer, France was struggling. A childhood friend of his,

Sylvie Lajoie, invited her to audition for a play she was directing. France seemed as if she might be interested, but it was hard to tell. Although she's been better since the shoplifting thing, his mom had suggested they have her meet a woman who counsels teens using horses. That might be something they could actually get France to go to, but who knew.

Maybe he could take the kids and his Dad to hike Mount Mansfield and for a swim in Lake Willoughby. He had loved it as a kid.

He lay on more speed as he thought about how 43 Winding Path Drive had been a great house for them. So many really good memories. He was thinking of designing their next home with more hidden doors and secret spaces and rooms of different heights and shapes. Maybe a sleeping niche recessed into a wall and storage above. That'd be cool, although Liz would say it'd be hard to change the sheets. He'd figure it out.

He slowed his pace back down. What a relief that she didn't blame him for their business crapping out and accepted that he'd never been unfaithful. It was hard enough to live with his own guilt about the stuff that had and hadn't happened, but he couldn't bear it if she thought he'd failed her.

Chapter 45

When Liz pulled into their driveway, it was more like revisiting a memory than coming home. Only a couple more days.

She stood at the sink and scrubbed, washing dusty vases and glasses before packing them for the movers. Was this move their choice, their failure, or simply exhaustion? Her dishcloth slowly rubbed the dishes submerged in sudsy water, then rinsed them under the running tap. A meditation in motion.

She's been so relieved that Pamela wasn't a threat that she didn't mind when the woman showed up at their 'everything must go" tag sale yesterday. They'd made $2,237.40, but it'd been really hard to see people walking off with bits and pieces of their past. She'd never do it again; no matter how much they needed the money, it'd all go to charity or the dump.

Utterly emotionally drained, Liz leaned her forearms on the edge of the sink, staring into the dirty water. Where would they go from here? Besides just away. She picked her head up to look out the window. From this point in time, it would all be new. She'd try to see possibilities like Dan did. A movement hooked her eye. Back from his run already? She stepped to the right to peer out, and her breath gapped in surprise.

In the sunlight, not ten feet from the house, stood the buck she'd seen in the woods last winter. His side was towards her: strong, protective, majestic. She could see a sliver of the white shag on his breast, his coat sleek, lush. Broader after his summer forage, he patiently watched her watching him. She and this woodland patriarch stood, immobile. She considering. He accepting.

Leaning against the edge of the sink, she let out a rattling sigh. Patriarch. Interesting choice of descriptor. But yes, he felt fatherly, just like she'd always thought of the stag in Dan's mural above her.

This acknowledgement nudged the child she'd once been to stretch and awaken as if from a long sleep, freeing her to ask for what she'd needed then: to be held, her head stroked, to be tucked into bed and read to, to receive consistent caring. It was the same need as during this latest fiasco: to feel safe. It was something she'd never really felt growing up, that time when feeling secure was so essential for a child and for the adult they would become.

She slowly backed away from the window, hoping the buck wouldn't leave, willing him to stay, to acknowledge her and respond to her need. Might he even walk over to her? Quietly, she opened the mudroom door, but he was gone. Her spirit sank. Her issues of abandonment roared higher, crackling around her heart. Driven by a sense of loss and an instinctual need for comfort, Liz took off toward her rock. She came around the corner of the house and spied deer scat, dropped like a trail of bread crumbs. She sped up, crossing Winding Path Drive, padding along with the pond on her left, avoiding twigs that might snap and warn the buck of her presence if he was still near. She scanned the woods to her right with the stubborn hope of seeing his retreating bulk.

She slowed as she approached the three birches that marked the last turn. Rounding their white, freckled trunks, her heart leapt. He was there, grazing in a small, grassy lea fifteen feet beyond the rock. She crept forward. His head flew up; he was motionless, assessing the danger. He saw her, sniffed for her scent. Liz opened her hands; her palms face out to him, fingers wide. Without thinking about what she was doing, she sent him feelings of fellowship, the trust inherent in love. His head bobbed, then he lowered his massive neck to resume grazing.

She worked to soften her breath and be calm to ease his mind, which served to quiet hers. She noted how much looser her emotions felt in his presence. She held them lightly, and was willing to open her grasp should her feelings squirm asking for the space to breathe.

As she climbed onto the rock, the granite's heat shot through the soles of her bare feet. Perched atop the crest, she alternated between gazing out over the pond and watching him graze. Time dissolved. Presence swirled and settled about her. A sense of grace rode the air from the stag to pool within her, while a core strength rose from the rock. The emptiness that had drained her for so long was filled. All that'd happened hadn't been a loss but a clearing of space to receive.

Resting in this sheltered hush, she noticed a shard of residual darkness tucked inside, an ache decades old. She sat with it in the sun and the insect hum. She opened to it, tenderly exploring what it might be. Pulling her gaze from the buck, she looked out over the pond. A frog leapt into the still water, sending a small stick floating on the surface, bobbing on the ripples. And then she knew. The raft of beliefs she'd clung to so tightly had in fact been the weight pulling her down. She wouldn't sink if she let go of those beliefs; sinking had never been the risk.

After living life tethered to the past and only skimming across its surface, this revelation felt fresh and bright with its offering of a better way.

Following one of Malia's suggestions, she took her childhood anger and imagined folding the resentment like a newspaper into a toy boat and then mentally setting her phantom ship of fury down on the pond to float from view.

Gratitude. Exhilaration. Peace. The sweep of release unbound these prospects. She could allow them, even invite them into her life.

A hoof stomped the dry, packed earth, drawing her attention. A flood of love coursed through her. She yearned to throw her arms around his plush neck, burying her face in his fur. At the thought her muscles relaxed, her nose filled with his sweet musky scent and she sensed the steady throb of his heart as if she had embraced his strength. And within this image, it was as much her late father's shoulder as the buck's flank she rested on. Her dad had loved her, and she felt that love, strong and pure.

A lightness Liz hadn't known since she was very, very young rekindled. She imagined sprinting through the woods in serpentine loops; swinging around tree trunks, her foot flight releasing the scents of dried leaves and pine needles into the rich summer heat. She felt the wild abandon of galloping off on the back of her buck. They raced a hawk though the woods' flash of light and shadow.

She smiled at her fancy, pulled her feet in and clasped her arms around her shins.

Heat shimmered over the pond. A mockingbird sang an original trill. Frogs croaked, basking among the cattails. "They are doing the best they can." She snapped her head up. The buck stood mute. It had been a voice within her that was not her own. Its meaning was clear. There had been no cruel intent.

It was as though her edges dissolved. She was the breeze, the water, the stone, the light. She simply was. Again, she looked out over the pond that had brought her such solace over the years and that she'd be leaving in two days. This sweetness, this freedom was its parting gift. Just as the buck's sentry imprinted its echo on her heart; her father's love, so hard for him to express in life, had reached out and guided her, had protected her during her recent struggle and growth. He had always been with her.

She thought of her parents, and all the people she'd judged as not having done enough to help her and her family, or as not having been compassionate enough. With brilliant clarity her new truth released her: *They are all just doing the best they can.* And then she gently added the corollary: *And so am I.*

Chapter 46

The new owners had bought the chandeliers, all of the appliances, the upholstered chairs, TV room couch and pool table, the tables Dad had made and the piano. Liz had checked with Duncan about selling the piano, and he'd said yes, but he hadn't played it since. If they'd kept it, it would have been put in storage at exorbitant cost for who knew how long and probably would have been damaged in its dormancy. He could use his grandparents' upright while they lived there, but the expression on her son's face told her that having his piano may have represented hope. It'd been a logical choice, but perhaps not the best one.

For their last dinner they would ever have in the only home they'd all shared together, Dan prepared a simple meal of corn on the cob and salad, with ice cream sandwiches for dessert. The candles were lit as always, but the meal was more subdued than usual, and afterward Dan suggested that they all go into the den.

Even though August was too warm for a fire, he built one anyway. He picked up Bassa, who had followed them in, petted him and then put him back down. "So what shall we do on our last night?"

France fumed, "Dad, do you have to say 'last night'?"

"Sorry." There was an awkward silence. He tried again. "I've already got some awesome ideas for the new place, but what do you guys want? It can be anything!"

Their youngest was unconvinced. "Nowhere will be as good as here." The subsequent quiet was punctuated by sniffles and throat clearing. Duncan's voice strained to be strong. "Daddy, can I hide something in my secret place, so they'll know I was here?"

Liz seized on this, "Great idea! Rituals are important at important times. Well, this feels like a very important time."

"What do we do?" France asked intrigued.

"Whatever we want I guess."

Dan stood, and in a solemn voice appropriate to an exalted ritual, said, "The Burgess family built this house. We leave behind the names we scrawled into the concrete foundation, but 'home' we will take with us because home is where we are." His voice flipped back to its usual enthusiasm. "Hey, why don't we each take a piece of this house with us and each leave something behind? Come on. Get up, people."

Each went to claim their singular token and then met back in the den to share their choices. Duncan had whittled off a tiny piece of the wall in his secret place. Chuck chose some strands of the carpet in the computer room. France took a splinter from her bedroom's turret window seat. Dan chiseled off a little bit of brick in the den's fireplace. And Liz had removed a paint chip from the stag in the great room's mural for reasons she didn't share.

Chuck studied the carpet strand as he rolled it between his fingers, "Why don't we leave a list of our favorite memories?"

"Yeah! We can hide it in my secret place like a time capsule."

They all agreed that this was a great idea. Dan put the smooth, lyrical music of Katie Drake on the sound system, and they scribbled away on the scraps of paper Chuck doled out. When everyone was done, they each shared what they'd written.

Chuck read, "Building the tree fort with Dad. Laying in the hammock with Mom and France while Mom read the first Harry Potter to us and Duncan napped in the playpen. The time Dad made me laugh at dinner, and I blew milk out my nose."

Duncan recited, "Pretending in my secret place. When a bat got loose in the house, and we all chased him with tennis rackets until he flew out the front door. Jumping in the big pile of leaves Dad raked, and building snow forts for snowball fights."

France remembered, "Having a FAB sleepover in the TV room and tickling Ashley's nose while she was sleeping so she slapped whipped cream all over her face. Following the string all over the house to my presents on my 10th birthday. Painting with Daddy in the studio."

Liz noted, "Playing board games here in front of the fire and playing Sparkle at dinner. Working in the garage office with Dad for Evergreen Designs. Watching lightning out our bedroom window with Daddy during a snowstorm. Daddy cooking dinner. Having bubble baths by candlelight. Bringing each of you home from the hospital."

Dan recalled, "Duncan playing Christmas carols while we sang with Gramma and Grampie around the piano and had hot cider and Christmas ginger cookies. Cooking dinner for the family. Family pool tournaments. Making paintings with France in the garage. Playing Yu-Gi-Oh! with Duncan. Building the tree fort with Chuck. Kissing your mother anywhere. I even liked mowing the lawn."

There was only the corn pot to wash; the rest went into the dishwasher. The kids had gone upstairs to bed. Liz's heart was still in her throat. Dan came up behind her and slipped his arms around her waist. "You are an amazing woman."

"Because I do dishes?" Her joke sounded more like a lament.

He nuzzled her neck softly, tickling the small, light hairs there. "Because you love me even though." Slowly his lips nipped and wandered until they found her earlobe. Her body began to burn with a heat that had nothing to do with August or menopause.

Chuck came downstairs. "Oh gross. Get a room." A quick u-turn and he headed back up.

"Not a bad idea," Dan quietly growled.

"Chuck will know what we're doing," she protested. Dan took her hand in one of his. His other index finger pressed to his lips. They snuck across the great room. He pointed up the bedroom stairs to indicate that Chuck was in the bathroom as she followed him into the library. He gently pulled the French doors closed and then opened the hidden panel in the wall. As she ducked into the darkened cavern, he brushed his hand along the side of her breast and across her back, then patted her bottom before following her in and pulling the door shut behind him. It was pitch dark inside. They tumbled into a thick nest of comforters and pillows. He pulled her top off over her head and undid her bra while she unbuttoned his shirt.

They reclined, rubbing their naked chests together, nipples erect, enjoying the smooth delight of skin on skin. Their kiss was open, wet, and consuming. She massaged his jeans where he was engorged with anticipation and moved quickly to release his zipper. His face nestled into the curve of her neck, lightly biting the intimate arc. When their clothes lay crumpled beside their bodies, the sense of bestowing and receiving touch was heightened by the absolute absence of sight in the utter blackness.

Here was another unexpected ritual, even more healing than the one they'd shared by the pond or the one with their children tonight. She felt him slide away and down the length of her. Her breathing grew shallow as his tongue and mouth browsed over and within her. Her mind could only flash between *don't stop* and *come up*. When he did rise up above her in the dark, nothing mattered but right now, this moment, this man.

She awoke and heard music. Her body felt stiff and cramped. She shifted and felt Dan naked beside her, but it was so pitch black she couldn't see him. She started to sit up, but Dan whispered directly into her ear, "It's Duncan. We better stay, or we'll scare him." She realized that they were in Duncan's secret place where they had made love. Then, she recognized the melodies being played so softly beyond the wall that they were almost a whisper. Their baby had gotten up in the wee hours of this August morning, in the middle of his last night in the only home he'd ever known, to quietly play Christmas carols.

Chapter 47

"Okay, if your clothes are packed, load up the car. Chuck, if you're done then you can help someone else."

Liz went into her bedroom closet and stood. Her head ached. She heard Dan downstairs talking to one of the kids; his words were muffled, but his tone was heroically buoyant in his attempt to keep their spirits up. Her morale strategy had been to keep them busy and moving ahead of their emotions.

She retrieved the floral tapestry bag from the nearly empty closet. Focus. Put one foot in front of the other. The movers would be here soon to pack up their remaining belongings.

Chopin rose through the floor boards and stopped. Then a snip of Bach. Silence. Briefly Liszt. Silence. Rachmaninoff. But no Mozart. She sat on the bed to listen. Duncan was playing the pieces more tentatively than usual, but it was good that he was playing again.

She regarded the bedroom's familiar Navaho-white walls; old friends that had witnessed the conception of her children, sheltered her from storms, kept her secrets, and now stood steadfastly around her splintering heart. They were like a jilted lover, formerly known so intimately in all shades of light, so often taken for granted, but soon belonging to someone else. She would no longer be able to open the door to this house without ringing the bell, or get a cup from the cupboard without asking permission, or even know where the mugs were kept.

The Rachmaninoff was now pounding. Duncan kept faltering, uncharacteristically. She rose from the bed and lifted her packed bag. She was halfway across the room when the playing stopped and didn't resume.

Dan yelled from downstairs, "Okay, time to hide the time capsule." France and Chuck assembled in the kitchen with twin dragging gaits. Liz picked up the time capsule from the table, a Tupperware container holding their handwritten memories.

Duncan crawled inside his secret place, followed by the rest of the family. All of the comforters and pillows had been packed in the car in order to rebuild Duncan's nest in his grandparents' shed, but the battery light was still there.

Having their bodies tightly packed together brought some comfort; no one wanted to be far from the others, their shared sorrow sewing their hearts together even as they were breaking.

Liz passed their memories back to Duncan, and Dan suggested tucking it behind the joists in the space below the bottom stair, then he said, "Make a huddle, hands in. Ready one-two-three..."

They all yelled, "Go Burgi!"

"Okay everyone out to the car." Liz ordered. "Bassa's already in his carrier and is probably freaking out." That was all it took to send Duncan blasting out of his secret place and running for the car. The older two followed him out. Then, their parents.

"We're good," Dan said.

"Always have been."

"Always will be."

Liz nodded. It didn't matter where you lived. Or what you did. Or even who you thought you were, she thought. Life doesn't have to be perfection. It's about embracing life even when it's falling apart. That's what made it rich.

"Mom! Chuck put his smelly feet on my side." France's screech easily reached them from the car.

"Your stupid makeup bag is where my feet are supposed to go."

Liz smiled up at Dan. He kissed her forehead.

"Ready, Mrs. B?"

"It's been really good, Dan."

"Has been. Will be." He swung the screen door open and then closed it behind them.

She said, "I've been thinking, maybe your yogurt company scheme isn't such a bad idea..."

Acknowledgments

This book is a collaboration with Bruce, who grazed nearby as I lay in the grass writing. The best magic for writer's block was kissing his velvet nose. Now a spirit horse, Bruce, I thank you and love you.

Deep gratitude to Doug, Ben, and Sam who support my every endeavor with love and enthusiasm. The two who were boys when this began have become young men with great integrity. xo xo xo

Thank you to my agent who adored this book from the first when it was not so lovable.

Thank you to Linda Cardillo at Bellastoria Press for conjuring a reality out of hope. Your intelligence, enthusiasm, clarity, and support are epic.

Thank you to my manuscript readers for your feedback and insights, and for your morale boosts when my confidence wavered. Priceless! Special shout-out to Audi Keller, Debi O'Neil, Margaret Orto, Susan Ricker, and Cyndi Saltzgiver. Thank you, Melissa Bonney Kane for drawing the Burgess' blueprint. And, to my *uber*-talented cover designer, Corrinne Hamilton.

Thank you to my all cherished friends and family whose love is the life blood of my spirit.

And, Thanks to You for reading this book. Enjoy!
May your Life be filled with Love, Hope, and Laughter.

It took 13 years of being woken by new plot ideas in the middle of the night, writing at Little League games (yes, I saw your home run), and editing during my cancer treatment to create this baby. And, now here it is!

NEVER GIVE UP ON YOUR DREAMS!

About the Author

Sharon Wright also wrote *Getting Started in Bonds* after a career in finance, which led to appearances on TV, radio and in the national press. Sharon is a Life and Executive Coach, often assisted by her horses north of Boston.

She is currently writing a book of comfort and inspiration for people ridding their bodies of cancer.

Whatever activity she is involved in springs from her belief that each of us is whole, unique, and capable of creating a life of joy, ease, and prosperity.

She is married to Mr. (W)right and her two sons are the Wright Brothers.

Visit her website at www.sharonwrightbooks.com

Photo: Selfie of the Author and her Muse, Bruce

Book Discussion Questions

1. What fears hinder Liz? What other characters are working through their fears? What fears limit your happiness or cause you suffering?

2. At what points does Liz show that she is shifting away from her habitual perceptions and responses, and beginning to broaden her viewpoint?

3. Did Malia handle Liz's talk of suicide well? What would you do if a friend told you that they were thinking of hurting themselves?

4. What are the positive and negative sides of the characters' personality traits? For example, Dan is creative but that also means his solutions may not always be practical.

5. Do you believe people can communicate with animals?

6. Why do you think people are more apt to show support for people when ill than when they are unemployed? What would be appropriate to say or do for someone out of work?

7. Which of the women would you be friends with?

8. Would you like being married to Dan? What about him might drive you nuts? Do you believe that he didn't have an affair with Pamela?

9. What actors would play these characters in the movie?

10. What would you do if you suspected a friend is the victim of domestic violence? An acquaintance? A stranger?

11. If your child shoplifted, how would you address it?

12. What do you think the Burgesses could have done when their business started to slow? Why do you think they didn't do that? Should they have sold the house sooner?

13. What are the advantages of staying home when raising children? Of working when raising children?

14. Why do you think women can be judgmental of each others' choices?

15. What is your metiér, your passion, i.e. the purpose that inspires your life and gives your life its juice?

16. When were you most frustrated with what was going on?

17. What was the funniest part in the story?

18. What affected you most?

19. Liz had trouble accepting her parents' personal failings. Should she have? Is there a time when not forgiving is better? Does forgiveness mean acceptance? That you condone the behavior? That you release them from responsibility? That you understand why they did it? What is forgiveness? Are there things in your life that you haven't been able to forgive? How does it affect you?

20. What are examples of love in the story? How do you express love? How do the people in your life let you know they love you? Does it matter if people say they love you out loud? Why?

21. The house is a silent character in the book. What is its influence? How do our attachments motivate us? Limit us?

22. Is there a physical place or mental image you go to when you need emotional grounding or balance, just as Liz goes to her rock?

23. What good memories would you write down to put in a time capsule?

CPSIA information can be obtained at www.ICGtesting.com
Printed in the USA
LVOW12s1106160614

390238LV00011B/132/P